DARK CROSSROADS

DEBRA DUNBAR

I was in my basement, staring at a spoon.

"The candles are lit. What's next?" I asked.

"Place the object in the center of your circle by walking the east-to-west line of the pentagram."

Thankfully the candles meant I could actually *see* the pentagram. Before I'd lit them, the basement had been dark as I imagined the grave to be—if a grave had a faintly luminescent outline of stones around a magical circle, a giant furnaced, and some broken furniture and rusty paint cans, that is. Weirdly enough, even in the darkness I could see Chuck's face in the spoon. Let me tell you, that was one of the creepiest things I'd seen outside a horror movie, and as a Templar, I'd seen lots of creepy things.

"There." I was now at the west quarter candle of my magical space, eyeing a smooth river stone at the center of the circle.

"A quick review," Chuck said, sounding an awful lot like one of my college professors. "Why six candles?"

I wanted to be a smart ass and reply "because that's what the ritual calls for," but I held back. When I'd been with Haul

Du, they'd only taught me to follow the ritual as outlined in various grimoires. They did encourage further study of symbolism and structure of a ritual with the more advanced mages, but with novices the idea was to get them to follow directions down to the last letter, and get used to channeling energy and controlling Goetic demons.

Chuck was making me deconstruct each ritual before I even attempted it, which meant there was a frustratingly long time before I got to actually try magic. I persevered because I understood why Chuck was taking this approach. After he'd met my mother and eyeballed her sword, he believed my Templar gifts would sometimes counteract a magical spell—or send it off in an unpredictable and possibly fatal direction.

I also persevered because Chuck was the only mage who would teach me. I'd been kicked out of Haul Du the moment they'd discovered I was a Templar and blacklisted from any registered magical group—which was basically any magical group. If I wanted to level up my magical skills, then I had no choice but to do it Chuck's way.

"The four corners anchor the magical space, but candles at the pentagram capture and hold. Using both sets a strong barrier, and holds the spell tightly inside, concentrating it. That's useful when the energy you're trying to read, or what you're trying to divine is faint. Six is also the number for harmony."

"And as a Templar…" Chuck prompted.

I glanced at my candles, glad that I'd bought long-burning ones because this lecture in the middle of my ritual was really slowing things down.

"Three is the most sacred of our numbers. It's the symbol of creation. It's the beginning, the middle, and the end. It's the Father, the Son, and the Holy Spirit. It's also a masculine number. Usually feminine numbers are considered Satanic, hence the symbolism of 666, but six on its own escapes the darkness of other female numbers. It's the first perfect number, therefore it is balanced. Two trinities. It is the only number that is both of the light and the dark."

"Good."

I squinted at Chuck, wishing he'd been able to perform this magical Skype spell on a larger utensil. I guess people serving time in prison couldn't be picky about what dinnerware they had access to.

"And you have the herbs?"

"Birch bark, rosehips, goldenrod, and raven's bread."

All those had been easy except for the raven's bread— otherwise known as Amanita muscaria or fly agaric. First, it wasn't an herb, it was a fungus. Second, even though it was supposedly common in North America—a large, bright red toadstool that grows in birch and evergreen forests—finding any in the wild was pretty much akin to that whole needle in a haystack thing. Most mushrooms could be easily bought over the internet, but given that this one was lethally poisonous in some doses, and intensely hallucinogenic in others, it was illegal—as in "Class A Drug" illegal. Chuck had finally needed to step in and help out by giving me the name of someone who sold the stuff over the dark web. I had purchased the raven's bread and hoped I wasn't on any FBI or DEA watchlist.

"And the ritual?"

This was where things got tricky. The usual words hadn't worked the first time we'd tried this, so Chuck had made me modify them to mimic a Templar blessing. In addition, I was using my sword as an aid instead of the athame I'd purchased that had never felt right in my hand.

"Light incense at the west quarter. Sprinkle on the crushed herb mixture, which you hopefully measured correctly, then build your energy. When you feel it peak, recite your incantation and direct both energy and intent in the words toward the object using your sword as an aid."

I knew all this since I'd practiced the ritual a few times, and memorized the heck out of it. I also had been meticulous in measuring and crushing the herbs, all while chanting to blend their properties and power. This better work because I'd put a ton of time and effort into it. And it would be an incredibly useful spell. Knowing what human owned something would be awesome. From there it was a small step to modify the spell to know who held something last, or even whose energy was within a radius of an object. I could even work to expand the spell to include whether the owner was human or supernatural. Next time I came across a soul trap, a charm, a bloody crime scene, I would have a spell in my arsenal that would cut mine, and Detective Tremelay's, job in half.

"Showtime." I breathed in for six counts then out for six counts, clearing my mind of all except for the spell I was about to perform.

I was already at the west quarter, so I just had to squat down and light the incense. It took a few minutes for the flame over the fragrant disk to die down, leaving a glowing round ember. Holding tight to my intent, I sprinkled the herbs on top, standing and stepping quickly back so I didn't breathe in anything that might end up with me in the hospital or running naked through the streets babbling about pink unicorns.

Even in the dim light I saw the curl of smoke rising from the incense disk. Suddenly, energy filled the circle, snapping tight to the confines of the barrier I'd established. The lines in the concrete glowed blue, the perimeter stones sparkling like stars. This energy wasn't from within me, it was gathered from the cosmos and held together by a magic I didn't quite understand, no matter how many books I read.

I admired the energy for a brief moment, then stepped forward to stand on the circle, willing my body to become just another conduit to its flow. It felt strange, like I was holding on to the hot wire of a cattle fence with one hand and gripping an icicle with the other. With a ragged breath, I slowly began to draw the energy into myself. There was a point where I wasn't sure I could hold any more, but still energy remained swirling about in the circle. Chuck hadn't covered this in his instructions and I wasn't sure what to do. Would the spell work if I wasn't holding all the energy? Would I explode if I tried to take in more than I felt I could hold? Unfortunately I wouldn't be able to communicate with my bodiless mentor until the spell was over, so I was going to have to make a decision on my own.

Hoping Dario didn't arrive tonight to find me splattered all over the basement, I eased more and more of the energy inside until I held it all.

Bloated was an understatement about how I was feeling at that moment. I'd gorged myself on Thanksgiving dinners before and not felt quite this stuffed.

Raising my sword, which I belatedly realized was the icicle-feeling item, I pointed it toward the stone in the center of the circle. Energy quivered at the edge of my hand, barely held in check and ready to race down the blade.

"Earth is to earth, and stone is to stone. Saint Anthony show me who calls this their own."

I was no poet, so I'd kept it simple and to the point. The original spell had lines of gratitude to everything from the four quarters to the elements, and individually called upon a host of deities. I had no problem performing spells that expressed gratitude to God's creations, but I figured Saint Anthony was the dude I needed for this particular spell, not Celtic goddesses.

I recited the incantation over and over until my vision

blurred and my skin heated, then I sent the energy down the sword in a huge bolt of white. The basement lit up like the sun, then just as quickly went dark. Temporarily blinded, I held still and blinked until my vision slowly adjusted. I was supposed to see something overtop the rock. With the spell modifications, Chuck wasn't sure if I'd see a person's face, or words with their name or both, but he said I should definitely have a sense of who owned the object in the center of the circle.

There was nothing over the smooth river stone—not the face of my beloved great grandmother, not her name, not even a crude stick figure. I was still so hot I felt as if I were in a sauna, but there was no sixth sense of who owned the stone.

"I don't think it worked." Think. There was no doubt in my mind that it hadn't worked. I'd spent so much time on this spell—time, money, effort. And I'd gotten nothing for it. Maybe this just wasn't a spell I would be able to work. Maybe this wasn't a Templar-compatible spell.

"Everything looked spot-on from my viewpoint," Chuck-in-the-spoon said.

I walked forward, thinking that maybe instead of a giant projected image, there would be something so small I couldn't see it from the edge of the circle. When I got close, I saw something flicking around the stone. It was dim, fleeting, and looked sort of like a distorted diamond shaped object that was a bright reddish-orange.

I went to pick up the rock and yelped, dropping it back to the ground and shoving my burned fingers into my mouth. The faint illusion vanished and I saw steam rise off the rock.

"What was that?" Chuck asked.

I took my fingers out of my mouth and flexed them gingerly. "I don't know. Looked like a red-orange butterfly or something. It wasn't very distinct."

"Well, that's clearly a success, but it may not have been the result you were hoping to get," he commented.

"No shit, Sherlock." I waved my fingers around, thinking an ice pack would be nice about now. What the heck had the spell delivered? It was supposed to reveal the owner of the rock, not it's fiery origins. Maybe this could be a useful spell if I wanted hot burning rocks to lob at enemies, but honestly it would be faster to just shove a bunch of stones in the fireplace if that was my intent.

I frowned, thinking about the spell and all the different iterations that could return. Owner. Who last touched the object. Where it was last.

"Remember when you did the identification spell on the soul trap and it initially returned the Argentinian mage instead of Dark Iron because he was the actual owner?" I asked. "Do you think instead of who owned it last, maybe my spell identified the original owner."

There was no mistaking the exasperation in Chuck's sigh. "It's a smooth rock. That's not exactly the sort of thing someone passes down for generations."

"My great grandmother gave it to me," I countered. "Maybe someone gave it to her."

It did sound ridiculous. It was a worry stone, a rock worn smooth by water and decades of oils from Essie's hand. But just as she'd given it to me when I'd gone off to college to soothe a troubled mind, perhaps her great grandmother had done the same to her."

"And the someone who gave it to her is what?" Chuck drawled. "A dragon? A fire elemental? A demon?"

Crap, I hoped not. It was actually better to believe the spell was a dud than think Essie stole, or was given, the stone from a demon.

"It would have been easier to just kill a chicken," Chuck lamented. "That spell works. That spell always works."

"I'm not killing a chicken. Besides you said that *wouldn't* work for a Templar."

Not that Templars were vegetarians and I'm sure at one time we'd killed plenty of chickens to stick in the dinner pot. Chuck felt the problem wasn't in ending the life of an animal, it was doing so for the purpose of a magical spell. I agreed because any sort of ritual killing was a line I wasn't going to cross.

"Let's move on and try something else," I suggested. "I really do want to perfect this spell, but maybe later when I've had a few more successes under my belt."

My confidence had really taken a hit the last few weeks, and I needed a win to show me that this course of study really was something I could do.

Chuck sighed. "Tell me what you've done so far—besides accidently summon a high-level demon and get yourself marked, that is."

Jerk.

"I can create null bags. Templars learn to create null spaces since we might be called upon to bring in an artifact. My keychain is spelled to blister vampires, but that's also a Templar thing since it's a blessing and not really a mage spell. As a Templar I can send wraiths and undead spirits back to their graves. I can create a globe of light. I can also sanctify an object and create a holy space. Oh, and my butter knife!"

Chuck's face in the spoon scowled. "You can conjure a butter knife? Like, if you need to spread some jam on toast or something? What in the world is that spell possibly good for?"

"No, I put a spell on a butter knife. At first it was a spell to harm vampires. Then I spelled it to open locks, which I'm particularly proud of I'll have you know."

Chuck didn't look impressed. "So what's on the top of your list? What spell do you want to try next?"

I thought for a moment. The ownership spell would have been handy, but there was something else that had been bothering me. Yes, I knew how to shoot, but throughout the centuries, our consecrated weapon had always been a sword. That had been pretty handy in the fifteenth century, but in the twenty-first, it was…well, it was bringing a sword to a gunfight.

Although it would be amazing to figure out how to bless a Glock and have the equivalent of a holy hip cannon, I was more concerned about not getting shot again.

"Can I do something to make myself bulletproof? I mean, I'd really love it if the spell could make me invulnerable to any sort of attack, but if that's too ambitious, then I'll take just not getting shot."

I watched the spoon as Chuck's face distorted in thought.

"There's a potion. It's a pain to make, but I think it would be compatible with your Templar alignment."

We discussed the ingredients and the preparations for the spell, then I signed off, which meant I stuck Chuck's spoon into an old Crown Royal bag and stashed him behind a rusty paint can. Then I picked up the worry stone which was now only room temperature, and went upstairs.

Working with Chuck was more difficult than my brief stint with Haul Du, and it wasn't just because he was a pain in the butt. He had a broad knowledge of different magical practices, but his main focus was in death magic. And, of course, that was the one practice I wouldn't do. Even if I was willing to cross that line, Chuck was fairly certain that my being Templar meant death magic wouldn't work for me anyway, so that left us sifting through the others, trying to figure out which spells could be modified, which ones would work as-is, and which ones were a definite "no."

Goetic demonology was compatible, but I wasn't about to go down that path without someone who specialized in that particular practice. Blessings and charms were compatible as were hexes and curses but wouldn't be as helpful as spells that did days of research in a few hours, or ones that could protect both me and others.

I got ready for work and walked to the coffee shop in the Inner Harbor, willing to brave the January cold rather than drive and fork out the exorbitant fees to park within a few blocks of the shop.

There was something about January that always seemed so bleak. The streets were bare of their holiday decorations and cheerful colored lights. The joy on people's faces just last month had been replaced by a grim sort of stoicism. *Just get through this month. Just manage to chisel down the Christmas debt a little. Just keep the heat on and don't get the flu,* seemed to be the silent mantra of everyone inside and outside the coffee shop.

We hadn't had a customer in over an hour. The sun had set, but I still had three hours left on my shift. I was tempted to text Dario and tell him to swing by, but I knew he had stuff to do as the head of his *Balaj*, and I was supposed to go over to his house later. We were doing this balancing game in our relationship, trying to figure out the perfect mix of work time, alone time, and together time. Now that I was on a more regular schedule at the coffee shop, and his small *Balaj* wasn't facing any immediate threats, we'd fallen into a pattern of spending three nights a week together, and at least meeting for dinner or something another one or two nights.

We could spend every night together if I moved in with him, but I wasn't ready for that. I liked being in my own home, with my magical space in the basement and my pets. I didn't want to wake up to a Renfield fixing me breakfast and hanging around the house. Plus, Dario's place had become a sort of home base for the *Balaj*, which meant at nightfall half a dozen vampires or more were in and out of his house until a little before dawn. It wasn't a home, it was a business, and the trade-off of having Dario with me most of his waking hours would be a severe decrease in intimacy in the time we did spend together. I wouldn't be getting just a nice home and a convenient way to see more of Dario if I moved in with him, I'd be getting an entire *Balaj*.

And where I was a little nervous about taking the next step with Dario, I was *really* nervous about becoming some sort of Templar house mom to a group of vampires.

Tired of hashing through all this mentally in the silence of the coffeeshop, I poured Brandi and myself a cup of Ethiopian Blend and leaned my back against the counter.

"So what's up with you?" She asked, sipping the coffee. "Any New Year's resolutions?"

I thought of Chuck and the failed spell this morning. "I'm on a bit of a self-improvement kick. Running with Fulk each morning. Practicing with my sword every day. Studying some…stuff with a mentor."

She nodded. "I enrolled in two courses at Towson this semester. I've been taking college on the ten-year plan, and I figured it was time to get things done, get a real job, and maybe eventually move into a bigger apartment."

I poured some caramel syrup and a dollop of cream into my coffee and stirred it. "What are you studying?"

"Biology. At first I had dreams of being a veterinarian, but then I realized by the time I was out of school I'd be forty. I'll probably end up a lab tech somewhere."

She didn't sound all that enthusiastic about the prospect. "If you could do anything in the world, what would you do?"

Brandi thought on that a moment, looking out the door with a pensive expression on her face.

"I really don't know. There's no job I can think of that sets my heart on fire. I just want something that pays decently, has regular hours and good benefits, something where I can occasionally chat with coworkers without getting yelled at. I want a job that doesn't suck the soul out of me."

"And when you get home?"

The pensive expression was replaced with a dreamy one. "Take off my shoes and my bra. Make plans with friends to go out. Watch TV. Game. LARP. Read comics. Hopefully find a cute guy who likes to do the same and marry him."

It sounded kind of boring to me, but I'm sure my life probably would be equally boring to her—well except for the demons, evil mages, vampires, and monsters part. That would probably scare the pants, or bra, right off Brandi.

"How about you?" she asked. "I mean, you've got this history degree, but you're here. Isn't there something you really want to do with your life? Either work, or in your free time?"

I'd refused to take my Oath of Knighthood for years now, left home and moved to Baltimore in an effort to figure out who I was and what I wanted from life outside of the Templar role I was born into. Ironic that here in this city I'd discovered myself, I'd found what really gave my life meaning was the very thing I was born to do. But my version of a Templar Knight was a bit different from what the Elders and our Order saw it to be.

"Fight the monsters. Protect Pilgrims on the Path. Safeguard the Temple and the artifacts that are held inside. Facilitate the dissemination of knowledge, both sacred and profane, that we've studied, collected, and catalogued for centuries."

"Always the paladin," she teased. "So your ideal life is LARPing and playing RPGs. Huh. We're not so different after all."

Brandi and I were both members of Zac's role-playing game. We met weekly, and next month would be my turn to host the group. I couldn't wait. Unlike my old apartment, my new place had ample street parking, no asshole land-lord, and no neighbors who made noise complaints every time I conducted a magical ritual or made out with Dario in the hallway. Plus if any of my gaming buddies had too many beers, I had an air mattress in the spare bedroom, and a comfy couch ready to accommodate an impromptu guest.

"Wouldn't it be nice if we really could LARP and play Anderon for a living?" She sighed.

"Yeah, until you roll a one and the demon you summon isn't Goetic and he marks your soul as his, then your best friend dies twice trying to rid you of the mark."

In real life, you couldn't just roll up a new character and rejoin the game. I felt a sharp twist in my chest as I thought about Raven. Russell, my necromancer friend, had tried several times in the last few months to contact her, but to no avail. She was gone. It was like she'd vanished from every plane of existence. I hoped that meant her soul was at rest, that she'd somehow been lifted up into heaven, but a knot of worry in my gut told me otherwise.

"Yeah, I guess you're right." Brandi sipped more coffee. "With my luck I'd be the dude in the red shirt that was victim number one of the dragon, demon, or whatever Big Bad we had to face."

Big Bad. It reminded me of the unknown horror the death mages had been trying to anesthetize with death magic, then soul magic. Chuck had been giving me little hints each month, but none of them were enough for me to have any idea what might be descending on Baltimore when the weather warmed a bit.

Brandi had been playing these games for far longer than I had, and although there were differences between the monsters in the players' manuals and the ones in the real world, there were also some shocking similarities. It made me wonder if the creators of these games had used research as much as their imagination.

"So what would be the worst Big Bad you'd ever want to encounter?" I asked. "Something that is pretty much immortal, that can be lulled into slumber by magic, but also by cold weather. Something that lives underground."

"Dragons."

I'd played with Brandi long enough to know she really had a thing about dragons. Not that I blamed her given how books and movies had been portraying them for the last century. I'd never personally encountered one, and from what I'd studied about them, I hoped I never did.

"Dragons mostly live in caves," I countered. And although there were a lot of dragons who didn't give two figs about weather, a few of them were definitely your typical reptiles in that they preferred warmer climates.

"Caves are underground," Brandi shot back.

She had a point. I made a mental note. "What besides dragons?"

"Undead. An army of wraiths or banshees or zombies or something."

That would totally suck, but outside of banshees, I think I could manage. Well…maybe. "Like how big of an army?"

Brandy waved the hand not holding the coffee. "Hundreds. Thousands. Everybody up and out of the grave."

"No one has the kind of magical power to raise that many dead," I told her.

"No one that you *know of.*" She tilted her head and gave me a side-eye.

I opened my mouth to argue, then thought. Russell had only been able to raise a couple dozen undead at a time, and he admitted he was a necromancer of middling talent. Would a high-level mage be able to raise hundreds? Would a truly powerful one be able to raise thousands? If so, why was he waiting to do so? What could trigger him to summon an undead army and attack a city? Did the Conclave that governed groups of mages know of any such necromancers? Would such a powerful person be off the grid, or someone even the Conclave was afraid of?

An undead army would definitely fall under the Big Bad heading, but a few things didn't make sense. Chuck had indicated that whatever it was had been contained and kept asleep by others, but that Fiore Noir had taken over the duties recently. If a powerful necromancer had been constantly thwarted for what I assumed to be centuries, then I'd think he'd either level up, or find something else to attack the city with.

"No. Not undead. A creature or a monster or something."

She shrugged. "Well, zombies *are* underground. Although I think they'd probably like cold better since they wouldn't decompose as fast. Unless it's an army of skeletons, then you're screwed at any time of year."

"It can't be undead, unless they're autonomous undead like a lich or ghoul. Think of something else." I mentally added lich and ghoul to my list, although I didn't think one lich or ghoul would be enough to warrant a group of death mages' attention. Plus neither liches nor ghouls liked hanging in packs. They were solitary creatures.

"A demon trapped inside a rock or something that's slowly degrading? A pissed-off demigod? Godzilla—which would be some sort of dinosaur that's been in stasis a gazillion years? Aliens that were cryogenically frozen, whose spaceship crashed here three thousand years ago, and due to global warming, they're thawing out?"

Wow. Brandi should be running her own games. The woman really had an amazing imagination. I'd made a list of potential Big Bads, but never thought to include frozen dinosaurs or aliens.

Dragon. What if it really was a dragon lulled to sleep over the centuries by some varying kind of magic? A dragon that would wake this spring, or earlier. But dragons were primarily in Europe, Asia, the Middle East, and Northern Africa, not in the Americas. They *were* territorial though. It was possible that a few thousand years ago one was forced to migrate here.

A dragon waking up after an abnormally long sleep would be hungry and grumpy. Plus if anyone had raided his treasures while he was dozing, he'd be more than grumpy. There was no way I could handle a dragon on my own. Even if Dario enlisted his *Balaj*, vampires wouldn't be much of a threat to a dragon. I'd need backup, especially since I wasn't about to resort to the techniques Chuck and his buddies in Fiore Noir had used.

If I needed help, I'm sure my family would assist, but the timing might mean some of them were unavailable. Right now, Mom and Dad were off on some Templar business in Italy. Roman and his wife were in France for the next two months with their family teaching at the Academy. Athena and her husband were available, but I hated to risk little Jet losing her parents before she'd even had a chance to really know them.

It wasn't like I could appeal to the Order. I mean, I *could*, but I doubted they'd provide any help. I'd not taken my Oath. I wasn't a Knight, thus they viewed me as a sort of child Templar who'd aged out of the system. Even if I *were* a Knight, I wasn't sure they'd help. I would need to phrase the request very carefully for the Elders to consider an attack on Baltimore to be something that required the Order's attention.

Brandi and I continued to talk about gaming. A grand total of three more customers came in between then and closing. We locked the door promptly at nine, cleaned the few things that hadn't been cleaned hours before, then went home.

The walk to work had been cold, but the walk home was worse. I clutched my coat snug around me, pulling my hat down farther over my face and ears. The wind grabbed my scarf and threatened to sweep it off and into the Patapsco River, so I knotted it again and tried to stuff it into the neckline of my coat.

A few blocks and I'd left the tourist area behind for a sort of no-man's-land area of Baltimore. During the day, this area was busy with people and commerce, but at night the streets were empty and the businesses shuttered. There was a shadowy feel about the place that made me grip my butter knife tight in my hand and wish I'd brought my sword with me. I'd gotten pretty good at the spell that concealed my huge sword from view, but it was still a pain having to find somewhere to stash it back in the storeroom while I was working. And pulling the scabbard straps around a bulky wool coat wasn't any picnic either. Maybe I was an idiot for leaving it at home, but I'd come to rely on my affiliation with the local vampire *Balaj* to keep any human gangs away. It irked me that the other vampires and their affiliates saw me as "The Boss's" property, but it *was* nice knowing I could walk pretty much any Baltimore street and remain unmolested.

In spite of the creepy horror-movie atmosphere, I made it home without incident. Stomping some frozen slush off my boots, I headed up my stairs only to stop abruptly when I saw the envelope on my poinsettia-print doormat. The wind hadn't blown it away. The light snow that had fallen a few hours earlier hadn't touched it. More amazing, no one had stolen it.

I reached down to pick it up, noticing the warm electric

feel I'd grown to recognize since I was practically in the cradle. A Templar blessing had safeguarded this note.

Eyeing my full name on the front I frowned. The handwriting wasn't one that I recognized. What Templar besides my family would be leaving a note on my doorstep?

Deciding this was a mystery best solved inside my warm home, I opened the door, shutting it tight against the cold as I took off my layers of outerwear and tried to avoid being knocked over by an excited dog, or tripped by the cat winding around my legs.

There was no way I could open this note and read it while my fur-babies were demanding my attention, so I set it aside and went about the nightly ritual of welcome with Gaia and Fulk.

It was a fairly brief ritual since both of them were hungry. Once I got them settled and happily munching on dinner, I returned to the note. With trepidation, I slid the card from the envelope and read.

Solaria Angelique Ainsworth – Elder Emmett Purcell requests an audience with you at your residence Tuesday at four to discuss your upcoming Knighthood ceremony.

Fuuuuuuuuck. And I really meant that word and not my dog's name, which was Fulk. Had my mother done this? Although she pestered the heck out of me to take my Oath, I couldn't see her stooping so low as to schedule the ceremony without my agreement. None of the others in my family seemed to care overmuch about my Knightless status, seeing it as a phase I was going through that would soon be over. I stared at the note, trying to decipher what was going on. Usually it was the prospective Knight that came to the elders to schedule their ceremony, not the opposite.

Feeling as if an anvil were about to drop on my head, I stuck the note back into the envelope and put it on my coffee table. I was pouring myself a big glass of cheap boxed wine when a knock at my door about gave me a heart attack.

It wasn't Tuesday and it wasn't four in the afternoon, but I still opened the door half expecting to see a stern-faced Elder Purcell standing there.

Instead of a Templar, the man at my door was a mage—a mage who hadn't returned my calls since that fateful Halloween night.

Reynard smiled that sexy, bad-boy smile that had made Raven fall in love with him, and I'll admit I wasn't exactly immune because instead of slamming the door in his face, I opened it wide and invited him in.

CHAPTER 2

"So what do you want?" I asked as Reynard sprawled on my couch.

The guy might be hot with a killer smile, but I wasn't stupid. He wouldn't show up out of the blue like this unless he needed something only I could provide. I knew he blamed me for Raven's death. Heck, I blamed myself for her death.

Trying to help me get rid of the demon mark was what had gotten her killed the first time, then assisting in the ritual to actually remove the mark is what got her killed the second time. Or got her spirit hauled across the veil somewhere. Again, I thought of Russell. He'd managed to contact her once on the other side. She was preoccupied with something, cutting off communication after a short, confusing message. He'd never been able to contact her again. He couldn't even locate her presence anywhere.

Reynard didn't know about me causing her first death. He, as well as everyone except a handful of people, had blamed the death mages for that. He definitely knew about the second one because he'd been there.

And when Balsur, the powerful sun demon who'd marked

me, had offered to restore Raven's physical body, give her life again, Reynard had jumped at the chance. I was pissed at him for being so willing to sacrifice me body and soul for Raven, but I understood. He loved her, and he harbored no such feelings toward me. It was an easy choice to make for a mage with the fluidity in his morals.

"I just wanted to see how you were doing. How was your Christmas?" Reynard asked.

It had actually been wonderful. Dario and I had exchanged gifts early since he wasn't able to leave the city to join me and my family in Middleburg. He'd given me a case of wine and two very nice "emergency beers," joking that he figured at the rate I was going through them, I might as well stock up. I'd treated him to dinner at a Haitian restaurant, which turned out to be not at all like the food on the island hundreds of years ago. But it had been fun, and the experience had prompted him to talk more about his life before he became a vampire.

That was probably the best Christmas present of all.

"You're not interested in my holiday celebrations, Reynard. Get to the point."

He smirked. "Not buying any of this are you, Aria?"

I rolled my eyes. "What gave you that idea?"

"Okay, okay." He put his hands up in surrender. "Come sit down. I've got something I want to propose."

I was pretty sure this proposal didn't involve a ring, so I sat in the chair across from him and waited. Before he could start, my cat and dog wandered in from the kitchen. It was then that I realized how odd it was that Fulk hadn't abandoned his food to come bark at the door and welcome our guest. The dog loved his food, but he never missed an opportunity to harass or greet anyone who knocked.

Where Gaia ignored Reynard and made her way to the

pillow in the corner, Fulk padded over to him, sniffed, then plopped down at his feet.

I frowned at the dog, remembering that Russell had said if Raven had been able to communicate through the veil by temporarily possessing the dog, it would leave an impression. Fulk wasn't all over Reynard, but he certainly acted as if he knew and trusted the mage.

"I'm willing to mentor you one-on-one and train you in magic," Reynard said.

A few months ago I would have jumped at that offer, but I already had a mentor, and as much of a pain as Chuck was, his experience was far more broad than Reynard's.

"Why?" I asked, deciding that was just as important as what he wanted in return.

"It's something I know you want."

I snorted. "What I want was to be part of a magical group. I notice that offer isn't on the table, so I'm assuming that this tutoring you're offering is going to be done in secret with you denying that you've been within five feet of me all year."

He ran a hand through his wavy blond hair. "Aria, you can't be part of Haul Du. You're a Templar. It's a conflict of interest. You can't take initiation vows with the order when you have prior, conflicting vows as a Templar."

When they'd discovered I was a Templar and kicked me out last year, that had infuriated me, but the last few months working with Chuck had made me realize Haul Du had been right. Whether I'd taken my Oath or not, I was still a Templar. There might be occasions when my mere presence would derail a ritual. There would be rituals I'd be unable to perform. And there would be rituals that I'd be duty-bound to sabotage. I had a higher calling, and never would be able to pledge myself to Haul Du the way they wanted.

I didn't need Reynard as a mentor, but there was something I might need from him in the future. He had taken over leadership of Haul Du when Dark Iron had "disappeared." There might be a time in the very near future when having the leader of a group of mages owe me a favor might be advantageous.

"If, and I do mean if, I agree to whatever the other part of your proposal is, then you owe me a favor."

His eyes narrowed. "I can't just blindly agree to some favor in the future. It needs to be specific."

This time I was the one that shrugged. "Take it or leave it. I figure if you drove to Baltimore from DC to visit someone you despise, then you're desperate. *How* desperate is the question."

"I don't despise you Aria." Reynard leaned forward, his elbows on his knees. "It's just...that whole thing Halloween. I'm ashamed of what I did. It was weak of me to even consider such a thing. I've worked with demons enough to know their ploys, but I still let one play me. That and whenever I see you, I'm reminded that Raven is gone forever. It's still an open wound for me. I loved her."

That was my Achilles' heel right there. He'd loved her, and I knew Raven had loved him. And it was my fault that she was dead.

But I wasn't about to let him see my weakness. And as much as Raven had loved him, I'd never fully trusted this guy.

"What do you want, Reynard. Better make this snappy because I've got somewhere to be."

"Two Haul Du members have been found dead in the last week."

It's a wonder there were any left at all since this seemed to be a regular occurrence lately. Most of them had died at the hands of Dark Iron, but a few had gotten themselves killed via demon. It was an occupational hazard in Haul Du —both death by demon and death by Dark Iron.

"People die. Can't see why that's my business."

I sounded horribly callous, but in all honesty, it *wasn't* my business. If they'd screwed up a magical ceremony, well that was on them. If they'd pissed someone off within the group, then that was on Reynard to fix as the leader. If they'd had a heart attack climbing the Metro stairs, or jogging to catch the bus, then maybe Haul Du should start hosting weekly aerobics classes.

They'd thrown me out. It was not my business.

"They were murdered."

Still not my business.

"Crime in DC really has gotten out of hand lately." Not that I was in any position to talk living in Baltimore.

"Murdered by another mage."

"You should get right on that then, as the leader of Haul Du." I glanced toward the clock, then toward the door.

"They weren't killed by another Haul Du member. Hellfire is back in town from Italy. Evidently he heard that Dark Iron had vanished."

Okay, that was somewhat interesting, but still not my business. "Who is Hellfire? And why would he want to kill these particular members of Haul Du?"

Reynard reached down and scratched Fulk on the head. "About ten years ago Dark Iron ousted Hellfire from Haul Du. He claimed Hellfire was performing activities that crossed the line into black magic."

A laugh burst out of me. First, a magical group that specialized in summoning demons, even Goetic demons, was pretty darned close to crossing that very fuzzy, vague line. Secondly, Dark Iron was hardly in a position to cast shade over black magic practices. I doubted the mage who'd bargained for use of a stolen soul trap and killed anyone he felt threatened his position had been different ten years ago.

Which made me think of something.

"So basically this Hellfire was a threat to him, right? Dark Iron was worried he'd be ousted?" I waited for Reynard's nod. "They why didn't Dark Iron just kill him?"

The look of shock on the mage's face was real. "Dark Iron could be a real ballbuster, and he was ruthless, but he wasn't a murderer."

I bit my tongue, letting that one slide by. I hadn't let Reynard know about Dark Iron's role in the murders of several Haul Du mages, or of his participation with the soul magic this fall—and I definitely hadn't told him about Dark Iron murdering Raven. All that information would just lead to questions that would in turn lead to suspicions of my involvement in Dark Iron's disappearance.

Murder, actually. I guess I shouldn't be throwing shade either.

"So this Hellfire is back from an extended vacation, and now that Dark Iron is gone, he wants reinstatement? Why is that a problem?"

"Because I'm not reinstating him," Reynard snapped. "He came with friends. He wants to take over control of Haul Du, and he's killed two of our members."

Ah, I understood now why Reynard were here after not speaking to me for months. He didn't have the power or charisma or both to hold Haul Du against this guy, and he wanted me to do…something or another to help him keep his position.

Fat chance. I didn't give one rat's ass who ran Haul Du. Not my business.

"Why would he go around killing off mages from the group he wants to lead? Doesn't seem like a good plan to me." I shrugged, knowing my nonchalance would piss Reynard off. "Are you sure they didn't die in a drive-by? Or screw up a summoning? Or off each other?"

"Hellfire had them murdered," Reynard snarled. "They

were strong supporters of Dark Iron. He's taking out powerful mages that might oppose him."

"Don't you guys vote on your leaders or something?" I asked. "Have a vote, then just deal with whoever, whatever the members want, whether that's you, or Hellfire, or Billy Jo Bob, or someone else."

"He's killed two of our members. He's going to take over by force." A muscle in Reynard's jaw twitched. "And I won't let him. I won't stand by while he turns our group into something like Fiore Noir. And I won't stand by while he kills off any mage that opposes him."

"And *you* want to make your temporary leadership of the group permanent." I gave him a hard stare. "This isn't about two dead mages or someone turning the group to black magic, this is about your ambitions, isn't it?"

For a brief second the mage appeared embarrassed, then his expression returned to the usual confident, sexy default. "I've been leading the group since Dark Iron vanished on us. I'm the better option over a mage who was ousted for dark practices. But this isn't just about my ambition, it's about the group. He *killed* two mages. And I'll be next on his list, no doubt."

I shouldn't care, but Raven was dead and she'd loved this man. Could I really sit here and refuse to help him when he'd just confessed he feared for his life?

He was a grown man, a mage. And he'd proven he wouldn't hesitate to toss me under the bus.

"So what does any of this have to do with me? What exactly do you want me to do?"

"Run security during Haul Du meetings. Track down Hellfire and his goons and get them out of DC."

There were a whole lot of problems with his proposal. "First off, I'm not a cop, a club bouncer, or a mafia hitman. I'm not tracking down some guy based on your claim that he's behind the deaths of two members of a group that kicked me out. And I've got no authority to kick him out of Washington, DC, or anywhere else. Secondly, you want security? Hire a rent-a-cop."

Reynard's eyes narrowed and I suddenly remembered he was more than just pretty-boy good looks. Not that I was worried. Even without my sword I could take him, or at the very least give as good as I got. He might have some additional magic on his side, but I had a few tricks of my own, and I knew I could physically out-fight him. Reynard was strong, but he hadn't spent as much time swinging a sword or jogging three miles every morning weighted down with a Kevlar vest and bits and pieces of steel armor.

"He's not good for Haul Du." Reynard hesitated, as though he realized I didn't give one flying fig about Haul Du. "And he's not good for DC."

"He's got plans for world domination, does he?" I tried to keep from laughing. "He'll start with Haul Du, take over DC, then the state, the country, and the world!"

The mage scowled. "I'm not exaggerating, Aria. I know you didn't like Dark Iron, but he was a good leader. He was strict about the group, but he also had rules about what we could say and do when it came to outsiders. We weren't allowed to summon demons or perform magic to harm others, or to break laws."

Of course Reynard didn't know that those rules hadn't applied to Dark Iron himself. Still, I held back from tossing him out the door and telling him not to come back. What if he was right? Baltimore was my town; the residents my pilgrims to protect, but could I sit here less than an hour away while people in DC suffered? While some crazy mage sicced demons on those who pissed him off, or whose bank accounts he wanted for his own?

But there was no proof that this Hellfire intended any of

that. There was no proof that he'd actually killed those two mages. There was no proof of any of this.

And ultimately, I didn't care who ran Haul Du. Not my business.

I walked over to the door and opened it. "No deal. Good luck with that whole Haul Du thing, Reynard. Have a nice life."

I guess I did hold a grudge about that whole willing-to-sacrifice-me-to-a-demon after all.

He stood and stalked to the door. "You'll regret this, Aria."

"There are a lot of things I regret in my life. This isn't one of them."

I slammed the door behind him, then I let Fulk out into the backyard to take care of business while I picked up my sword to practice.

What if Reynard was right and this Hellfire was some sort of horrible evil Sauron dude? What if he killed Reynard, unleashed demons on DC, started killing anyone who stood in his way? I'd been joking about the whole world domination thing, but now I was starting to worry.

Reynard wouldn't have come to me unless he had no other choice.

But if he was right, then what could I really do? I had minimal magic skills. I hadn't taken my Oath, so I didn't have the strength of the Order behind me, and I was pretty sure they wouldn't care about two mages duking it out for power in DC. I had sword skills, but while those worked well against vampires and other supernatural baddies, a sword, no matter how blessed, didn't protect me against bullets or magical spells.

And if they summoned demons... I could maybe handle one or two, but dozens?

My intervention in this whole thing might not make any more of a difference than me staying in Baltimore and praying. There might be the same death toll either way—maybe more if my presence meant the war was drawn out longer than it would have been if Reynard and this Hellfire just went at each other fast and hard.

The more I swung my sword, the more the muscles in my arms and torso ached, the more I felt that this issue in DC wasn't going to end up in unicorns, hugs, and roses—not that unicorns were all that sweet. They weren't particularly kind to virgins in the physical sense as legend would have it. From my research, unicorns were just as much the judgmental beings as angels were, only on a lesser scale. Whether you'd had sex or not was less important than what sin was in your heart and in your past.

But unicorns were the least of my worries. I was filled with anxiety over what kind of monster the death mages had been spelling to keep at bay, and there was a note on my table commanding me to meet with an Elder about the fact that I was the oldest Templar who'd not taken their Oath.

I lowered my sword, panting and dripping with sweat. Leaning it against the fireplace bricks, I went to the back door and let Fulk inside. Then I grabbed a a tall glass of water and headed upstairs for a shower.

CHAPTER 3

I was still mulling over whether I'd made the right decision in kicking Reynard out as I made my way to Dario's house.

We'd taken to alternating where we spent the night, and I'd discovered there were pluses and minuses to each option. My house meant we had uninterrupted time together—well except for Gaia and Fulk. My house also meant our time together tended to be rather short, and sometimes cancelled at the last minute. Upon awakening at sunset, Dario needed to feed. Then he needed to take care of *Balaj* matters. Frequently those *Balaj* matters meant he didn't arrive at my place until after midnight. Sometimes I got a few texts delaying. Sometimes I got an apologetic call cancelling.

Thankfully those hadn't come as often in the last month. Dario had proven his ability to hold the territory, albeit with some Templar help, and coordinated attacks from outside the city had stopped. His priorities had shifted from defense to building and consolidating relationships with the *Balaj*'s human crime partners, and evaluating their investments.

I climbed the steps to Dario's Federal Hill house and

instead of not-so-thinly-veiled hostility, I received a nod as the vampire on guard stepped aside to allow me to enter. That was a change as well. Taking out a master vampire had earned me quite a bit of respect among the *Balaj*. There had been holdouts but even those vampires changed their minds about me after I defended their innocence in the death of a Templar Knight, then fought with them to oust the mercenary vampire group who had been responsible for the murder. Some of them may never like me, but at least they were no longer openly hostile.

"Hey, James. Sleep well?" The vampire grinned as he bowed, a remnant of his human mannerisms from two hundred years ago. He'd shown up a week after we'd taken care of the mercenary group, frightened but hopeful that Dario would keep his word and bring him into the *Balaj* as a reward for turning on his former colleagues.

As if Dario would ever go against his word. James had once helped the *Balaj* when they'd been under Alban as a Master, and that debt alone would have bought James sanctuary even if he hadn't provided us with the vital information we needed to take down the mercenaries as well as the mage who'd hired them.

"The Boss is in the kitchen," James said, sweeping his arm as if I didn't know where the kitchen was by this time.

Dario's house was a gorgeous mix of historic architecture and modern, somewhat industrial furnishings and artwork. I loved it and I would have seriously considered moving in with him if it hadn't been for all the vampires.

The entire *Balaj* along with their blood partners and the family's Renfields came and went like the place was a well-furnished bus station. Actually, there wasn't a lot of leaving unless someone was heading out to patrol or had an assignment from Dario. Their reduced numbers meant there was no need to go trolling for random blood donors unless a vampire was hungry for something different. The *Balaj*'s list of regular donors—most of them junkies—was more than enough to provide for the family's blood needs.

I cut through the living room, weaving my way around the vampires sprawled in chairs and across the rug, greeting those who I was particularly friendly with. Four more vampires were in the dining room, playing Parcheesi while several humans chatted in the corner. I heard Dario's laugh and smiled as I followed the sound into the kitchen, where I forced the smile to remain on my face.

Opal was rinsing some sort of leafy greens and putting them in a pot of boiling water, swearing to Madeline on all that was unholy that the other woman was going to absolutely love whatever it was Opal was fixing. Balin stared at the greens, his face a mix of stoicism and horror. Madeline looked as if she were about to start a long walk to the gallows. Dario stood next to a can that looked as if it held bacon grease, amused by the whole thing. The reason for my sudden drop of mood was the human woman standing a little too close to him, fresh fang marks on her neck.

Erica. Lenora's former blood partner and the highest ranking human in the *Balaj*.

Idiot that I was, I couldn't help but be jealous of her relationship with Dario. I was his girlfriend. I was the one he had sex with. He held *me* as I drifted into sleep. I was the one he texted as soon as he awoke. I was the one who fought by his side, who he confided in. I was the one he loved. I shouldn't feel this twisted knot in my stomach every time I saw or thought about Erica.

She'd lost her vampire partner, the woman she loved. Dario took her blood and refreshed her mark to honor Leonora and Erica's status in the *Balaj*. That was the extent of their relationship.

But looking at the marks on her neck, I couldn't help but

remember what it felt like to have that vampire venom coursing through my veins like a drug, sending me into ecstasy. My only blood experiences had been painful and traumatic, blood rape by a vampire I eventually killed, but I still remembered the intensity of feeling that venom brought.

I wanted that with Dario, but I didn't want the physical dependence that came with it—the addiction. And although sometimes in bed I asked him to bite me, he always held off, wanting my consent to be during a moment of sober reflection and not in the heat of passion.

I didn't want to be Erica. I didn't want to be the highest ranking blood partner of a *Balaj*. I wanted more. I had more.

It wasn't just the addiction Dario's bite would bring that worried me. It would change our relationship. Blood partners were adored, protected, coddled. If the inevitable happened and a vampire slipped and took too much blood, Dario had mandated the partner would be turned. No more dead humans, he'd said. Those who were important enough to be beloved of one of the family should not suffer death at their hands. There were times I almost convinced myself that would be a good life for me.

But it wasn't the life I wanted. I was a Templar and as much as I'd chafed about taking my Oath, there was no escaping my need to serve my pilgrims. I did that far better alive and not addicted to vampire venom, no matter how seductive that life sounded.

"Hi Babe." Dario's eyes met mine and his smile deepened, turning my legs into jelly.

"Hi." I crossed the room and kissed him. It wasn't enough of a kiss to make it look like we were on the set of a porno, but enough of one that those watching—including Erica—knew what we shared.

"Want dinner, Aria?" Opal asked. "I'm making spinach. It's Mom's recipe."

"Run for it. Save yourself," Balan intoned drily.

I liked spinach, but our family mostly ate it raw in salad, or creamed as our vegetable side. I wasn't sure about boiled.

Opal must have seen the doubt in my face because she giggled. The woman had never left the '70s behind, continuing to wear tube tops or peasant blouses and psychedelic-colored tights or patched bell-bottom jeans with platform clogs. Her natural hair was either teased out into a perfectly round afro, or gathered into a poof on top of her head. Today it was the latter, a rhinestone studded pick stuck through the base of the poof.

"I'm just wilting it in the salt water," she told me. "Then I fry it up in bacon grease. Trust me, you're gonna love it."

"You sold me on bacon grease," I replied. "Virginia isn't exactly Deep South, but I grew up below the Mason-Dixon Line. Butter and bacon grease are staples in our kitchen."

"See?" Opal wrinkled her nose at Balan. "Aria approves."

"Yes, but this is the human who eats Fruit Loops out of the box," Madeline interjected.

I scowled at Dario and punched his chest playfully. "You told her that?"

He laughed, the sound rumbling through me. "I like to think I embrace the modern world, but calling hardened sugar 'breakfast' is something I will never understand."

Opal gave the spinach a quick stir before scooping a spoonful out and putting it onto a towel-covered plate. I watched her pat it dry and drop a piece into a frying pan of bacon grease. It sizzled, and a wonderful smell filled the air— at least I thought it was wonderful. It was clear that Balen and Madeline did not.

"How are the magic lessons going?" Dario asked, turning my attention from the spinach.

"The find-ownership spell was a complete bust," I told

him. "I think I should shift focus to something like deflect bullets."

"Need me to be the guinea pig?" Opal asked cheerfully. She'd helped out in the past when I'd needed to test spells on someone who wasn't easy to kill. The vampire was enthusiastic about the whole thing, reading spell books as I worked, and suggesting all sorts of modifications. She would be a perfect test subject. If I made a potion, I wouldn't need to worry about it poisoning her, and if the spell failed, a bullet wound wouldn't do more than cause her a minor, temporary injury.

"Maybe," I replied. "I won't be ready to test anything for weeks, and I'll need to clear it through Dario."

He shifted behind me and I got the feeling my borrowing Opal might be an issue. I wasn't sure why, since he'd readily volunteered her several times before. He'd always seemed happy to help me and give one of the *Balaj*'s youngest vampires something productive to do.

His arm slid from my waist to my hip. "We'll be back to try the spinach later," he announced. "I need to talk with Aria in private for a bit."

That had become his code for "Don't disturb us unless the house is burning down, and pretend as if you can't hear everything we're saying or doing."

Another disadvantage of Dario's home becoming *Balaj* central was that private time was never really private. I was pretty sure even with super sensitive vampire hearing, the others couldn't hear every word of our conversations, but I was willing to bet they knew exactly when we were getting it on. I hated that, even though everyone had been very circumspect about our disappearing upstairs for hours at a time.

I headed for the stairs, but Dario steered me to the living room, clearing it with a glance. I wasn't sure where all the vampires vanished to. They were probably all piled in the kitchen, pretending not to be listening in to what we were saying.

I turned in his arms, this time giving him a kiss that did belong in a porno. He gripped my rear, pulling me up against him. One hand roamed up my back to grip my hair, holding my head as he took over. I rocked myself against him, wet and ready to get naked and make love on the couch. Screw it if the others heard.

All too soon he broke the kiss, easing me away and leading me to the couch, where he pulled me down onto his lap.

"How was your day?" He nibbled on my ear after the whispered words and for a second I forgot all about the question.

Then my day came roaring back like a dash of cold water.

"Well, I found this on my doorstep this morning." I pulled the little embossed card out of my pocket and held it out.

He stared at it. "It smells like Templar. Not you or your family though."

"It's from an Order Elder. Elder Emmett Purcell to be exact." I shoved the card back into my pocket and leaned against him, resting my head on his shoulder.

"And what does this Elder want?" His voice rumbled in his chest, and his hand rubbed my back.

I felt so safe in his arms like this. I just wanted to stay here, to feel his arms around me, breath in his spicy cinnamon scent, feel the coolness of his skin against mine. I snuggled into him, feeling the sharp edges of the card in my pocket.

"He wants me to meet with him and set up a time to take my Oath." I sighed. "I figured it would eventually come to this. It's been years since I should have taken my vow. Evidently their patience has run out."

"What happens if you say no?" Dario asked.

I shrugged. "Honestly I don't know."

It's not like they could force me to take my Oath. I'm sure there would be repercussions though. Maybe even for my family.

I hated the thought of my family paying for my decision. I doubted the Order would reduce their stipend, but they could start giving them the shit jobs. And they could penalize my family for supporting me in any way. None of that really jived with what I knew of the Order though. I assumed they'd continue to pressure me while declaring me to be basically excommunicated.

We sat in silence for a while, Dario still rubbing my back.

"Penny for your thoughts," I murmured to him.

He held out his hand. I didn't actually have a penny, so I dug in my pocket and gave him a dog treat still in there from this morning.

He tossed it through the dining room and into the kitchen where it bounced off the back wall. No one said a word, although I was pretty sure the vampires noticed a dog treat whizzing like a bullet past them from the living room.

"I was thinking about you shoving that card up the sender's rear end," Dario commented dryly.

I smirked. "Ainsworths would never be so impolite."

He snorted at my response.

"Well, at least not to a Templar Elder," I amended.

"I take it that means you're going to meet with him?"

I nodded. What else could I do? I might not have taken my Oath, but I was still a Templar. I'd been brought up to respect the Elders, and refusing a request to meet would be very disrespectful. Added to that, my parents and siblings were all Knights. It wouldn't look good on our family for me to thumb my nose at the leaders of our Order.

I didn't really have a good reason *not* to meet with Elder

Emmett Purcell. I wasn't on bad terms with the Order or the Elders. I hadn't done anything to piss them off, and vice versa. My refusing to take my vow so far wasn't a snub as far as the Order was concerned. They just saw me as a little eccentric, a late bloomer. I was pretty sure the Elders didn't comprehend how someone might never take their vows. They most likely viewed my not-a-Knight state as temporary, and something that was my parents' problem, not theirs.

My parents hadn't called to give me any sort of heads-up, although they were out of the country at the moment. It wasn't just politeness that was driving my decision to accept the meeting request, it was also a large dose of curiosity.

Reaching into my pocket, I pulled the card out again, holding it as if the thing were going to give me cooties. The front had an embossed, crimson Templar cross, the back a swirled cursive that I was sure had been written with an expensive fountain pen.

"Four on Tuesday," Dario commented. "Is he going to demand you take your vow right then in your living room, or do you have time to think about it?"

"Taking the Oath usually involves a ceremony in front of witnesses, so I doubt he's going to corner me in the kitchen and knight me." I stuck the card back in my pocket. "I'll hear what he has to say, then probably stall until my parents get back and I can talk to them about it."

"I'm pretty sure I can guess what they're going to say," Dario drawled.

So could I. Mom made no bones about the fact that she wanted me to take my vow yesterday, and although Dad had been less vocal on the subject, I knew he agreed. We were Templars. This is what we did. This is what I was born to do. My destiny was as inevitable as death and taxes as far as my family was concerned.

I thought back to my visit during Thanksgiving. I'd chafed against giving my Oath to an Elder of the Order, but really the covenant was with God. And if they wanted me to take my Oath so badly, maybe I could bargain assistance against the Big Bad, just as I was doing with Haul Du. Having a group of mages at my back would be useful, but not nearly as useful as having the might of the Templar Order to support me in defending the city and my Pilgrims.

"This isn't the worst of my problems," I confessed. "Reynard showed up tonight before I came over."

Dario stiffened. "What does that jackass want?"

He'd made it clear what he thought of the mage, and hadn't understood why I'd bothered to reach out after the mage had thrown me under the demon-bus. I'd tried to explain that Reynard was my only connection to Raven, the only other person who I knew was suffering her loss just as much as I was. Eventually I'd realized he was right. It was better to mourn alone than try to be friends with someone who didn't care about me at all.

"Reynard wants my help with something."

Dario practically vibrated with anger. "Of course he does. That self-centered, shallow dick-for-brains never does anything unless it benefits him somehow. I know you loved your friend, but she had lousy taste in men."

I chuckled, once more thinking how amazing it was to be curled up in Dario's arms, on his lap, talking over all these things with him.

"It seems some old Haul Du member has returned and wants to take over the group. Allegedly he's killed two members in his quest for Haul Du's leadership position, Reynard wants my protection and for me to get the usurper out of town. In return he's offered to tutor me."

The vampire made a growling sound low in his voice. "Your *protection*? And what amounts to a hit on a mage? This is the kinda shit you go to a vampire *Balaj* for, not a Templar."

I wasn't thrilled about Dario reminding me of what he and his vampire family did as part of their business plan.

"He didn't come right out and tell me to put this guy six feet under, but he sure as heck implied that. Get him out of town included making sure he stayed out of town and was no longer a threat. And how that happened wasn't something Reynard was worried about."

"I really hate this guy." Dario gave me a rib-bruising squeeze. "He wants you to be his hired muscle and take out the competition, and as your reward you get the benefit of his somewhat questionable expertise? Please tell me you didn't agree to this."

"Dude…squishing the breath out of me here," I gasped.

"Sorry." Dario let up on the crushing grip and kissed the top of my head.

"No, I didn't agree to it. I threw him out and told him it wasn't my problem."

"Good girl."

"But… He said it's going to turn into a mage war with collateral damage. He said this guy was into dark magic, that Dark Iron threw him out years ago because of his questionable practices." I snorted. "Can you imagine how horrible this guy is for Dark Iron to consider his practices questionable?"

Dario buried his face in my hair. "He's lying. Reynard wants you to help him and he knows what buttons of yours to push to get that. I wouldn't be surprised if he didn't bring up Raven and wax poetic on how she would have wanted him running Haul Du."

"Now *that* I wouldn't have believed." Raven loved Reynard, but she knew his faults. She'd told me once that he wasn't a leader, that he'd never sacrifice his personal goals for others. Looking back, I knew that was true. He was happy to sacrifice me for a chance to bring Raven back, but I doubt he would have put his own soul on the line.

It made me mourn my friend even more. She *did* have shitty taste in men. I wished she was still alive so I could encourage her to dump his ass and date someone else instead.

Like Balen. Or Tremelay.

"I'm glad you told him no. And if you ever feel the need to stick your sword through him, I'll be there to help with the cleanup." Dario's arm tightened, this time gently. "Oath. Potential mage war. Unknown Big Bad. Disappointing results of your spell. Which one's keeping you awake at night?"

I sniffed. As if he didn't know. "All the others are an issue because I'm trying to get my ducks in a row for whatever is about to descend on us. If I take my Oath, will the Order send help? If I support Reynard, will Haul Du assist? Will I ever be able to cast some decent magic spells or have to fight this thing off with my sword and a butter knife?" I laughed, suddenly thinking of something. "Wouldn't it be ironic if I worried myself sick over this and the Big Bad turned out to be nothing and Fiore Noir was just killing people and harnessing the energy of their souls for their own gain?"

"And Chuck is just messing with you," Dario added.

I scowled, on a role. "Maybe the Big Bad is only a fluffy adorable bunny."

Dario chuckled. "I watched that movie with you where the cute bunny was a murderous monster. You shouldn't discount fluffy bunnies. Maybe it's a unicorn."

I shuddered. "I'd rather it be a murderous Monty Python bunny. Unicorns suck."

His hand stroked my hair. "Any idea on when this murderous bunny is going to descend on us? I know you said spring, but then Chuck was hinting if it was a warm winter…"

There was something tense about Dario's question so I shifted around to face him, straddling his lap. "He's still hinting it might come before spring. Why?"

"Timing is going to be a bit dicey and I just want to make sure I'm available to help you."

I tried to read him, but the vampire had that blank, poker-face expression that let me know I really wasn't going to like what he had to say. "And you might not be available because…?"

"Finally things are relatively stable in our territory. We've got an opportunity to expand the *Balaj*—and we desperately need to grow our numbers. We're at risk being so small in such a large city. Winning against the Philadelphia group and beating back those mercenaries has bought us time, but I don't know how long this peace is going to last."

I knew exactly what he was talking about. Yes, they'd picked up James from the mercenaries and brought him into the *Balaj*, but they'd need to turn as many humans as they could and make sure they had time for both the new vampire to gain control and some minimum of power, and for the sire to recover the significant amount of power it took to turn a new vampire. It was a balancing act. They needed to turn as many as they could, but not so many that they left the *Balaj* vulnerable due to the weakness of their strongest members.

"Why you?" I asked, although I could guess at the answer. "Why not let Madeline, Balen or one of the others turn someone while you protect your family?"

"First, this is my *Balaj*. Those who I turn will be especially loyal to me and I need that. Right now no one would dare challenge me, but in a few decades, when we're stronger, someone might. I need to build a group of those who I can completely depend on."

I nodded, although that hadn't worked so well for Aubin. Leonora, Dario and others of his own had turned against him in the end. I guess much like a child overthrowing a parent, the circumstances had to be dire for that to happen.

"Plus, as I've mentioned before, there's a hierarchy to these things. It's an honor to be the first turned under a new leader. *And* it's an honor to be turned by the leader."

Yep, I knew exactly where this was going.

Erica. Leonora's blood partner. I'd tried to forget that Dario had been taking blood from her, and renewing her mark. It drove me crazy, but I'd kept the jealousy bottled up inside. This was how the *Balaj* honored her as Leonora's beloved. And it was how Dario honored the Mistress he'd loved and served, even though their relationship had been far from smooth. She'd given her life for the *Balaj*, and Dario felt duty bound to make sure her blood partner was taken care of, that she was honored by having her blood taken only by their new leader, and that when the time came to turn new members, she'd be first in line.

And she'd be turned by the highest ranking vampire in the *Balaj*—Dario.

I had to trust him—trust that this was nothing more than respect for both the human and his former Mistress. Still, I hated the thought of her living in his house, giving her blood to him. I hated the thought of the intimate relationship that would develop between them when he turned her. Parent and child wasn't exactly the right descriptor, because although Dario was very paternal toward Bella, other vampires seemed to have a different sort of closeness to those they'd sired.

But that was my problem, not his. This was who he was, and although I always made it clear when his responsibilities and duties didn't sit right with me, ultimately I had to either love him as he was, or break things off.

And I was too far gone to break things off.

"Will I be able to see you during the process?" I should have been asking how long it took, when he'd be able to help his *Balaj* if needed, to help me if needed, to resume the happy routine we'd fallen into of sleepovers, dinners out, and the occasional evening with friends. But I was in love with this guy, and the most important thing to me was that I wouldn't need to go months without seeing him.

"Not the first week. It wouldn't be safe." He ran his hands up my waist to rest under my breasts. "I'll be out of it. She'll be dead. There will be a lot of blood. I don't…I really don't want you to see me like that, Aria."

His hands cupped me, his fingers spanning my breasts and brushing against my nipples. I leaned into his touch.

"When then?" I hated the thought of Erica coming to life as a vampire and opening her eyes to see Dario with her. I wasn't sure what happened at that point. Did she drink from him? Him from her? Did they share a blood donor? Did they share more than that?

Trust. We'd agreed on emotional fidelity as well as sexual fidelity. If I couldn't trust Dario to keep that promise, then I had no business being with him.

"I will have Opal come to get you as soon as I'm ready," he promised.

That wasn't good enough. "When? Two weeks? Four weeks? Two months?" I pressed my palms on his shoulders and rocked my hips against him.

Dario sucked in a breath, his eyes darkening as his pupils dilated. "I want to say two weeks, but there's no real formula to these things. Sometimes it takes longer, and I owe it to Leonora to make sure this goes right."

I nodded. This was one of the traits I loved in Dario. He

cared so deeply. When he loved someone—either as a friend, a family member, or a partner—he put every ounce of his being into supporting that person. And if something happened where he couldn't be there, then he was honest and up front about it.

"I'll be waiting for you." I leaned in to kiss him, pulling away just as he started to take charge. "But when are you scheduling this event? Can we go out to dinner first? Celebrate?"

I had an idea brewing in my mind. I was going to make sure while he was in a coffin, or whatever, with Erica that his thoughts were one hundred percent on me.

"Absolutely." He tried to pull me against him, but I resisted. Which basically meant he let me resist. With his vampire strength, if he wanted to hold me tight, there wasn't much I could do other than start throwing my Templar powers around which wouldn't end well for either of us.

"This bothers me. You know that, right?"

He lifted one hand to my face and cupped my cheek. "I know. There are things you do that bother me. You're still in that role-playing game with the man you dated, and I know he still has feelings for you and that you find him attractive. You're a Templar, and I worry that there might be a time when your duties and mine are at cross-purposes. I worry that you may find my responsibilities as leader of the *Balaj* to be more than you want to deal with, that my being a vampire will eventually spell the end of our relationship. I worry that I'll never get the chance to taste your blood, that you'll refuse to allow me to turn you and that one day I'll have to watch you die and be lost to me forever."

That was far more than Dario had ever confessed to me before. He'd let me see how much he cared, how much he not just wanted, but loved me. But he'd never told me with such emotion the things he feared.

And now that I'd heard them, I realized they were pretty much the same things I feared.

I leaned forward. "I trust that there's nothing between you and Erica, and I promise to support you and your *Balaj* whenever you feel the time is right to turn her."

He closed the distance between us, kissing me lightly. "Let's go upstairs," he suggested against my lips.

I heard a laugh from the kitchen, then Opal called out that the fried greens were ready.

"I've got a better idea," I told him. "Let's go to my house instead."

Dario drove my car, practically squealing the brakes as he pulled up to the curb. We raced up the stairs, barely paused to greet Fulk and Gaia, then ran up to my bedroom.

I'd barely stepped foot into the room when he'd spun me around, pushing me against the wall and kissing me with a desperate hunger as he tried to undo my jeans.

"Let me." I laughed and pushed him away, worried that he was going to rip the things in his haste.

"Strip show. I like this."

I slowly unzipped my pants, easing them over my hips and wiggling to make them drop to the floor. With equal care I unbuttoned my shirt, continuing to shimmy in time to some silent music.

"A little faster," Dario complained.

I stopped, pouting a bit, then slid the shirt off my shoulders and down my arms with agonizing slowness.

"I'm gonna make you pay for this, you know," he growled.

"Really?" I hooked my thumbs on my cotton underwear, wishing I'd thought to wear the sexy ones instead. I didn't think Dario cared from the way he eyed me as I pushed them down one inch at a time.

"Time's up." He stepped toward me and I squealed, rushing to pull off my bra.

I barely gotten it off before he pushed me back onto the bed. Bending forward, he traced the various scars across my chest with his mouth, drifting to my left breast, fastening his lips on the nipple and sucking hard. I squirmed with the intense sensation, but his hands came up to my waist, holding me still.

"I want you," I rasped out, but he ignored me, bringing his hand to my other breast, flicking my nipple in rhythm with his mouth on the other side.

I moaned, deciding to stop trying to rush and just enjoy the ride. He scraped his fangs against my sensitive bud, and I felt the tightness coiling between my legs.

Just when I thought I was about to come, he stood, yanking off his pants and pulling his own shirt over his head. Scooting back over top of me, his hands slid between my rear and the sheets, gripping me as he positioned himself at my entrance. His eyes met mine, and I reached out to touch the cool skin of his cheek.

He tilted his hips forward, barely entering me. With one smooth motion, he pushed all the way in as he leaned down to claim my lips with his own. As he moved, increasing his rhythm, I felt my pleasure begin to build. Reaching around him to dig my nails into his ass, I gave in to the orgasm that rolled over me, shuddering and gasping as I came. Dario's thrusts grew erratic, and his mouth left mine. He buried his face into my neck and I felt the scrape of fangs, the pinch of sharp teeth almost breaking my skin as he thrust one last time, his muscles tight.

Then he relaxed against me, kissing my neck and whispering something I couldn't hear against my skin.

"I love you," I told him.

Pushing himself upright and rolling to the side, he looked down at me. "I love you too."

"Love me enough for a second round," I teased, knowing how quickly he recovered.

"Absolutely." His fingers lightly followed sensitive skin from under my arm down to my wrist, then he yanked his hand away.

I jerked in surprise then glanced down at the Templar tattoo on my wrist. "Sorry."

The ink had been sanctified and the artist a Templar who'd blessed the artwork as he injected the ink into my skin. At the time I'd thought it just another symbol of my faith, my birthright, my destiny, but the tattoo had some magical properties. It burned the undead. Dario had always been careful not to touch it beyond that one time he'd intentionally gripped my wrist to make a point, but as we'd gotten familiar with each other's bodies, he'd clearly let the fact that I had what amounted to a branding iron on my wrist slip his mind.

"Does that always burn you?" I asked.

He shook his head. "No, but I'm very aware of it on your skin. It's not a problem." He grinned. "There's plenty of non-sanctified skin for me to concentrate on instead."

As if to prove his point, Dario ran his fingers down my waist with a light, feathery touch that was almost ticklish. I felt him rise and twitch, his cock brushing against my thigh, and I grinned. Round two, here we come.

* * *

AFTERWARD DARIO LAY BESIDE ME, his eyes closed even though I knew he wasn't asleep. I traced the crucifix scar on his chest that I'd inflicted months ago, not knowing it was him in the room and panicked that a vampire was trying to attack me in the dark. There were other marks I'd made during that fight as well, but this was the most defined.

He'd teased me that it was a brand, that I was his, that it was a mark of Templar ownership forever on his body. My tattoo didn't leave a lasting mark when it burned his fingers, but *this* had.

And the symbol I'd drawn on my neck in clear nail polish had killed a powerful Master vampire. Magic had its uses, but Chuck was right—I shouldn't discount my Templar gifts.

Placing my hand on his chest, I snuggled against him and closed my eyes. A Templar and a vampire. We were an odd pair that probably shouldn't be in love. But I guess there was a first time for everything.

CHAPTER 4

I was getting used to waking up alone.

I mean, I'd spent years waking up alone, but the few times I'd had a boyfriend, this didn't tend to be the norm. At first it had bothered me that Dario was gone when I awoke, but honestly it was bothering me less and less. Now that it was winter, there had been times when I'd actually been able to rise with him, sometimes even having that amazing sleepy morning sex and sharing a cup of coffee before he'd had to head off to his daytime shelter. Lately he'd needed to head out between seven and seven thirty. Days that I opened, that meant we got up together. Days I worked afternoons or evenings, he let me sleep in.

This morning I'd awoken hearing the faint snick of the front door closing. A few seconds later, Fulk bounded up the stairs and jumped onto my bed, drooling on my face as he stood over me.

"Seriously?" I eyed the alarm clock. "Give me another hour, Fulk. Just one more hour."

The dog bounced off the bed and just as I felt myself beginning to drift off he was back, dangling a leash on my forehead. I heard Gaia meow, then the rumble of her purr as she shoved Fulk aside and butted her head against my chin.

"Okay, okay." I scooted my four-legged family members aside and crawled out of bed, shivering as I threw on my leggings, a sports bra, and a long-sleeved lycra shirt. The old boiler in the basement hadn't been doing the best job of keeping up with the cold, but this morning seemed chillier than usual. Rubbing my arms, I checked the thermostat in the hallway. I'd set it for sixty-five degrees, but in spite of that, the temperature read fifty-eight.

Ugh. Reaching down I put my hand near the vent and felt the cool air pouring out. It was below freezing outside. This was better than nothing, but clearly this heating system was on its last legs. I'd need to call the property management company later this morning once they opened. They'd been responsive when I'd needed a repair in the past, and I was confident that one call would get me a repair today or at least some heaters to help out until whatever part they needed came in.

My pets were glued to my side, nearly tripping me as we all headed down the stairs. I poured Gaia some food, then sat down on the couch to lace up my running shoes. Fulk glanced at the bowl of cat kibble and whined, but he knew that his food would need to wait until after we were done with our morning run.

Once my sneakers were on, I strapped on the Kevlar vest that Detective Tremelay had given me, then slapped on some armor elbows and knees before tossing an oversized jacket I'd picked up at Goodwill over the whole lot. A hat and some gloves later, and Fulk and I were out the door, our breath clouds of steam as we jogged down the empty street.

The weather this year had been typical Maryland according to my coworkers at the coffee shop. Sixty degrees one week. Forty the next and ten the next. There would be weird days of warmth followed by icy weather where the wind off the river made me feel as if I were in the arctic.

One mile in and I didn't feel as if I were in the arctic. Sweat wetted the hair at the nape of my neck, rolled down between my breasts, and dampened my gloves. I pushed my hat off my forehead and peeled the gloves off, sticking them into my pockets. Fulk kept pace beside me, his tail wagging and his tongue protruding as he panted happily. My dog was solid muscle, a bull terrier who, in spite of his short hair, could handle any temperature Baltimore threw at him.

Two more miles and I was regretting my expanded running routine. I'd started out at three miles, but now I was up to six and adding weight to my run each week, in an attempt to improve both my cardio fitness and my strength. My legs were killing me. I was sweating like I was in a sauna and unzipped my coat in an effort to cool down. The vest felt like I had a wall of bricks plastered to my chest and back, and my breath burned in my lungs. Still, I persevered, the thought of coffee and breakfast keeping my feet moving at a steady pace. My watch beeped the turnaround and I dropped down to a fast walk, pushing the button to mark the mile before I headed back home.

Something whizzed past me and instinct kicked in. I spun and went to drop to the ground, but was too slow. The bullets felt like I'd taken two blows to the chest from King Kong. I struggled to inhale, pain turning my vision white as I felt my body hit the sidewalk.

Fulk snarled and yanked free, tearing across the road with the leash bouncing behind him. I couldn't gather the breath to call after him, but I did manage to roll myself behind a parked car as another bullet hit the sidewalk where I'd just been.

More shots. I fought through the pain in my chest and got to my knees so I could pull my sword from the scabbard. Not that it would do much good against bullets, but if this son of a bitch hurt my dog, I was going to slice him to bits before I allowed myself to bleed out on the pavement.

With an agonizing inhale, I got to my feet and ran across the empty street, heading for the sound of Fulk's angry barking. A light came on in one of the row houses as I squeezed down the narrow space between it and the one next door. The dirt pathway led past the backyards and into a rear alley that allowed residents access to parking spots and dilapidated garages. As I staggered down the alley, I realized there was no more gunfire, and that Fulk's deafening barks meant if he was hurt, it wasn't bad.

My dog was at the end of the alley, jumping at a tall wooden privacy fence.

"Hey boy." I knelt down beside him, keeping my sword handy just in case. Fulk had a bloody streak along his shoulder. The wound wasn't serious, and I couldn't tell if it was a graze from a bullet or if he'd cut himself on something, but it didn't look deep enough to require stitches. His muzzle was also red, as were his teeth, but I was pretty sure that blood wasn't his.

"Good boy. Good boy." I patted him, grabbed his leash and stood, eyeing the scrapes on the gray of the weathered fence. Some of them were clearly Fulk's claws as he tried to go over. The others looked like boot scrapes.

Whoever had shot at me, Fulk had got to him before he'd had a chance to reload. The guy had taken off, no doubt worried that the noise of gunfire and barking dog would bring any residents out to investigate or make them dial 9-1-1.

I headed back the way I came, stopping in the narrow passageway to pick up the brass casings. They went into my pocket to examine later. I'd turn one or two over to Tremelay when I filed a report, and the rest I'd use myself. That ownership spell had been a dismal failure yesterday, but maybe this time I'd get lucky and be able to identify my attempted assassin before he, or she, managed to kill either me or my dog.

So much for early morning jogging. I leaned against a car to catch my breath, dreading the three mile walk to get home. By the time I got there I'd need to shower and get into work. There wouldn't be any time to call Tremelay and file a report or to do any magic work until after my shift ended—unless I could manage to squeak in a quick call to the detective during my break.

"You okay?"

I glanced over at the row house with the light on and saw an elderly man peeking through a partially open door.

"Yeah." I smiled over at him. "Thanks for checking on me."

"Wasn't gonna." He shook his head. "You hear gunshots around this neighborhood you're better off hiding in the kitchen, but then I heard that dog barking and figured I should look. I'd be real upset if a dog got shot."

But less upset if a human got shot. Not that I blamed him. In this neighborhood most of the humans that got shot were participating in a risk-filled and illegal profession.

"Fulk's okay too." I reached down and patted my bull terrier.

The man blinked. "Glad to hear it. You and your dog Fuck be safe now, you hear?"

I didn't correct him. Instead I told him to have a nice day and began the long walk home, making sure I took a different way and stayed alert.

CHAPTER 5

I had a lot of time to think as I walked the three miles home. I had assumed the vest Tremelay had given me had once belonged to his wife since it was clearly sized for a woman. That meant it was probably around five to seven years old. My Templar training was mostly in archaic weapons and not modern warfare, but I had done a good bit of shooting growing up in Virginia, and I'd been interested enough in ballistics to have learned more than the average citizen.

The bullet casings in my pocket were nine millimeter. That and a forty-five seemed to be the go-to pistols from what I'd gleaned from hearing Tremelay talk about crime in the city. The vest was Kevlar with panels that had thin metal plates for added protection. It wasn't exactly lightweight, but it wasn't SWAT-team or military issue either. If I'd had to guess, I'd probably put it at Level II, which meant I was very lucky I wasn't lying dead on the sidewalk or in serious medical trouble. If the shooter had used a different bullet, or a rifle, I'd probably be dead, or dealing with internal injuries at the very least, instead of just some painful bruises.

The shooter had been in the passageway across the street from me. I'd been the only one on the street that early in the morning. Had I really been the intended target? I doubted this was a case of mistaken identity, since I ran this route every morning and hadn't ever seen another person out and about. Maybe this was some sort of gang initiation rite and I'd just been a convenient target, because I couldn't imagine someone would want me dead.

Well, I *could* imagine a few people who'd want me dead. Most of those people would probably think twice for two reasons. One, I was a Templar and even though I wasn't a Knight, the Order would still not look kindly upon my murder, and my family definitely would descend on Baltimore like a pack of Valkyries to avenge me. Two, Dario had made it very well known that anyone who messed with me, either vampire or human "business" partner, would face a very drawn out and gruesome death.

But I'd potentially pissed off a few people who wouldn't be deterred by angry Templars or vampires. Some of the Fiore Noir mages, for example. Then there was that mage from Argentina who hopefully hadn't found out I'd disabled his extremely valuable soul trap.

And if anyone had found out I'd killed Dark Iron… I'm sure he had friends who might want to avenge his death. I couldn't imagine the guy having friends, but even the worst of humanity had people who loved them.

My mind flicked back to Reynard's visit. He'd said I'd regret saying no to him, but killing me wouldn't exactly help his cause. Plus I didn't see Reynard as the type to hire a hitman just because I refused to help him.

Maybe this had nothing at all to do with me?

If it *were* an assassination attempt, then why use a handgun and not a sniper rifle from a rooftop? Unless the killer *was* worried about angry Templars and a vampire boyfriend and wanted to make it look like I got killed in a random drive-by, or got caught in the crossfire of a gang fight. It's not like that would be a stretch in this section of Baltimore where these neighborhoods saw regular violence.

The last mile my thoughts blurred as my adrenaline wore off and pain and fatigue set in.

Great. I had to work a long shift today and I felt as if someone had whaled on me with a baseball bat. Fear crept around the edges of the steady ache in my chest and stomach. Had someone really wanted me dead? And here I'd gone running off after them with nothing but a sword as a weapon and my vest for defense. Against a gun. Once again I thought about how useful it would be to have an amulet that would deflect bullets. The vest didn't cover my entire body, and after being hit with two bullets, I wouldn't want to rely on its continued effectiveness.

Could I afford a new vest? My birthday wasn't for a few months, but if I was going to be shot at, maybe I should consider dipping into the account my parents had been making regular deposits to. It seemed like the best solution to what was most likely an immediate problem. It would be beyond foolish to go around without any sort of protection while I saved money for a new vest, or tried to figure out a spell that actually worked.

I'd get a new vest. And in the meantime, this one was better than nothing. I'd also need to curtail my morning runs, or at least vary my route. Would the shooter try to take me out on the way to work?

I shoved down the sudden panic, and tried to concentrate on my breathing. Only a few more blocks to my house. Then I'd get a hot shower and call Tremelay on my way to work. Hopefully he'd have some good ideas on how I could protect myself. Hopefully he'd quickly apprehend the guy. Hopefully this whole thing had nothing to do with me, and I'd just been in the wrong place at the wrong time.

As I rounded the corner to my house, I was surprised to see an old woman dragging a black suitcase up the cracked sidewalk. Elderly homeless weren't exactly a rare sight in this neighborhood, but this woman's black wool coat was fairly new and clean, and the babushka around her hair looked to be Burberry. She was hunched over, cursing up a blue streak as she hauled the suitcase along.

Even if I hadn't recognized the Burberry scarf my sister had given her for Christmas, I would have still known her from the curse words filling the cold silent morning air.

My great grandmother Essie. Although what she was doing dragging a suitcase down a Baltimore sidewalk was beyond me.

"Gran! Hold up." I slowly and painfully jogged up to her, taking the suitcase from her hand as she stooped to pat Fulk and receive his doggie kisses on her gloved hands.

"What happened to your pup?" She exclaimed as she ran a gloved hand over the cut on his side. "Poor boy! Did he hurt himself? And he's got blood on his mouth. Did you kill a rat, sweetie? Oooo, my good boy killed a rat, didn't he?"

I normally didn't like to lie to Essie, but I really didn't want her to know I'd been shot. And I *really* didn't want my parents to know I'd been shot at. I might be twenty-six, but if any of my family got wind of this morning's events, I'd be home in Middleburg faster than I could draw my sword.

"Yes, Fulk is quite the rat killer." I shifted the suitcase to my other hand and walked beside her as she marched onward. "What are you doing here, Gran?"

The suitcase felt like it weighed a thousand pounds. I was glad we weren't far from my house because I was in no condition to be lugging this thing down the street. Actually, Essie wasn't in any condition to be lugging this thing down the street either. I couldn't figure out why my elderly relative was two blocks from my house in the early morning hours. She lived with my parents in Middleburg, although I wasn't sure whether they would have left her there in our palatial mansion with servants to assist while they were out of town, or if they would have sent her to Athena or Roman.

"Since when do I need an excuse to visit one of my great grandchildren?" she demanded.

I totally didn't buy it. A few of my relatives had shown up unannounced, but that hadn't been the norm for me or for any of my family.

"It's early in the morning—a freezing cold morning in January. I know you know how to text and use your cell phone. Why didn't you call me first? What if I'd been working early and hadn't been home?"

She shrugged, bending to give Fulk another pat and continuing toward my house. "I wanted to surprise you. If you hadn't been home I would have broken into your house, or maybe gone and visited one of your neighbors until you got home. Neighbors are always friendly to a little old lady."

One more block. One more block, then up a few steps, *then* I could sit down and relax before attempting a shower. Did I have some aspirin in the bathroom? How many could I take before I suffered liver damage, because I had a feeling this was more than a two-pill kind of injury.

Wait. How the heck did Essie get here? "Did you walk here from Middleburg or something?" I asked my great grandmother.

She snorted. "Maybe I flew."

I eyed her. "And walked here from BWI? Or did you mean you flew on a broom or that you sprouted wings or something?"

I hefted the suitcase, only managing to raise it a few

inches off the ground before regretting the motion. "How long have you been walking with this thing?"

"Since I left. And I'm here because I need to be here. When you're as old as I am, you learn to pay attention to intuition. Besides, I've been at Athena's house at least six times in the last five years. It's time for me to visit you."

I tried to catch my breath, blaming my exhaustion on being shot and not the stupidly heavy suitcase I was dragging down the street. My great grandmother had some magical skills which seemed to have been handed down through the generations of her Hungarian family, but still she was by my estimation well over a hundred years old. She might be sharp as a tack, salty as a sailor, and able to pound a tennis serve like Venus Williams, but she was still an elderly woman who I viewed as fragile—and more valuable than any antiquity or manuscript in my father's vault.

Most people never really knew their grandmothers, let alone their great grandmothers. Essie was my Yoda. Everyone else saw her as an eccentric, slightly scary, wise woman. I saw her as something more. Which is why I was actually happy she was here for a visit.

I dragged her suitcase up my steps and unlocked my front door, ushering her inside. "Gran, why are you here? Seriously. I'm thrilled that you would want to visit me, but why now? Why with no notice? Do Mom and Dad know you're staying with me? Because I didn't get any heads-up that you'd be hanging out in my spare bedroom which has nothing but an inflatable camping bed."

Essie snorted. "I've slept on worse. Straw mattresses. Blankets on piles of dung. Frost covered ground. Homeless in this century have it better than they did in the old days."

I unsnapped Fulk's leash and grabbed a paper towel, wiping the blood off his muzzle then heading into the kitchen. "Gran, I'm not about to let you sleep on a blanket over dung. I just want to know what's up, and who I need to call about your whereabouts."

Essie followed me into the kitchen, watching as I put the paper towel in a plastic bag to give to Tremelay, then dug a bag of dog food out from a cabinet.

"Why is it so cold in here? Don't you have heat? Aria, are you out of money? I know how you feel about taking money from your parents, but I can loan you some if you need to pay the electric bill or buy some firewood or something."

"The furnace is acting up." Crap. One more thing I needed to do. Call Tremelay. Call the property management company. Figure out a spell to make myself bullet proof, then perform the spell that had failed yesterday on the bullet casings and hope it worked this time.

I realized that Essie had neatly avoided my question. I poured some kibble into Fulk's bowl, pushing Gaia aside when she insisted that she hadn't been fed. "You're welcome to stay Gran, but I'm not really set up for guests. There's no real bed. No actual bedroom furniture. I'm happy to host you until my parents get home, but I don't have much to offer you. Maybe it's best that you go stay with Athena. Or with Roman."

"Nope. I'm here and I'm not leaving." She looked around the kitchen. "Is that air mattress blown up? I'm thinking I might need a bit of a nap or something. The trip here wore me out. I'm not as young as I used to be, you know."

"Yes, but it probably needs a bit more air." I sighed and went back into the living room. Grabbing her insanely heavy suitcase, I began to wrestle it up the stairs, wishing I could take the day off work and nap myself—preferably after taking some of the leftover narcotics from the last time I'd visited the ER.

Thankfully I'd been too lazy to deflate the air mattress from when my mom had been here a few months ago, so all I had to do was top off the air so it wasn't too squishy, then wrestle a fitted sheet over it. Gran was out of her clothes and in an oversized T-shirt that read "I've got the perfect body—in my freezer" by the time I got back with sheets and blankets.

"I hate getting old," she complained as she helped me arrange the bedding. "It's just ridiculous that I haven't died yet. Did I tell you it took me thirty minutes to pick a piece of paper off the floor the other day? This body doesn't work like it used to. Damn near thought I was going to end up toppling over onto the ground and having to push that beeper-necklace your father gave me last year."

"You still have the beeper, right?" I envisioned her falling down the stairs while I was at work.

"I think it's in my suitcase somewhere." She sighed. "I know. I know. I promise I'll put it on once I get done with my nap."

After I got her all settled in, I finally went to take my shower, carefully shedding clothing as I went. The oversized Goodwill parka had two holes in it and was torn where I'd slid along the sidewalk. I didn't bother looking too closely at the vest, because the moment I removed it I saw blood on my T-shirt.

"No, no, no," I chanted as I stripped and looked in the mirror. Thankfully I was not perforated by a bullet hole, but there was a horrible bruise on my left breast and another on my abdomen. The one on my stomach was also decorated with a round mark where the force of the bullet had abraded my skin enough for it to bleed. I took a fast shower, opting for dry shampoo rather than spend time I didn't have drying my long dark hair. Once done, I cleaned up the abrasion, dressed, and downed a few over-the-counter pain relievers.

Then I took a first aid kit downstairs to take care of Fulk, and called my sister.

"Athena, Gran is here." I glanced up at the ceiling, hearing a thump and what was clearly a curse word in another language.

"In Baltimore?" Athena let out a curse word, but hers was in English. "She went up to bed last night, then was nowhere to be found this morning. I called the police. There's a Silver Alert. They even brought in some search dogs to try to track her."

"Search dogs?" It was a huge mystery to me how Essie had gotten from my sister's home to mine. She clearly hadn't walked the whole way. Bus? Hitchhiking? Maybe she took an Uber. I could absolutely see her installing the app on her cell phone and using Dad's credit card number. He'd be surprised when he got his statement and saw the three-figure Uber bill. Or maybe not. He'd had more time to accept his grandmother's oddness than I had. Nothing about her probably surprised him at this point.

"Yes, search dogs—although they were of no use whatsoever. Essie must have spelled her stuff, because every time we got something for them to sniff, they backed away terrified. I'm talking howling, peeing on the ground, whites-of-eyes terrified."

I stifled a laugh, wanting to know that spell. Good for Essie. Hmm, maybe I was more like her than I wanted to admit.

"Anyway we've been looking everywhere," Athena continued. "Jet missed her Templar Tots lesson this morning because I was driving around all the strip clubs, liquor stores, and massage parlors."

Knowing Gran, those were good places to look. "Did you let Mom and Dad know?"

"Are you kidding me? I'm not telling Mom I lost Gran. Besides, they're in Italy. It's not like they could do anything to help find her."

I winced, thinking that she was right. Somehow Mom and Dad managed to keep Gran occupied and happy, but when they went away she had a history of going off and doing crazy, dangerous things. We all remembered the last time my parents had left her alone only to return and discover that Essie was in the Amazon Jungle, sweating it out with some natives who thankfully regarded her as an honorable wise-woman and were treating her as if she were a goddess. No doubt that's why Athena had been tasked with taking care of her this time.

"Well, she's here. How long are Mom and Dad supposed to be gone?" I knew they'd be back by Easter since I'd been already told I was to appear for a family dinner, but beyond that I had no idea.

"Four to six weeks." Athena laughed. "Have fun with Gran! I'd say to make sure she takes her meds, but it's always hit or miss with her. Oh, and she's been insisting she needs medical marijuana lately, so be ready for that."

My sister hung up. The marijuana didn't bother me, and honestly under any other circumstances I would have loved having Gran visit. But four to six weeks? And me being shot at while jogging this morning? What if the weather warmed up and this Big Bad popped out of the woodwork? Admittedly my great grandmother had a lot up her sleeve, and I had no doubt that in her day she had been a formidable witch, but she *was* well over a hundred and far more fragile than she appeared.

I eventually decided she'd be safe for now, napping upstairs while I was at work. When I got home I'd give Roman a call and see if he wouldn't come pick her up to relocate her to his own house. Maybe he could bribe her with something fun like theater tickets.

I was going to be late if I waited any longer, so I headed out, opting to drive and fork out the outrageous parking fees at the Inner Harbor rather than walk and risk being shot at again. On the way I called Tremelay, thrilled that I went to his voice mail.

"Hey. Someone shot at me when I was jogging this morning. I've got the casings if that helps at all. Oh, and Fulk bit him. I've got the blood bagged for you, so hopefully you can get DNA or something off that. Swing by work if you need them right away."

I hung up and by the time I was pulling into the parking garage, he was calling me back. I seriously thought about not answering, but it was better to talk to him now than have him come in and interrupt me during working hours.

"Ainsworth," he barked as I answered the call. "What the hell happened? Who shot you?"

"If I knew that, you'd be scraping his remains off the sidewalk," I replied. Actually that wasn't true, but it sounded good.

"Was it a drive-by? Did you get caught in a drug deal gone bad? What was the address?"

I gave him the address as I got out of my car, pulling my scabbard and sword over my shoulder, just in case I needed it. "There was nobody out but me and Fulk. Someone shot at me from one of those narrow passageways between row houses. That's where I found the casings. Nine mil. He shot at me, then at Fulk who ran after him while I was down."

"Down?" He interrupted me. "*Down?*"

"I'm okay. Just bruised. I've been jogging with that vest on —the one you gave me—and it took two of the bullets. The others missed."

"The vest… What hospital are you at?"

I winced, knowing he was going to yell at me for this one. "I'm not at a hospital. It's just bruises and some scraped up skin, so I showered and headed in to work. I can drop the casings and the paper towel with the blood on it by the station or your house after my shift if you want. I put them in separate plastic bags. Oh, and I only gave you two casings. I wanted to save the rest for a spell."

I heard Tremelay let out a long, very noisy breath. "Ainsworth, you need to go to the hospital. You could have cracked a rib. You could have internal bleeding."

"If I start peeing or throwing up blood, I'll go to the hospital," I vowed. "In the meantime, I've got some caffeine deprived citizens that need a good latte. Text me where to drop the evidence. Bye."

I hung up to the sound of his cursing, pulled open the door of the coffee shop, and got to work.

CHAPTER 6

"Your *grandmother* was walking down the street?"

"Great grandmother," I corrected Petie. "And yes, she was walking down the street with a suit-case. Seems she left my sister's house sometime last night and made her way by mysterious means to Baltimore by early this morning."

This had been my excuse for being a few minutes late. Believe it or not, Essie was a far better excuse than explaining I'd been shot while out for my morning jog and was only alive because I'd happened to be wearing a bullet proof vest at the time. Unfortunately I'd had to give all sorts of strange excuses for switching shifts, being late, or leaving early in the last six months since picking up my sword and defending the pilgrims of Baltimore. An unexpected elderly relative descending on me in the early morning hours went over much better than yet another a-vampire-chewed-my-neck story.

"You never expect what grandmas are gonna do." Chalese shook her head. "Girlfriend probably took an Uber to your house and they dropped her off a few blocks too early.

Maybe that baby of your sister's was keeping her up all night or something. A woman's gotta have her beauty rest, you know?"

"Well, she's not going to get any beauty rest at Aria's with that hot boyfriend of hers hanging around every night." Anna laughed.

Chalese shrugged. "I'd take a banging headboard over a baby crying any day."

"She said she's here to help me." I looked down at the order on the cup Anna handed me and pulled the coconut milk out of the mini fridge.

"Maybe she'll cook for you," Petie offered. "Didn't you say she was Hungarian? Man, I love their food."

"Paprika chicken," the customer at the countered chimed in. "And Goulash. Not that weird stuff they call Goulash up in New Jersey where it's macaroni noodles and spaghetti sauce, but *real* Goulash."

I hadn't recalled Gran ever cooking anything when I was growing up, but then again we'd always had servants in our house. They either cooked, or Mom or Dad did when it was something special. I'd need to ask Essie when I got home if she could make me something Hungarian, because Goulash sounded really good about now.

"Maybe it won't be so bad," Anna told me as I tamped the espresso down. "We've got game night at your place next week. We could roll up a character for her, or let her play an NPC. Or is your grandmother more of the bingo type?"

Essie was hardly the bingo type. Actually I could see her having fun in our game. Anna had a good idea. If Roman couldn't come pick her up this week, maybe I could have her as a sort of temporary player next Wednesday. It would keep her from getting bored hanging around my house.

I knew what happened when Essie got bored. She ordered weird stuff off the internet, found herself in questionable chat rooms, and also found herself in questionable establishments all the way across town.

I finished up the iced coconut milk latte, and swapped places with Chalese as Anna got ready to clock out. Lately I'd been the one manning the machines, but I knew to step down to a higher level of expertise. Chalese made the best coffee, and I was happy to run the register while she worked her special kind of magic at the espresso bar.

Petie headed out with Anna, leaving me and Chalese for the afternoon crowd. Things slowed down after an hour and I was able to check my texts and make a quick call to my brother Roman. He and Hilda had taken the boys to Disney World and were in line for a ride when I called. It seems that not only had Athena not let our parents know that she'd lost our great grandmother, but she hadn't informed our elder brother either. He was relieved that Gran was okay, and said he'd be glad to have her stay at his house—in two weeks when they got home from their vacation.

I told him to call when he'd returned and got back to taking coffee orders, wondering what the heck I was going to do to entertain Gran for the next two weeks. Actually, it was more about keeping her out of trouble. And what should I feed her? Half the time I didn't even eat a real meal myself. Most of my actual nourishment came from when Dario took me out to eat, or from the leftovers I brought home. I guess I needed to start thinking about meal planning and ensure that I had things like sandwich fixings and microwavable entrees for when I was at work. It's not like Gran could live off that giant bottle of Fireball under my sink and the random leftovers in my fridge.

Well, maybe she could. Although Gran was just as snobby about her booze as my mother was, and I didn't know how she'd take to a liquor that was more cinnamon than whisky.

Things got unusually busy as the sun set. I got Dario's

wake-up text and quickly responded that I'd call him when I was off work, not wanting to get into an involved conversation about my new houseguest when I was busy. I especially didn't want to tell him about being shot at via text either. The evening went by quickly, and I calculated how much time I'd need to wrap up here, drop off the bullet casings and bloody paper towel with Tremelay and, no doubt, file an actual formal report. Then I'd have Dario meet me at home, tell him about the day's events, then get busy on a spell while he, no doubt, went out to try to track down whoever shot me and kill him.

Oh drat. Essie. Hmm, maybe I'd order something delivered by Door Dash, and tell her and Dario about the shooting over tamales and black beans. With any luck, I could be working on my spell before midnight. With any luck, either Tremelay or Dario would have caught the shooter before I could even light a candle. Tremelay had a bit of a head start, but if I were a betting woman, I'd put money on Dario finding the guy first. He had connections, a vampire's keen tracking senses, and he'd be motivated by anger. I knew Tremelay would be personally motivated as well, but Dario took my safety as seriously as only a possessive master vampire would.

It was nearing closing time, and Chalese and I were about to start our clean-up when I realized the woman who'd bought a double espresso with a twist an hour ago was still sitting off at the corner table. She was a tall woman who looked to be in her mid-forties with auburn hair pulled up into a messy bun. I'd thought she was one of the white-collar downtown people swinging by for some caffeine after work from her navy-blue pants suit and heavy statement jewelry, but now I wondered. She didn't have a purse, or any sort of briefcase. She'd had cash in her coat pocket, but I doubted she had much else.

The woman looked up and caught me staring. Her brown eyes held the authority of a high-powered executive, or a cop, or a Templar, although I hadn't seen the trademark tattoo on her wrist when she'd paid.

I smiled, and the one she returned was stiff and artificial.

"You know that woman?" Chalese inclined her head, her mouth in a grim line. This was getting to be a regular occurrence. The first time, the loiterer was a Boo Hag trying to gauge where I stood on their race. The second time, it was a plague demon who'd left both my coworkers with a nasty case of food poisoning. Both times the person lingering long after their beverage was completed had been waiting for me, and I got the impression this woman was as well.

Deciding to take the bull by the horns, I left Chalese to clean out the pastry case and went over to where she was seated.

"We're getting ready to close. Is there anything else I can get for you?" I figured I might as well be polite, just in case this was an actual customer.

"Are you Knight Solaria Angelique Ainsworth, Templar of the Baltimore area?"

Yep, she was here for me, but since she'd addressed me as a Knight, she clearly wasn't from the Order.

"That's me. Full-time Templar, part-time barista. Another double espresso in a go-cup, perhaps? Maybe a scone before we pack them away and you leave for the night?"

"What is your relationship with Haul Du?"

I froze, wondering who the hell this woman was. I'd thought Reynard had said Hellfire was a guy. Unless he had an amazing disguise spell, this wasn't the rival mage.

"I studied with them less than a year, and they kicked me out when they discovered I was a Templar. So basically, I have no relationship with them." Chalese banged an empty pastry tray, letting me know in her not-so-subtle way that she wanted a little help in closing prep. "Look, you need to get to the point or schedule some time to meet with me when I'm not working—preferably at a place where you're picking up the lunch tab."

The woman blinked at me, her face conveying obvious shock before she composed herself. Yeah, demanding lunch wasn't exactly something a Templar Knight would do, but then again, I wasn't a Knight. Although I'd probably end up being one by the end of next week if that Elder had his way.

"Where is Dark Iron?"

The woman's question sent a spike of fear through my chest. What did she know? How? No one besides Dario knew I'd killed Dark Iron. Well, I had kinda told that priest, but I hadn't named the mage and I couldn't see him outing me, especially since it was kinda-sorta a confession.

Crap. If Chuck could kill a chicken and determine who owned an object, or who had handled it last, then maybe this woman had the ability to divine the identity of a murderer. Was she a necromancer like Russell who summoned Dark Iron's spirit and learned what had happened?

Suddenly secrets weren't so secret anymore.

"I've got no idea," I lied. "I don't exactly socialize with the guy."

There. Hopefully I was either convincing enough or she believed that a Templar Knight couldn't lie. All I had to do was be vague and pretend as if I didn't even know the guy was dead.

"But you do socialize with Reynard," the woman informed me. "He was seen at your residence last night."

Another bang of the pastry tray saved me from having to respond, which was a good thing. I was shocked that this woman or her colleagues had been conducting some sort of surveillance on my home. Had she listened in? Probably not or she would have heard that I wasn't a Knight, and would have known that Reynard and I weren't exactly on friendly terms right now.

"I'm working." I grimaced over a Chalese, waving to let her know I was on my way. "We'll need to continue this discussion at another time. You obviously know where I live, so feel free to stop by during daylight hours. Or call me to set up a meeting."

The woman knew my address, so I was betting she knew my phone number as well. Could she tap my phone? Listen in to calls? Not that I used the voice feature of my phone all that much, but I did send a lot of texts that I'd always assumed were private.

I left the woman and helped my co-worker clean up for closing, thinking about cybersecurity and wondering who the heck this woman was. Once we'd locked up, I walked Chalese to her car, sword in hand, then made my way up a level in the parking garage to my own vehicle. By the time I got to Tremelay's house, I was beginning to think I'd jumped to conclusions about someone trying to kill me. Nothing had happened since this morning. Surely if someone wanted me dead, they would have tried to take me out heading to or from work. If they knew enough about my routine to know when and where I jogged each morning, then they would have known my work schedule as well.

Known my routine. Had it been that woman in the coffee shop asking questions? She'd most definitely been watching me and my house, but why shoot first, then ask questions later?

No, it was probably a gang initiation thing. I was freaking out and making a big deal over nothing.

Maybe, but I was still going to have Tremelay look into it, and I was still going to try my spell and see if I could identify who'd shot those bullets.

Tremelay took my statement and took both the casings

and the bloody paper towel, then continued to insist I go to the hospital and get myself checked out. I barely made it out of his apartment without having him inspect my boob and stomach. I promised him I'd run by the emergency room or at the very least let the *Balaj*'s physician-on-call check me out if needed, then headed home. I'd need to order some food, see how Gran was doing, and text Dario. Then get started on my spell. The whole day was turning rather chaotic, and as I headed up the steps to my house, I peeked in my living room window and realized I had company.

Hopefully this company wouldn't be staying for dinner.

CHAPTER 7

Opening the door, I found my great grandmother in the living room, sitting across from the woman from the coffee shop. Gaia was curled up on the rug. Fulk was nowhere to be seen. Gran was wearing a red and orange muumuu that made her look as if she were being burned at the stake, or burned on my couch. The woman sat in the most uncomfortable chair in the room as if she were on trial for capital murder, a coffee cup gripped tightly in her hands.

"There you are dear," Essie said in a grandmotherly voice that was completely unlike her. "We have a guest."

"I see that." I turned to the woman. "This isn't exactly daylight hours."

What. The. Hell. I was immediately on guard, my hand going to the sword in its scabbard across my back. I stopped just before I drew it, realizing it probably wouldn't be a good thing for me to skewer a woman in my living room.

It wasn't myself I feared for, it was Gran. She sat across from the woman as if she were about to pick up her knitting or bring out pictures of her great-great grandkids. Gran was a powerful witch, but she was so old. Maybe her magic had faded with age. Maybe she was no match for this woman across from her. All I knew was that I needed to protect her at all costs.

"It was important that I speak with you tonight." The woman went to lift her coffee cup to her lips, only to set it hurriedly back down on her lap. That's when I realized her hands were shaking.

She was afraid. If interrogating me didn't unsettle her, then I doubted the presence of my sword across my back would. No, I was pretty sure the woman was terrified of my great grandmother. What had Essie done prior to my arrival, because right now she seemed absolutely frail and helpless sitting on the couch with her delicate-boned hands folded in her lap.

"Go ahead then and ask your questions," Gran said in that strange elderly voice. "One of us needs to be in bed, and one of us has a booty call on his way over. I'll let you guess which one of us is which."

I smothered a laugh and took a seat next to Essie. "You said you were looking for Dark Iron? Well, I'm afraid I can't help you because I have no idea where he is."

That was *not* a lie. I'd called in Dario and he'd taken care of everything for me. I really *did* have no idea where he'd disposed of the body.

The woman set her coffee cup on the table and leaned back in her chair. "See, I think otherwise. I think you know exactly where Dark Iron is."

I leaned back as well, attempting to stall. "Before I consider answering any of your questions I'd like to know just who the hell you are."

A muscle twitched in her jaw and she eyed my great grandmother from the corner of her eye. "Grand Magus Golden Hemlock, Justice of the Conclave of Mages."

I tried really hard to breath evenly. A Justice. A Justice

from the Conclave. The group that regulated mages wasn't known for their speed in addressing matters, but once they got moving they were pretty much like the theoretical object in motion. The fact that they sent a Justice, a Grand Magus, meant they were taking this matter *very* seriously.

"And you're here looking for Dark Iron? What did he do this time? Slander the wrong mage? Send a demon after someone? Steal another mage's spell book?" I studiously kept my voice even, injecting a note of boredom into my tone.

She tilted her head, watching me in a way that made me think I'd completely failed at my little act. "Tell me about your interactions with Dark Iron—both when you were in Haul Du, and when you'd been evicted from the organization. That must have made you angry—him finding out who you were and removing you from the group."

Crap. Double crap. What had made her suspect me in particular? I was sure there were other people besides me who Dark Iron had pissed off. Either way, I needed to move this woman's suspicion as far away from me as possible— even though I wasn't exactly sure what Golden Hemlock knew and didn't know.

"Dark Iron was a self-centered, arrogant asshole, and I'm not the only person who thought so—both inside and outside of Haul Du. I only stayed with the group because I had become friends with a few of the members and I was eager to learn Goetic magic. As a Templar, it's one of the few magical subsets that mostly lines up with my vows."

"But he kicked you out, and forbade any of those mages you'd called friends from speaking to you, or associating with you, ever again," she replied.

A wave of emotion swept over me. Sadness. Isolation. Feeling adrift and without purpose. Being ousted from Haul Du had hit me hard. Having Raven not return my calls had hit me harder. But Raven had come around, and I now had a purpose. *And* I was learning magic once more, although that seemed to be a rocky path for me to travel.

I shrugged. "It was one of their rules, and I broke that rule. I understand why they wouldn't want to allow Templars into their organization. There's too much room for conflicts of loyalty and interest. Dark Iron is an asshole, but I don't particularly blame him for kicking me out."

"But in spite of your being blacklisted from the group, you continued to contact one member—Raven." Golden Hemlock lifted an eyebrow. "She died, and now her lover, Reynard, has been seen visiting you."

"Yes…" Damn. What did she know? I felt like I was walking through a field of landmines here, trying desperately not to blow myself up.

Essie laughed. "What, you mages aren't allowed to share a shot of whisky and reminisce about a lost friend? That Dark Iron is an asshole. It's one thing to kick out a member and tell the others they can no longer share confidential information with her, but I don't care how powerful that dickwad was, he had no right to tell people who they could be friends with."

Go Gran.

I leaned forward, deciding to play ignorant of everything. "Why are you asking all this? Are you thinking that I'm conspiring with Reynard about something? Or that I'm involved in whatever is going on with Dark Iron? Surely you can't believe that I, a Templar, would be involved in any of that?"

She considered that, doubt a brief flicker across her face. "Did the Order have any issues with Dark Iron or with Haul Du? If so, please let me know now because that would change the entire focus of my investigation."

She thought I was a Templar Knight. And that was the

very thing that would have been on my side in this situation. For the first time since I came home, I relaxed.

"I'm afraid I can't answer that question, but I can encourage you to address your inquiries to the nearest Elder."

If I were a Knight and involved in any sort of conspiracy or action against a member of Haul Du, then it would have been at the direction of the Order. And she was right. If the Order had instructed someone to kill a mage, the Conclave would need to take that matter up with the Elders and not with the individual Knight.

Of course, I wasn't a Knight, and the Elders wouldn't have the foggiest idea who the heck Dark Iron, or Haul Du was. It was a bluff, but the Order moved just as slowly as the Conclave when it came to inquiries, and they didn't respond to phone calls, e-mail, or even a handwritten letter. Golden Hemlock would need to track down an Elder and speak to him or her in person. Then they would need to look into the matter and get back to her—a process that had been known to take months even in urgent matters. Time was most definitely on my side here.

"But if you need my help in some other matter..." I needed to extend a bit of an olive branch here. There was no sense in my getting a reputation for being uncooperative with a Grand Magus from the Conclave.

Essie snorted. "Stupid Templars. I charge for my information. No sense in giving anything away for free. Always get *something* in return, I say."

There was a long, drawn out silence, then the Grand Magus sighed. "I formally request information of you, Knight Ainsworth. Dark Iron was under investigation for theft and he has vanished. We believe foul play may have been involved. I will most definitely inquire with one of the Elders, but if you know anything about the alleged theft by

Dark Iron of a soul trap, or his disappearance, I would be grateful if you'd share it."

I needed to be very careful to give her enough information to appear helpful, but not so much that the trail led back to me. "Tell me about the situation, and I'll give you whatever information I have."

She told me about the soul trap and that the owner had claimed Dark Iron was the thief. The two alleged witnesses had sadly perished in a building accident with several other mages before there had been a chance to question them. Inquiries to Dark Iron had gone unanswered, and when she'd arrived this week to question him in person, she'd discovered that no one had seen or heard from the mage in months.

"Do you believe Dark Iron had anything to do with the two witnesses' deaths?" I asked, trying to shift her suspicions elsewhere. "Is there a possibility that he was aware the men were going to testify against him, and took actions to silence them?"

"It's possible," Golden Hemlock grudgingly admitted. "But it's also possible that the deaths were just an unfortunate accident. I have no proof that Dark Iron was involved in that. In fact, our investigation shows it was most likely retaliation from another magical group who had a contentious relationship with Haul Du and those mages in particular."

Oh, the perfect scapegoat!

"Fiore Noir. I remember there was some back and forth between the groups late last September. Three Haul Du members died while blessing a building—their deaths reported as accidental, but several believed Fiore Noir was responsible. Two other Haul Du members later died at the hands of a demon they had summoned for revenge. I know the last incident because that demon became *my* problem."

The Grand Magus didn't appear too concerned that I'd had to clean up that particular mess. "My investigation reveals that you provided information that helped bring the Fiore Noir members to justice. I personally believe you may have been involved to a greater extent in that situation."

I tried once more for the enigmatic smile. "Again, that is a question best addressed to an Elder."

She waved a hand. "Either way, I'd like to know any information you might have on Dark Iron's involvement, either positive or negative, with Fiore Noir, and if you have recovered any magical artifacts in the area."

Hopefully she'd blame the whole thing on a mage war between the two groups and close the inquiry. Dark Iron had been working with them, but no living Fiore Noir member knew about that. Well, except for Chuck, and he was locked up in Jessup.

"Fiore Noir was performing death magic with human sacrifice," I told her. "They were also performing soul magic with human victims using a soul trap. There were those who believed that Fiore Noir acquired the soul trap, either legally or not, from Dark Iron."

"Did you or the police recover this soul trap?" She leaned forward, her expression eager.

"No," I lied. "There was evidence leading me to believe a soul trap was definitely used, but one was never found at any of the scenes or at the homes of those Fiore Noir members who'd been arrested."

She blinked and I knew she was connecting the dots. Soul magic. A stolen soul trap. Dark Iron the accused thief and also possibly involved with the group using a soul trap. If I were sitting in her place, I'd be thinking either Fiore Noir did away with Dark Iron to avoid any future blackmail, or that the mage who had accused Dark Iron of stealing his soul trap had tired of waiting for the Conclave to act and took care of matters himself. Or that with both the mage and authorities closing in, Dark Iron had vanished with the soul trap to wait for things to cool off.

Although the latter wasn't all that believable to anyone who knew Dark Iron. That arrogant prick would have stayed and manipulated things so Fiore Noir took all the blame and he walked away clean. That's what he'd been trying to do when I killed him.

She knew I'd been involved with bringing Fiore Noir to justice and cleaning up the mess both they and Haul Du had left behind. If I'd been a Templar Knight and killed him as part of my holy duties, then Golden Hemlock would have no recourse. As a Knight, my actions would fall under the purview of the Order. And just as possible crimes committed by active duty service people fell under the armed forces judicial system, my actions would fall under the protection of the Templar Order. She couldn't touch me. The justice she would have delivered had I been a mage or an ordinary citizen wouldn't be allowed. She'd need to walk away, declaring it all a Templar matter.

But I wasn't a Knight. That had been a proud, defiant statement for me for years, but now I sweated just thinking of the corner I was being backed into.

If it came out that I'd killed Dark Iron, I was going to be in trouble. It all came down to which group I'd rather be in trouble with. As a non-Knight, the Order might refuse to vouch for my actions. Just as the vampires delivered death sentences, so did the Conclave, although life in a moldy dungeon would most likely be my punishment. More likely, a bloody fight between the Grand Magus of the Conclave and my family would be my future, as well as a long, drawn out feud where the Order kicked my entire family out and refused to support or back them.

Or I could go rogue and run for it, protecting my family

and trying to live off the grid, defending myself from the Conclave if they caught up with me.

The other option would be for me to take my Oath. There was still no guarantee that the Order would vouch for me and my actions, but any punishment I faced would be through them. It wouldn't be much better than the punishment I'd face with the Conclave, but at least my family wouldn't be involved.

Who was I kidding? My family would totally be involved. They'd never stand by and allow me to be stuffed into a dungeon for the rest of my life.

I took a deep breath and squashed down the panic. That's what this was—nothing but foolish panic. The Order wanted me. This was my bargaining chip. I'd wanted to use a promise to help me face the Big Bad as my bargaining chip, but if Golden Hemlock was as good an investigator as I thought she was, I might need to adjust my strategy.

Either way, all roads right now were leading to my taking my Oath. And that idea made me more than a little nauseous.

"When is the last time you spoke to Dark Iron?" she asked, as she fingered a charm on her bracelet. I felt the tingle of magic, then Essie reached out to touch my hand and the magic slid off me like water on oil.

"When he kicked me out of Haul Du."

"You haven't seen or spoken to him after that?"

I hate lying. I sucked so bad at it, but I could hardly confess to the last time I'd seen Dark Iron and not go into the details of that encounter.

"No."

Her eyes searched mine and she released the charm on her bracelet. The tingle of magic in the air died, but Essie kept her hand on mine.

She nodded and stood. "Thank you for this information,

Knight Ainsworth. I will definitely contact an Elder about any official Templar actions in this matter."

I hid a wince and walked her to the door, feeling as if I were playing out a chess game in my mind and planning defensive moves six steps ahead.

She hesitated at the door and turned to me. "I'd still like to know what the subject of your meeting yesterday with Reynard was."

"Merely a social visit. He was Raven's boyfriend, and I was close with her. We try to keep in touch since her death." I ushered her out the door, and waited there until I heard her footsteps fade.

Did she think Reynard's ambitions regarding Haul Du might give him motive to kill Dark Iron? Did she also wonder if Hellfire's recent arrival might be suspicious?

I wanted her to think either the Argentina mage who'd owned the soul trap had killed Dark Iron, or that Fiore Noir had. Preferably Fiore Noir. Preferably a member of Fiore Noir who was dead and couldn't answer any questions. I wanted this all to go away. I wanted Golden Hemlock to fly back to wherever she'd come from thinking both the theft of the soul trap and Dark Iron's disappearance had been resolved in a way that didn't require any further justice. Then I could save my chip with the Order and use it for Big Bad instead of to defend me against a charge of murder.

It was getting late. Dario was blowing up my phone with texts asking where I was and if he should meet me at my house instead of his. I hadn't eaten anything since a piece of pound cake at the coffee shop for lunch. I didn't feel comfortable leaving Essie here alone for the night, and my head with spinning with everything that had come down on me in the last twenty-four hours.

Vow. Possible assassination attempt. An unexpected

houseguest. A potential murder charge with me being boxed into a corner of unpleasant choices.

One thing at a time. I texted Dario as I turned back to the living room, telling him to come over to my house and to pick up food for three. Hopefully that would give me some time to dig my shield out of my armor bag and paint some protective sigils on it. If there was someone out there trying to kill me, then I'd need to start carrying my sword *and* shield while jogging. And wear my damaged Kevlar vest until I could order a new one off the internet.

"Did you kill that asshole mage she's looking for?" Grand asked me in a cheerful tone of voice that most elderly relatives would have used to ask about how your day went.

I hesitated, knowing I couldn't lie to her and knowing that I really didn't want to. Of everyone in my family, Essie was the least judgmental—probably because of everyone in my family, she was the only one who wasn't a Templar. Things others found morally questionable, Gran found admirable. Plus she was family, and I knew how much that meant to her. She might not hesitate to throw anyone else under the bus, but Essie would never betray her family. Ever.

"Yes, I did."

"I'm proud of you. And I'm assuming fanged, dark, and handsome took care of the body?"

I bit back a smile at her description of Dario. "Yes, he did."

"Good. That means no one will ever find so much as a fingernail. Vampires are particularly good at disposal."

They were, and I had mixed feelings about that fact.

"Dark Iron stole that soul trap and traded its use for the elimination of those who knew about it as well as others he wanted dead," I told her, not sure why I felt the need to explain myself to the one relative who was least likely to be concerned about my reasons for murder. "He killed Raven. He flat out murdered her because she'd figured out what he was up to. He killed her, then posed her like one of the Fiore Noir victims for me to find. She fought him. She warded her soul, and in retaliation he sliced her to ribbons." I choked back tears at the memory.

Essie stared at me with her dark eyes. "Dear, I've got no problem with anything you've done. You don't need to explain your motives to me."

But I did. "I confronted him and he laughed about it. We fought, then he put down his weapons and turned to walk away. I had nothing that would have resulted in a conviction in human court, nothing that would have brought him to justice through the Conclave. He was going to get away with everything, so I stabbed him in the back with my sword—I stabbed him *in the back* with my consecrated sword."

I'd told all this to a priest, but it hadn't felt as much of a confession as me telling it to my great grandmother.

Essie shrugged. "Back. Front. Up his ass with a pike. Doesn't make any difference. Some people need killing, and you've got to get it done any way you can."

"It *does* make a difference," I insisted. But somehow over the last few months, my feelings of guilt over what had amounted to an execution were fading. Templars were no longer supposed to judge—that was left to God—but we *did* judge every time we went out to kill Chupacabra, or a sand wyrm, or a pesky troll. How was *that* any different from judging a human as a threat to society and ending his or her life?

Protecting the Pilgrims on the Path. God was the only one who could judge a soul, but as God's swords, as His hands of justice, perhaps we *were* tasked with judging the physical life.

I shook my head, because that was a slippery slope that had led to what we'd become during the Crusades, when we'd slaughtered men, women, and children in the name of God.

What was done, was done. And I couldn't be feeling too terribly guilty over it if I was weaving lies left and right to avoid paying for what I'd felt was my own crime. The world was a better place without Dark Iron alive and walking the streets. My faith had been shaken in the last few years, but I was beginning to rediscover it—starting with the faith that God would guide my hand when delivering my own sort of justice, whether that was toward demons, undead, non-humans, or humans.

"I have seen so many die in my life," Essie said softly. "So *very* many. It has made me numb to death to see the wheel of life turn over and over. None of us know the future, Aria—not even me. All we can do is hold fast to what we believe is true, and take action. In the end, that God of yours will decide if your motives were acceptable or not. Stop over-thinking everything and embrace who you are and what you were put on this world to do."

I'd heard that so many times in my life, but I hadn't expected to hear it from Essie. "Be a Templar Knight. Serve the Order until my death," I recited.

She sniffed. "Fuck the Order. Be the Knight your God wants you to be, and tell those pricks you'll serve them if you feel like it. You've got more important things to do than sit around and take orders from a bunch of wrinkled old assholes."

I smiled, thinking she might be right about that.

’ll give Dario credit; he didn't call or send any panicked questions in response to my last text. Instead he showed up at my door half an hour later with a dozen containers of food.

I'd found my shield and had decided to use a Templar symbol of blessing instead of sigils. To keep from messing up the classic lines of the red Templar cross, I'd begun applying the symbols using clear nail polish.

Aesthetics were important if I were going to walk around the city of Baltimore carrying a sword and shield, and I knew from experience that the symbols would be just as powerful in clear nail polish as they would with red.

Dario's face lit up when he saw me. I gave him a kiss and took the bags from him, before stepping aside so he could enter and see my guest. It warmed my heart to see him hug Essie, kissing both her cheeks and telling her how pleased he was to see her. I waited for him to finish his greeting, then promptly dragged him into the kitchen while I told Essie dinner would be ready in just a moment.

"How long is she here for?" Dario whispered. His hand ran down my back to rest on my ass, and I knew he was wondering how this was going to affect our sex life. I didn't like his *Balaj* hearing us doing it, and neither of us wanted my great grandmother to hear us right next door to her bedroom.

"A couple weeks until Roman and his family get back from Disney World," I whispered back.

Dario pulled three plates out of the cabinet. "Should we get a hotel room?"

"I don't want to leave her here alone. She's over one hundred years old."

The idea appealed to me, but skipping out on Gran seemed terribly rude. No, we'd just have to suck it up and be celibate for a few weeks…or learn to be super quiet in the bedroom.

He sent a glance toward the living room. "So how about we rent a hotel room and don't stay all night? She'll be safe for a few hours. Doesn't she have one of those beeper things I've seen advertised on the television?"

I elbowed him. "Yes, but I'm not going to be in a hotel screwing your brains out while my great grandmother is laying on the floor with a broken hip. I'm putting up with Erica and your responsibilities toward her so you need to just deal with my responsibility toward Essie."

He sighed. "I'm sorry. My mother taught me to revere our elders, to always put their needs first, but it's been a long time since I've been human and elderly vampires don't exactly need our care. I'm proud of you for looking after her. And I'll help any way I can, even though I'll be suffering some severe blue balls for the next few weeks."

I laughed. "Do vampires get blue balls? I mean, you all aren't technically alive. Half your organs don't even work like they did when you were a human."

He gestured toward his crotch. "The important organs work, as you well know."

"Yes, I know." I reached a hand toward Dario, running my palm down his side to his hip. "Sorry. If I had my way we'd be eating this in bed."

"Umm. That sounds amazing. Rain check for two weeks from now?"

He went to pull me toward him and I backed away. "Rain check. Now let's eat before the food gets cold."

Dario frowned, looking around the kitchen. "Speaking of cold, did you turn the heat down for some reason?"

Crap, the furnace. I had completely forgotten to call the property management people. Hopefully it would hold out or *all* of us would be getting a hotel room tonight.

"The furnace is acting up. It hasn't been above sixty-three in here for the last few days. I'll call in the morning and get it fixed."

"Should I call out for pizza?" Essie shouted from the living room. "I'm starving in here. If you're going to fuck, then hurry it up so I can eat."

Dario laughed, kissed me, then grabbed the plates and utensils and headed into the dining room. I snatched up a bunch of spoons to dish out the food and grabbed the bags. Dinner at my parents' house—even casual dinner—was a fancy affair, but today we were going to pass around containers of Italian food family-style.

That *was* fancy in my house. Usually I just ate right out of the container.

"Aria's got troubles," Gran announced once we'd each dished out our food. "I'm thinking you need to kill this Golden Hemlock mage and dump her body in the Bay."

Dario's fork stopped halfway to his mouth. "What?"

"No, don't kill her." I scowled over at Essie. "Golden Hemlock is a Grand Magus from the Conclave. She's investigating Dark Iron's disappearance and came to question me."

There was a disturbing gleam in the vampire's eyes. "So I *should* make her vanish? I don't want her thinking you had anything to do with his…disappearance."

I rolled my eyes. "Gran knows. And no, you don't need to kill her. I can handle it. No one but the three of us and your *Balaj* knows what happened to Dark Iron, and I intend to keep it that way. Hopefully Golden Hemlock will blame his disappearance on his involvement with Fiore Noir or something and go away in a week or two. It's best for us all to just keep a low profile and let the trail go cold."

Sheesh, I sounded like Tremelay. Actually I sounded like a vampire—which was more than a little disturbing.

"By the way, what did you do to make a Grand Magus, a Justice of the Conclave, scared of you?" I asked Essie.

She snorted. "The bitch showed up throwing her weight around. I told her to be respectful. She did some hocus-pocus. I laughed then did some hocus-pocus of my own. Then she got *real* respectful, so I invited her in and got her a cup of coffee."

Now Essie was scaring *me*.

"What sort of hocus-pocus did she cast?" If the woman had magically assaulted my great grandmother, I was gonna have to bring that up with whoever the heck she reported to.

"Hell if I know. Whatever it was, it didn't work."

I caught my breath. A Grand Magus cast a spell against my great grandmother and it *didn't work*? A Grand Magus was visibly afraid of my great grandmother? My whole life Essie had been quirky and odd, the sort of woman who dispensed shocking statements side-by-side with shadowy wisdom. Her magic had always been little stuff—making toys dance across the room, lighting the fireplace with a wave of a finger, refilling her glass of whisky without touching the decanter. She redirected tennis balls in a different trajectory from where she'd hit them, sent croquet balls through every hoop on the course. The woman gardened like every finger was green, and trained the squirrels and finches to eat from her hand as if she were Snow White.

"Did I mention how much I like your great grandmother?" Dario commented.

I ignored him. "What did you do to her?"

Essie grinned. "Just a parlor trick. These silly mages. It's all eighty million spell components and a bunch of Latin. All you have to do is shuffle three walnut shells around with a pea under one and they're freaked out. I'm glad you're not like them, Aria. You're a Templar with everything that birthright brings, *and* you're my great granddaughter, with everything *that* birthright brings as well. That's unexpected. The two don't usually blend together, you know. Heck, none of Tarquin's and my children *or* grandchildren got my gifts. That you would…it gives me hope that maybe things will be right with the world. It gives me hope that maybe fate will smile on me and mine once more."

That was very flattering, but still didn't blind me from the fact that Gran hadn't answered my question.

"What sort of shell trick did you pull on her, Gran?"

She waved her hand and took a quick bite of her manicotti. "It was nothing. You need to tell vampire-hottie here what happened to you on your jog this morning, though."

I sucked in a breath, wondering how Essie had known.

"Blood on your dog," she told me. "Blood on that shirt you were wearing, too. I did some laundry this afternoon because I refuse to be the sort of person who arrives at my great granddaughter's house uninvited and doesn't bother to help out at all. That's when I saw the holes in your coat and the blood on your shirt."

I felt the weight of Dario's stare, but Essie's words

suddenly shifted my thoughts and fears in another direction. "Where's Fulk? Where's my dog?"

I shoved my chair back with enough force to knock it over and ran to the back door, hoping he was out in the yard. Gaia had been in the kitchen with Dario and me, but I hadn't seen Fulk since I'd gotten home. How could I have not noticed? I was a terrible doggie momma to not have wondered where he was earlier. Here I'd been eating and talking, and my dog might be dead somewhere, or running through the neighborhood humping other dogs, or at the animal shelter.

"He's up in your room sleeping," Gran shouted after me.

I leaned against the door jamb and breathed, willing my heartbeat to slow.

"He was agitated all morning, jumping at the door and growling," she continued. "I gave him a little something to make him sleep. No need for him to wear himself out, injured like he was. I told him I'd keep watch and protect the house, and that he needed to rest up so he could protect you on your jog tomorrow morning. From attacking rats, you know—the ones who've got teeth sharp enough to bite clean through your winter coat."

I felt weak from the adrenaline receding from my veins. Giving my arms a quick shake, I went back through the dining room and up the stairs. Sure enough, Fulk was curled up on my bed, snoring away. I sat down beside him, running a hand over the scabbed cut from earlier today. He opened an eye, yawned at me, then went back to sleep.

Tears stung my eyes. It had been a hard day, and the fear that something might have happened to Fulk had put me over the edge. All I wanted to do right now was curl up with him and Gaia and sleep until dawn.

I felt the warm familiar buzz of vampire aura, and from

my peripheral vision saw Dario enter the room. He sat down beside me, rubbing my back.

"Everything okay?"

I nodded.

"What happened with these rats on your jog this morning? Were they rabid or something? Wererats? Monster mutant rats?"

I took a breath, then I stood and pulled my shirt off. "There were no rats. Someone shot me when I was out for my morning run."

Anger poured from him—anger and fear. "You were shot."

It suddenly hit me. I could have died. I'd been saying that all day, but it never really sunk in until now. It was one thing to face down summoned spirits, evil mages, murderous Boo Hag, and vampires. It was another thing to be out jogging and be shot. If I hadn't been wearing that vest, I would have died. Somehow that was far more terrifying than to die while battling someone or something. Killed without even realizing I was in danger, before I even had a chance to defend myself.

But Dario was actually shaking with rage. This wasn't the time for me to have a meltdown.

"I'm okay." I reached out a hand to touch his chest. "They're just nasty bruises. I've been jogging while wearing the Kevlar vest Tremelay gave me for the added weight. And Fulk chased the shooter off."

"Where?" he snarled. "Why didn't you let me know? I could have sent a crew out to track him."

I stepped into him. "Because it happened at dawn and by the time you were awake, any scent would be mixed up with dozens of others. I called Tremelay and made a report. I also gave him some of the casings and the blood I wiped off Fulk's mouth. He'll give them to his lab, and I'll do a spell on the casings I kept and see if I can determine who it was."

He touched the purple and green bruise on my stomach then trailed his fingers gently up to touch the one right above where my bra ended.

"I'm okay," I whispered, not liking the look in his eyes.

The darkness and anger faded, leaving only fear. "You could have died, Aria. You could have died and I wouldn't have been able to help you. I wouldn't have even known until tonight. I would have woken up to hear that you'd died."

He pulled me close and held me carefully, burying his nose in my chest.

"I know," I whispered into his hair. "We'll find who did it, and they'll go to jail. It probably wasn't personal. The guy probably wasn't specifically targeting me. I'm sure it was a gang initiation thing and I was just in the wrong place at the wrong time."

He gently kissed the bruise above my bra and pulled back just far enough to meet my eyes. "It doesn't matter. He'll never see the inside of a jail cell. And if this *was* some sort of gang initiation, then his gang is about to be exterminated as well."

I should have argued, should have been shocked at the violence in his voice, but I wasn't shocked and I didn't argue.

"No more jogging unless you're doing it at night and I'm with you." His voice was firm, making it clear he would brook no argument.

"Wait." I held up a hand. "I'm not becoming a prisoner in my own house just because some idiot decided to unload a pistol in my direction."

"No jogging. And you, your great grandmother, and your entire menagerie of pets are moving into my house. I'll assign a Renfield to drive you to and from work, and to guard the coffee shop while you're there."

"Wait, whoa there buddy. I'm not becoming a prisoner in your house either. I'm not some helpless damsel, remember?"

A muscle in his jaw twitched. "No you're not, but you *are* helpless against bullets, remember?"

"Not all that helpless," I argued. "I've got a Kevlar vest, and I'm going to take my shield with me. Sword, shield, vest. I'll be fine."

"A shield." He stared at me in disbelief. "What are you, Captain America or something? You're going to be pinging bullets off your shield? This isn't a comic book, Aria. I'm not joking."

"I'm not joking either." My voice was getting loud, but in my defense, his was as well. "My shield is over an inch of titanium alloy. It's the same shit they use in combat aircraft. I'll admit it's not quite Captain America grade, but it's damned close."

"Repeated hits and it'll have zero effectiveness," Dario shouted. "Same with your damned vest."

"I'm covering it with symbols of Templar protection," I shouted back.

"That's just the shield. You're not coated in the stuff. A decent sniper with a rifle will take you out before you can even raise your shield and that vest of yours isn't going to do shit against a rifle round. You're not jogging. You're not leaving this house without me or one of my family to protect you. That includes work, visiting your friends, or anything. Do I make myself clear?"

I was pretty sure the neighbors two blocks away could hear us at this point, but I didn't care.

"Oh, crystal clear. But since I'm not your blood slave, I don't have to obey your orders, Master."

It was a low blow, but I was pissed.

He reached out and grabbed my arms, tightening his grip just short of hurting me before he realized what he was doing and pulled away. With a snarl he stood and left the room. I heard the front door slam before I could blink.

I took a few calming breaths, alternating between wanting to smash something and wanting to cry. He had a point. I was vulnerable when it came to bullets, and that scared me. But when scared, I'd rather do something proactive than hide out and wait for someone else to resolve the situation.

My job was dangerous—the Templar thing, not making coffee. There was always a risk that someone might want to take me out. I couldn't live my life in fear, hiding behind Dario, or hiding behind anyone for that matter. I'd been scared for him many times, but never once had I ordered him to hide in my house and not come out until I took care of the situation for him.

Damn it. Just when I thought we were at a point where he respected my decisions and my abilities, he turned back into some overprotective vampire.

I put my shirt back on and went downstairs. Essie was still at the table, eating. She put a few spoonsful of something from a container onto a plate and slid it over to me as I sat.

"You know he's retracing your jogging route right now, trying to track down who shot at you." Essie handed me a fork. "Eat. Then finish the symbols on your shield."

"He wants to keep me locked up somewhere safe," I told her, ignoring the food. "He wants to move us all into his house and have me not go anywhere without him until he catches this shooter."

Gran chuckled. "Yeah, I heard. I'm pretty sure everyone within half a mile heard. He's afraid and he doesn't want to lose you. He loves you and he has no idea how long he'll have you in his life. And he's angry at himself that he can't protect you during the day."

I poked at the linguini with my fork. "I get it. But I'm not moving in with him because of that. And I'm not letting some nutjob with a gun be the reason I no longer jog in the morning, or go to work, or go get groceries."

"I wouldn't mind moving in with him," Essie grinned. "All those hot vampires hanging out around his house? They can bite me all they want—and do other things as well."

I shook my head, knowing she was more than half serious. "I lost my temper. I told him I wasn't going to be his blood slave, and I called him Master. He's worked so hard to change that culture in his *Balaj*, and here I was throwing it in his face the first time we get into an argument."

Gran snorted. "I'm sure that wasn't your first argument, and I'm sure it won't be your last. And trust me, those words hurt you far more than they hurt him. He's probably had some lurid fantasies about you being his blood slave, tied to the bed with nothing on and calling him Master."

I bit back a laugh, realizing she was probably right. I was the one that had issues with that, not him. He'd made changes in his *Balaj* because of me, not because it bothered him all that much.

I ate, fed my pets, finished working on my shield, then watched a movie with Gran. After she went up to bed, I sat on the couch with Gaia and Fulk, hoping Dario would come back.

Finally around six in the morning, he texted me.

Sorry. You win. You always win. Tracked scents all night, but came up with nothing. Please be careful tomorrow, and please text me that you're okay come sundown.

Right. I was absolutely not winning and we both knew it.

I will. Oh, and please make sure the guards you're assigning to me introduce themselves. Some strange guy starts following me and I'm likely to stab first and ask questions later.

I waited a few moments for his response.

I love you.

He wasn't denying he'd be sending someone to guard me. Guess he felt there was no sense in lying about it.

I love you, too. Master.

I giggled as I added the last, wondering if Essie was right. His reply was immediate.

Stop. I won't be able to even walk with this hard on. Wish I had time to swing by for a quickie. Earplugs for Essie?

I laughed, told him I'd see him tomorrow night, then went upstairs wondering how soundly Gran slept, and if I could somehow soundproof my room. Two weeks was going to feel like forever.

CHAPTER 9

I woke up at my usual early hour. Gaia and Fulk were begging for food as usual. What wasn't usual was the heavenly smell of coffee and bacon wafting up from downstairs. I normally didn't eat anything until after my run, but this smelled amazing. Might as well have a leisurely breakfast before I headed out for a jog fully armored and carrying both a sword and a shield.

Dressing with haste, I ran down the stairs, nearly tripping over Gaia in the process, to find Essie in the kitchen. She even had food in Gaia's and Fulk's bowls, and the two made a beeline for their breakfast.

"Gran! What are you doing up so early?"

She turned and handed me a cup of coffee. "Couldn't sleep and figured I might as well get up. When you get to my age you never really sleep. It's more like short naps throughout the day. I'm lucky if I get two hours in a row at night."

I sipped the coffee and eyed what was on the stove. It looked like a frittata, and that reminded me of something.

"Can you cook goulash? We were talking about it the other day at work and I've got a craving."

She gestured for me to sit and slid the frittata onto a plate. "I never had much interest in learning fancy cooking skills, and it's been a long time since I made goulash."

I smiled as she cut a piece of the frittata for each of us and sat down. This was nice. I'd gotten used to just grabbing something to eat after my run. This was the first real breakfast I'd had outside of my trips back home.

"I'd have thought you would have been taught by your mother," I commented as I dug into the frittata. It was amazingly good. I had no idea where Essie had gotten fresh spinach and roasted red peppers, or where she'd gotten the cheese, bacon, and eggs for that matter. Had she gone shopping? Knowing my great grandmother, she'd probably gotten a Peapod delivery or something yesterday while I was at work.

"I never had a mother," she replied with a shrug.

I paused mid-bite, realizing I knew very little about Essie's life before she'd married my great grandfather. All her stories were of the two of them, and all I really knew about her past was that Tarquin had met her in Hungary, and that she was some sort of witch with innate magical ability.

"Did you grow up in foster care?"

"I lived on the streets for a while, then fell in with a nomadic group. I was with them about five years, then parted ways in Budapest. That's where I met your great grandfather, you know."

I knew. It was a romantic story. They were both on a train. Essie was a stowaway trying to keep one step ahead of the conductor. About to be discovered, she quite literally ran into Tarquin who agreed to hide her in his cabin. A whole lot more than hiding happened in the cabin and the rest was history. I'd grown up hearing tales of how they'd worked together across Europe, how Tarquin had married her in Prague and brought her home to a disappointed family. She'd definitely rocked the boat with her independent and quirky ways, but the pair had never wavered in their love for each other. Their arguments had always been short, and passionately resolved. My great grandfather had died before I was born, but I'd seen pictures of him—a handsome blond man with bright blue eyes. From the way she talked about him, I can imagine how devastated Essie must have been to lose him. She'd found happiness in a life without her husband, but it was clear that a part of her had died with him.

"I don't remember much about when I was a child." Her gaze grew distant. "It was so long ago that I'm not even sure I ever was a child. So very long ago…"

I ate more of the frittata while Essie lost herself in the past for a few moments. Then she shook her head and smiled. "I might not be much of a cook, but goulash I can definitely manage."

My mouth watered at the thought. I'd leave Dario a message and tell him he needed to not miss dinner tonight. Then we'd have the makeup sex I'd been dreaming about all last night. I didn't care if Gran heard or not, makeup sex was definitely going to happen.

"So what are your plans for today, dear?" she asked. "Do you need to go to work?"

"I'm off today, so I'm going to go for a run, then try a few spells." I also needed to connect with Tremelay and see if he'd discovered anything about the shooter, and to let him know whatever my spell may have revealed about the incident.

"Be careful on your run today." She reached down and patted Fulk. "And you too, pretty boy."

"He's staying here today." Fulk would definitely be handy to have on my run since I was pretty sure he could sniff out the shooter blocks away and provide me with an early warning growl, but I didn't want to risk him getting shot.

Hmm. I needed to get a Kevlar vest for Fulk as well as a replacement for mine. Yes, I would definitely need to dip into the parental account for this purchase.

"Can I watch you doing your spell work?" Essie looked excited at the prospect and I didn't see any reason to say no.

Gran's magic was different. Haul Du and the other mages I'd encountered used specifically worded incantations, key materials, and rigidly outlined processes to harness the energy that everyone carried inside themselves and create magic. Some people never were successful. Others had very moderate success. Only a few were truly mages. With Essie, magic just happened. But she was so incredibly knowledge-able. She was the one who'd told me how to disable the soul trap, and I'd used the same technique to kill a master vampire. She'd spent decades by her husband's side. She knew magic. She knew Templars. Maybe she'd be the one to figure out how to combine my Templar abilities and the magic that Chuck had been trying to teach me.

"Actually, I'd love it if you could help," I told her. "So many traditional spells don't work for me, or they have unin-tended consequences."

She nodded. "Because you're a Templar. Tarquin was limited in what he could do as well. Although it wasn't just him being a Templar that hindered him. I loved the man, but he was absolutely shit when it came to magic. Incredible with a sword, but he couldn't so much as unlock a door without a key."

I blinked in surprise. Heck, even I could do that. I'd been spelling my butter knife to do that for months now.

Gran waved her fork at me. "You're very lucky, girl. You've got his sword arm and my magic."

"I'm nowhere near as good with a sword as my great

grandfather," I told her. "And I've been told my magical ability is pretty average."

Essie snorted. "You're young. Humans. Everyone expects potential to instantly become expertise. It takes time. It takes practice and failure and pain to achieve success. You may be average now, but if you work at it, you've got the talent to be better than Tarquin. Better than me in some ways."

This was like a motivational seminar. Affirmation from my parents, from teachers, from Dario hadn't moved me like these few words from my great grandmother.

"I've been working on a spell to identify the ownership of an object, or who handled it last," I told her. "I don't want to summon a Goetic demon for this or kill a chicken, so my mentor and I modified a spell. It didn't work last time I tried it, so maybe you can see where it went wrong?"

I went over the spell in great detail while Essie nodded thoughtfully. When I told her what had happened with the rock, she started to laugh.

"The problem isn't with the spell, sweetie, it's with your interpretation. The heat? The fire? That's my essence. That's me."

Oh sheesh. "Well, knowing the essence of who owned or handled an object isn't going to help me one bit," I complained. "I was hoping for an image of the person and a name written in smoke. And an address, if that isn't too much to ask."

Essie was laughing so hard by this point I was worried I might need to call for an ambulance. I got up and refilled our coffees, then sat back down as she composed herself.

"First, you've got the wrong spell for that sort of thing. Secondly, you don't need all that crap. All magic needs a channel to focus and direct it. Some people need a convoluted channel with a dozen herbs and certain stones and phrases said a certain way. You don't need that kind of channel."

"And you don't need a channel at all," I commented.

"Exactly. But you're young. You'll get there in time. But you still don't need all that crap you just told me about. You're not these hocus-pocus fools you're trying to learn from. I don't know exactly what sort of channel you need, but I'll help you figure it out."

I wasn't sure I had that sort of time. "I'd love that, Gran, but today I need to find out who shot me, otherwise Dario is probably going to insist I go into some kind of vampire protective custody."

"Well, you're not going to get the answer with that spell," Essie said.

I sighed. "Maybe I should just summon a Goetic demon, or kill a chicken."

She chuckled. "I heard what happened the last time you summoned a demon. I'm thinking for now you should stick with banishing the demons and save summoning for the future. And as for killing a chicken, unless you're planning on adding that to the menu tonight, don't bother."

This just sucked. I wanted to find this guy. I wanted to find out why someone had shot me, and take steps to make sure it wouldn't happen again. I wanted to go back to my morning jogs with Fulk, my daily routine. I wanted to prove to Dario once more that I didn't need him to cover me in bubble wrap and hide me away, that I needed a partner not a protector.

Essie stood and grimaced as she put a hand to her back. "Go for your run. I'll let your pup out back to do his business and stretch his legs while you're gone. And when you get back, we'll work on the spell. Together."

* * *

Jogging proved to be much more difficult than I'd imagined. The bruises on my stomach and chest made every deep breath a bit painful. I slowed down—way down—realizing that besides my injuries, I was carrying the extra weight of a shield this morning.

Thanks to Essie's breakfast, I was out later than usual and for once I wasn't the only one on the sidewalks and streets. A few people waved as I went by, asking if they were filming a new Avengers movie in the neighborhood. It was a good idea. Avengers in Baltimore. I'd totally watch that.

I wasn't foolish enough to think that I could jog the whole six miles today, so instead I decided on four, and that I would take as many walking breaks as I felt I needed. By the turn-around at two miles, I was feeling much better and emboldened by the commuter traffic, I decided to do one more mile. Turning left, I headed down an alley and toward a more commercial section of town, thinking there would be safety in numbers.

Too late I realized that the alley was a bad choice. I stopped, ready to turn back when I heard the noise of a car behind me. I didn't even look, I just took off running as fast as I could, hooking the shield around my arm.

There was nowhere to jump onto a fire escape ladder, no heavy metal dumpster to use for protection. The only way I'd survive this was if I made it to the end of the alley before the vehicle behind me caught up. I'd feel like an absolute fool if I was racing like crazy away from some guy just cutting down the alley on his way to work, but at least I'd be a live fool and not a dead one.

Two strides in and I realized I wasn't going to make it. Duh. It's not like I could outrun a car, even if I hadn't been injured and lugging around a sword and shield. I couldn't outrun it, but the alley wasn't all that narrow.

And there might not be a metal dumpster, but there was a row of big, blue recycling bins to my left.

Spinning around, I grabbed two and tossed them into the alley. Bottles and plastics scattered everywhere as the huge bins toppled onto their sides and spilled their contents right in front of the oncoming car. The driver swerved on instinct, then decided to plow right through it all. As he corrected to come toward me, I heaved two more bins in front of him, lobbing a smaller one into the windshield of the car.

Then I ran the opposite direction, narrowly avoiding getting clipped by the rear-view mirror. The driver screeched to a stop, slamming the car into reverse.

Fuck this.

I jumped to the side, yanking my sword from its scabbard and flipping it around to reverse the grip. Then I smashed the heavy pommel into the driver's side window.

Spidery cracks feathered out. The safety glass held, but the driver flung up his arm on instinct and jerked the wheel, smashing the rear end of the car into the brick wall of the building to the right of the alley.

I was pissed, and the combination of that plus adrenaline made any discomfort from my injuries vanish. Like some psycho superhero, I jumped onto the hood of the car and smashed the pommel of my sword into the windshield right in front of the driver's face.

He might be brave enough to try to run a jogger down, but he certainly wasn't brave enough to face a crazy woman trying to bust through his windows with a medieval weapon. The guy yelled, flung open the driver's side door, and tried to make a break for it.

With the magical power of adrenaline still coursing through my veins, I leapt off the hood of the car and ran after him, whacking him across the back of the head with my shield before he'd gone more than ten steps.

The man fell to the ground, rolling over onto his back and holding his hands over his face as he screamed.

I reversed the grip on my sword. "Stay down fucker, or I'm going to shove the pointy end of this right through your chest."

He held out his hands. "Okay. Okay. Don't kill me. Please don't kill me.

To my credit, I didn't kill him. Instead I called Tremelay, who personally came out because he was concerned that a responding patrol officer might take exception to a jogger holding a would-be attacker in place with a sword.

"Ainsworth. Really? What's next? Are you going to start jogging in full plate mail? Ride down the MLK on a horse with a lance?"

"Could happen." I missed horseback riding. Was my back-yard big enough for a pony? Probably not.

I'd tried interrogating the guy before Tremelay had arrived, but hadn't been able to get much out of him. All I'd learned was that this was supposed to have been an easy job, and that whatever "they" were paying him, it wasn't enough to deal with this shit.

I'd also learned that he had no idea about me being shot yesterday. And I believed the guy. Dudes who wet their pants because you were pressing a hefty sword against their chest tended to tell the truth.

Which meant that someone had it out for me, and that someone was hiring people to take me out. They wanted it to look like an accident—a random gang shooting, or a random hit-and-run. These things weren't exactly uncommon in large cities, especially Baltimore. And the fact that my enemy wanted this to look like an accident meant they were worried about retaliation.

Either Templar retaliation, or vampire retaliation.

"I take it you're pressing assault charges against this guy?"

Tremelay looked down at the pathetic dude lying on the blacktop.

I waved a hand at the wrecked car behind me amid all the recyclable garbage. "What do you think? He tried to run me over. Even tried to back up and run me over when he didn't get it done the first time. How about charging him with attempted murder instead?"

"Think that's a bit of a stretch, but I'll have to talk to the DA." Tremelay nudged the guy with his foot. "How about you stand up and I cuff you and read you your rights."

"How about this woman gets her sword out of my chest," he snapped. "I should be the one pressing assault charges here. Did you see what the crazy bitch did to my car? And she damned near gave me a concussion with that shield. Who jogs with a sword and shield anyway? You should be arresting her."

Tremelay rolled his eyes. "Can it, asshole. This crazy bitch has saved my ass enough times that I trust her over you any day. Now come on. Stand up."

I put my sword back in its scabbard and stood at the ready while the guy rose and Tremelay cuffed him. Once the detective had read the man his rights and stuff him into his police car, he turned to me.

"You coming down to the station sometime today? I'll need you to sign a statement on this guy, and I've got a few things to go over with you on your little incident from yesterday morning."

I caught my breath, hoping that between the shooting and this guy we could find out who seemed to have a hit out on me.

"Let me go home and clean up a bit first," I told him, thinking that I also needed to leave my sword and shield behind, and maybe dress in something that didn't look like I was headed into a combat zone.

"Make it after lunch," Tremelay told me. "Say two or three. That okay?"

I nodded, and watched as he climbed into the police car and drove away. Then I headed back home, adrenaline totally worn off and completely feeling not only my injuries from yesterday, but the effects of all the whoop-ass I'd dealt out this morning as well.

CHAPTER 10

My basement stairs definitely weren't ideal for a century-old woman. I had to help Essie down the rickety wooden steps one at a time as she cursed and lamented her age the whole way. She'd only been with me here for a day, and already I felt closer to my great grandmother than I had growing up in the same house as her. Helping her down these stairs, I understood her frustration. To have been young and physically fit, then in what seemed like a blink of an eye, be unable to do certain things unassisted? I'd be cursing as well.

As soon as we cleared the last step, I guided Essie to the chair I'd brought downstairs for her. She sank into it gratefully and caught her breath as I showed her the magical space that had made me so eager to sign the lease on this house.

She squinted at the circle. "Someone put a lot of work and energy into that. Very nice work."

I beamed, happy that she confirmed how I felt. "Do you think it's part of my channel?"

Essie pursed her lips. "I think having a space that resonates with you is helpful in channeling your magic.

Whether it's a space like this, or out in the woods, or kneeling in a church only you will know."

I hadn't thought of that. Templars of old found their strength in prayer and in a holy space, but our modern Order seemed to have lost that practice. We still prayed. Most of us attended church occasionally. But the building itself had somehow lost its significance to us. I looked down at the circle, at the lines, symbols, at the embedded stones and metals. I'd always associated this with magic, and I did feel the flow of power here, but maybe this wasn't the only place I could summon my magic. I'd have to think about that a bit because it was a whole lot easier for me to find a church in the city of Baltimore than a charged magical circle.

Now that I'd brought my great grandmother downstairs and settled her in for the ritual, I wanted her to meet Chuck.

"Gran, this is my mentor." I pulled the spoon from the Crown Royal bag and touched it to the circle, waiting for Chuck to respond.

"Your mentor is a piece of cheap flatware?" Essie shrugged. "Could be worse, I guess."

About that time Chuck made an appearance. I expected Essie to shriek or jump like my mother had, but instead she just frowned.

"What's that old man doing in your spoon?" she asked.

"What's that old woman doing in your ritual space?" Chuck responded.

"Chuck, this is my great grandmother, Estera Ainsworth. Gran, this is Chuck. He's in prison right now and can't mentor me in person, hence the spoon."

"Most mages use a mirror for this kind of spell," she commented.

"It's a little easier to slip someone a spoon during visitation than a mirror," he shot back. "I've made arrangements with most of the guards here, but I don't like to push it too far."

Gran turned to me. "Think you could find a mentor that isn't doing time, Aria? I mean, if he's a decent mage, then he shouldn't be behind bars."

"Trust me, I could leave if I wanted," Chuck snapped.

Essie shrugged. "If you say so. Okay, Chuck. Do your mentoring. Let's see what you got."

"Why is your ancient relative sitting in on our session?" Chuck turned to look at me, distorting his imagine in the spoon.

"She has her own magic," I tried to explain. "And she's been around Templars for more than eighty years. I need her help. I need both of your help."

I'd added the last knowing how miffed Chuck got when he felt I wasn't being suitably appreciative, even though this whole thing *was* his idea.

"Well, I don't want her here. Get rid of her, or I'm not going to help you."

Whoa. What was it about Gran that had Chuck so pissed off?

"She doesn't need your help anyway," Gran told him. "She'd do better without you. You're slowing her down. You're trying to fit her magic into your system and it's not going to work."

"Me or her," Chuck demanded.

I hesitated, not wanting to offend either of them.

"Well, you both go right ahead then. If you change your mind, let me know." The mage's face vanished from the spoon.

I didn't have time to deal with his hurt feelings today, so I went ahead and repeated the spell process as I'd done before, putting the bullet casings from yesterday morning into the center of the circle. Essie made the occasional hmmm noise. Right before I began the incantation, Essie stopped me.

"Yep. It's definitely too much," she insisted. "I can see what your mentor was trying to do, but it's absolutely the wrong approach."

"You mentioned earlier this morning that this was the wrong spell," I reminded her. "Is there a different one I should be doing? Or modifications to this one? Or…." I held up my hands, feeling completely overwhelmed here. I'd always had an experienced mage guiding me before—a mentor from Haul Du, or Raven, or Reynard, or Chuck. Even with Essie here, I felt like I was going it alone.

"You're overwhelming your senses," Gran insisted. "Yes, all this crap you're doing isn't going to get you the results you want, but you don't need a new spell with more crap. Just pick one or two things that you've already got here to help you focus on what you're trying to achieve, and go with that."

My gaze shifted between the herbs and the candles. "Which should I pick, though? What's most important?"

"I'd suggest ditching the herbs." Gran pursed her lips. "They limit you and you don't need them."

I grumbled a few choice words about how much money I'd spent on them then, gathered up the herbs, and gently placed them aside, just in case she was wrong and I *did* need them for the spell.

We went over each of the spell components and the ritual itself in great detail. At the end of a half hour I found myself standing in the middle of the circle holding one of the bullet casings trying to decide whether I should use a symbol for fire or water for the spell.

Gran had said her element was fire. I was betting that Chuck's was water. But what was *mine*? I thought for a second, then went upstairs and came back down carrying the cat's litter box. "I'm using this. If it doesn't work, then I'll try fire."

"Cat litter?" Essie burst out laughing. "Your element is *cat litter?*"

"Well I didn't have any potting soil or sand to use as earth," I told her. "I'm going to perform kitty litter magic. You did say it's about the symbolism and not the actual substance, so this is what I'm using."

Essie shook her head with another laugh. "You're absolutely related to me, girl. Did you clean it out first, or are you going to read the shooter's name in cat turds?"

"I cleaned it out first." It was time to change the litter anyway. I just hoped that Gaia didn't need to use it until I was finished.

We both fell silent. I lit a center candle then turned off the lights. Gran had tried to get me to do away with the candles, but I'd insisted on them. After so long performing magic through complex rituals, I felt that I needed at least some sort of ceremony to focus and prepare myself.

After lighting the candles at the five points, I hesitated. There needed to be something else. I didn't feel ready. I felt as if there was a part of the rite missing, no matter what Gran said.

Approaching the litter box, I found myself wishing I'd brought my sword downstairs. That would complete the ritual. That would be the perfect melding of ceremonial magic and Templar powers. But since I didn't have the sword, I used the one symbol of my faith and my purpose that was with me always—the tattoo on my wrist.

Touching the crimson ink, an electricity coursed through me.

"All-knowing Almighty who guides my sword and safeguards the souls of the faithful, show me who fired this bullet. Reveal to me their name and their face I pray, so that I may deliver your justice."

The red Templar cross on my wrist glowed. I felt the energy swirl around me. Gathering it, I sent the energy into the bullet casing and dropped it down into the cat litter.

There was a crackling and popping sound, then the litter exploded upward. I gasped and jumped backward, trying to shield Essie from kitty-litter projectiles, but instead of blasting beyond the circle, the litter hung above the center candle like a granular gray cloud. Then it shifted and twisted, revealing a face and a name.

I'll admit my first thought was that I needed to start using colored kitty litter so the face didn't appear as a black-and-white photo. That was quickly followed by elation that the spell had worked. A magical space. Candles. My tattoo. And a box of cat litter.

Maybe I didn't need Chuck after all. Maybe I didn't need anyone but myself, my magic, and prayer. I'd been fighting the combination of the two abilities, haunted by a belief that ceremonial magic somehow tainted the faith-based abilities I'd been born with. How wrong I'd been. How wrong all those who'd held the same opinion and influenced me had been. There was so much more to being a Templar than swinging a sword and banishing undead. So. Much. More.

"Henrietta Aliette," I read the words in the cat litter. I hadn't expected that the shooter had been a woman, which was a sign of just how ingrained patriarchy was in our society. But even though I had her name and her face, I still had no idea where to find her or why she'd shot at me.

But at least I had something for Tremelay to go on.

"Excellent!" Gran cackled, sounding very much like a witch at the moment. "What do you want to work on next now that you've succeeded in this spell?"

Hmm, there was so much I wanted to do, but one thing came to the forefront of my mind.

"I want a spell to call my sword to my side, no matter where it is," I announced.

"Like that smoking hot blond guy in the Avengers movie does with his hammer?" Gran sighed. "I'd so hit that. I'd rock that man's world. He'd combust with all the action he'd be getting."

I held back a laugh as I envisioned poor Chris Hemsworth's Thor worn to exhaustion by a century-old woman. Poor guy wouldn't know what hit him.

"Have you *seen* those movies?" I asked her. "His hammer smashes through buildings, and cars, and priceless art objects as it travels in a straight line from wherever it is to his hand. I really don't want to randomly impale people with a flying sword, and my sword isn't exactly Mjolnir. It's going to end up broken and bent, or at the very least dulled, by smacking into the side of a building on its way to me."

"That would be hysterical," Gran said. "I'd pay to see that."

"A dented, broken sword isn't going to help me," I argued. "And I'd be horrified if I hurt or killed someone in summoning my sword to me. I just want it to come back to my hand if I'm disarmed. That sort of thing."

"Too bad you can't just store it in the veil and call it from there when you need it," Gran commented.

I shot her a sideways glance. "Even if I could place a physical object in the veil, I really wouldn't want my sword where every ghoul and demon could snatch it up and use it."

She made a clucking noise. "The veil isn't just one big place, it's thousands. A small space can be segmented off and sealed for private use. At least that's what a sorcerer told me three thousand years ago. Although he may have just said that to get under my skirt."

I didn't want to know if the sorcerer was successful or

not. Besides Essie's wild imagination about history and timelines, she tended toward TMI when it came to her sexual encounters—both real as well as fictional.

Still…if such a thing were possible, it would include spirit-worker specific magic, which wasn't something I'd ever done. It was something I assumed I'd never be able to do. But was that right? I'd gone into Goetic magic assuming that was the only form that would mesh with my Templarness, but what if I'd been wrong? We banished demons, but we also sent the undead back to the grave. Perhaps magic in the spirit realm was something I should consider. But in the future—other spells were more important for now.

"I'm going to start with just calling my sword into my hand, then save the storing-things-in-the-veil for when I've got the time to research it," I told Essie.

How much energy it would take to move a sword a few inches as opposed to across the room? Did distance matter? Could I craft the spell so it didn't just work on my sword, but on other objects as well? How would I specify the object? By name? But what if I was tied and gagged, or otherwise rendered speechless? What if it was pitch dark and I couldn't even see the object I wanted?

This was going to take a lot of thought and research. Far more than I had time for this afternoon.

CHAPTER 11

J was getting ready to head out to see Tremelay when the doorbell rang. Jumping up, I ran to answer it. Essie had ordered Chinese delivery and I was hoping there would be some leftover for when I got back. One of the benefits of having my great grandmother stay with me is that she evidently had a limitless credit card—courtesy of my father, I assumed. Where I was reluctant to accept help from my parents, having Gran buy me food and other goodies felt perfectly acceptable. It was a grandparent's role in life to spoil their grandchildren, so I didn't argue at all when Essie called Peking Palace, and placed a huge order.

There was a delivery man on my front stoop. There was also a man carrying a toolbox, and another guy who looked as if he were an active duty Navy SEAL.

You'd think I'd be more excited about Mr. Buff, but I was in a hurry. Shooing him aside, I held out a five to the delivery guy as a tip and took the bag. The smell of fried food hit my nose and my stomach growled. Maybe I'd grab a few egg rolls to eat on the road.

"I need to check that," Mr. Buff told me as he snatched the bag from my hand.

"Like hell you do," I replied. "Mitts off the fried rice or I'll run you through with my sword."

Unfortunately I didn't have my sword, nor did I have a spell to call it to me yet.

"Can I go in?" Toolbox Man complained, giving Mr. Buff a quick, respectful glance. "I'm here to fix the furnace."

Holy crap, the furnace! It had been cold this morning, but I was either too busy to notice or I was getting used to the cooler temperature in my house because once again I'd forgotten to call the property management people. How the heck had they known I was having heat problems?

Dario. Duh. Yes, it was high-handed of him to arrange for the repair, but I *did* appreciate him remembering and taking the initiative. It would have been disastrous if the furnace died completely with Gran here. So instead of scolding him, I was going to thank him for his consideration. He'd probably die of shock, if he wasn't technically dead already.

"I need to see ID and call it in," Mr. Buff told him. "Just because you've got a logo on your shirt and a sign on your truck, doesn't mean you're who you say you are."

I glared at Mr. Buff, who was quickly losing his appeal. "Just who the hell are you anyway?"

"Terrance Lincoln." He fixed me with a steely gaze.

Damn. Bod. Cheekbones. Chin—with a cleft in it. Dark eyes. Golden brown skin and a cleanly shaven head. And he had that smolder down pat. Whew.

"And why exactly are you here, Terrance Lincoln?

His eyebrows lowered. "To keep you safe. You're not eating this food until I inspect it, and I'm not letting this repair guy in until I check his ID. I've been hired to make sure nothing happens to you, and that's exactly what I'm going to do."

I was going to murder Dario. Forget thanking him, I was going to flat out stake him tonight. Stake him.

My sword was across the room, but I had another weapon to use—one I'd realized was just as formidable.

"Gran! There's a hot guy on the stoop that is trying to steal our lunch!"

I heard her huffing and puffing as she shuffled her way across the living room floor.

The repair guy dug his wallet out of his rear pants pocket. "Look, buddy, I'm on the clock here. You need to hustle this up or I'm going to have to bill you for an additional hour."

Dario's two projects were clearly conflicting here. It would be really funny to have to tell him that my furnace didn't get repaired because Mr. Buff, the guard he hired, wouldn't let the guy in. But before Repair Guy could even yank his driver's license out, Gran was by my side.

"Give my great granddaughter the food, or suffer the consequences."

I don't know what it is about an elderly woman, but when they delivered a threat, it was taken seriously. This six foot five dude who was built like a tank took a step back and handed the bag to me as if it contained live explosives.

"It's my job—"

"You think my great granddaughter can't protect herself from a delivery boy and a furnace repair man? You think my great granddaughter can't tell if food is poisoned or not? *My* great granddaughter, the Templar, the mage, the woman who banishes the undead, who protects the pilgrims of this city against all who would do them harm? You keep your incredibly tight ass out there and watch for snipers. If you're nice, maybe I'll send an eggroll out to you."

Gran motioned for the repair guy to enter as the delivery man ran for his car. Then she slammed the door in Mr. Buff's face.

Taking the bag from my hand, she opened it. "Ooo, did they give us extra eggrolls? I think they did."

* * *

"THIS FURNACE IS as old as me." The repair guy stood up and wiped a bead of sweat from his forehead. He had nearly run for it after seeing the ritual space down in the basement, especially since I hadn't cleaned up the candles or the kitty litter. I'm pretty sure the guy thought I was sacrificing cats down there or using their feces for some arcane rite.

"Will it need to be replaced?" I glanced up the stairs, thinking of Gran. "How long will that take? Can you get it to keep going until it's replaced? Or get us half a dozen space heaters—the kind that are safe to run while I'm at work?"

The man pursed his lips and narrowed his eyes, giving him a cartoonish expression. "I can keep it going until the part comes in. Won't be more than seventy in the house though."

That was a heck of a lot better than what it had been. Gran hadn't complained, and for someone her age she seemed to have quite the internal metabolism, but I still worried about her being warm enough if we had a cold snap.

"How long will it take for the part to come in?"

The repairman still had that scrunched-up expression on his face as he stared at the old boiler. "Couple weeks? I'll tell the property management company to send a few heaters over just in case." He handed me a business card, finally settling his facial muscles into something more normal. "They said for you to call me direct if it goes down again. Twenty-four seven. You don't got heat at three in the morning? You call me and I'll haul my ass over here right away."

That was a pretty impressive, and pretty expensive,

service for what really was a cheap slum rental property. I pocketed the card and escorted the repairman out, noticing that Mr. Buff was still outside, no doubt hoping to scare potential snipers off with his intimidating presence.

Closing the door, I pulled the card out and set it on the fireplace mantle. "Guy says to call him day or night if the heat goes out," I told Gran.

"Hmm."

That was her reply. Hmm. I'll admit I was thinking the same thing.

"Interesting how the property management company psychically knew I was having furnace problems," I said.

"Uhhuh."

"And that we had a repair guy here first thing in the morning. We're getting space heaters, and they're probably paying through the nose to expedite delivery for the part."

"Yup."

"I wouldn't be surprised if we end up with an entirely new furnace before spring."

"Maybe you should hint to your boyfriend that you really need central air while you're at it. And a complete bathroom remodel with heated marble floors."

I sighed. "I had my reporter friend check on the property owner, *and* had my detective friend check on him. I seriously thought this place wasn't owned by the vampires."

Gran shrugged. "Maybe loverboy bought it after you signed the lease. Maybe the owner is a front and he's owned it all along. Either way, you'd think he would have steered you to a nicer house in a better neighborhood."

I would have been suspicious of a nicer house in a better neighborhood in my price range. No, Dario had clearly set this one up. He'd somehow found a house with a permanent magical space in the basement, and knew I wouldn't be able to resist. How long had he sat on this place waiting for me to either decide to move or get evicted? Had he hired a mage to create the magical space, or had the house already had it when he bought it? How long did he think he could keep this from me?

"Adeyemi Properties." I shook my head. "A shell company, and some dude he probably pays monthly just to have his name on the deed. Vampires. They're like mafia with pointy teeth."

Gran smiled fondly. "Yes, they are. I like your boyfriend, though."

"He's a vampire. He'll live forever while I'll age and eventually die. Mom and Dad would rather I be in love with a human." I snorted. "Preferably a Templar human."

"Well, we don't always get to pick who we fall in love with. And that vampire of yours is a hell of a lot better than ninety percent of the humans I've met—including Templars."

"Still…" I thought about the whole immortality thing. I thought about the blood thing. There were a lot of major hurdles in the path of this relationship, and neither Dario nor I couldn't ignore them forever.

"Most times one partner outlives the other," Gran said softly. "Sometimes by decades. Sometimes by centuries."

I winced remembering how long she'd lived without her beloved Tarquin.

"And as for the other issues…." She shrugged. "Well you need to stop whining about them and face them head on. You're a Templar. You're a mage. You've got my blood in your veins girl. Time for you to use it." Essie turned around and headed for the stairs. "I need a nap. Go do whatever you need to do today, and tell that pornstar out front that he better not wake me up before noon. Unless he's climbing naked into my bed, that is."

* * *

THIS WAS RIDICULOUS. I was contemplating sneaking out of my own house to evade Mr. Buff. I was a grown woman, a Templar. It was bad enough that Dario secretly owned my house and was making sure I had better-than-usual response from the property management people, him sending a guard to my house just because someone may or may not have shot at me on purpose was taking things too far.

Actually, I kinda liked the better-than-usual response from property management thing. It wasn't like Dario was letting me live here rent-free. And if he were truly the owner, he *did* have a responsibility to make sure major appliances and the heat were working.

As for Buff, I knew he was worried about what happened while I was out jogging. Heck, I was worried too. I could have died if I hadn't taken to running with a Kevlar vest on. I could have died today if I hadn't gone all berserker and scared the piss out of that guy trying to run me over. But Dario putting a jacked-up guard outside my house and having the man interrogate food delivery guys and repair people was really annoying.

Nope. I wasn't going to sneak out of my own darned house.

Strapping my sword onto my back, I walked out and immediately encountered Mr. Buff.

"Where do you think you're going?"

He stood in front of me and I contemplated shoving him down the stairs. Not that I could, but I still contemplated it.

"Out. Gran's napping, so keep it down out here." I didn't tell him the rest of her message.

Buff still blocked my way. What would happen if I called the police? Or drew my sword and skewered him?

"You wearing your jacket?"

I knew he wasn't referring to the parka I had on. "Yes, I'm wearing the Kevlar vest." Maybe now he'd let me by.

"Boss sent a new one. You shouldn't wear one that's been damaged."

It would have been nice to know that before I'd put my parka on. He was right, though, so I followed him to a huge black truck with what I was sure were illegally tinted windows. Buff handed me a vest, then stood guard like he was in a war zone while I pulled my parka off, and quickly changed out tactical gear. This one was way heavier than the previous one and I barely managed to get my parka over it. Looking at my reflection in the truck's tinted windows, I realized I looked like a bloated tick.

"It'll protect against pretty much anything outside of a nuclear weapon," Buff proudly told me.

"How about if your boss sends me one that's lightweight and doesn't make me look like a linebacker?"

He chuckled. "Next time whoever's gunning for you might not rely on a pistol to do the job."

He reached out to take my damaged vest and I held it out of reach. "Nope. I'm keeping this one."

And I was having a few words with Dario tonight about all this. I'd wear this for now just to get away from Buff, but I wasn't working at the coffee shop in this bulky, million-pound thing, and I definitely wasn't putting it on every time I wanted to go to the fricken grocery store either.

I started toward my car and realized Buff was following me.

"You're not coming. Stay here and watch my house."

"Boss said to keep you safe, and that's what I'm doing," he replied.

I stopped in front of my car and turned around to glare at the man. "If you follow me then I'm going to sic the entire

Baltimore City police department on you. And your boss won't be getting any sex, which means you'll be fired. Why don't you make sure no one plants a bomb around my house, and I'll tell your boss that you never left my side all day. Deal?"

He looked at me in my overstuffed parka, a sword strapped to my back, and slowly nodded. "Deal. Do not get killed though. If you so much as get a hangnail, the boss will kill me."

He wasn't joking. One more thing I was going to take up with Dario tonight. "Understood."

Tremelay was at the station as usual, filling out the endless reports that being a police detective seemed to require. Honestly it was Kafkaesque the amount of paperwork the guy did in relation to the cases he handled. But his administrative duties meant he was usually at the station when I needed to see him and not driving all over the city to crime scenes.

As luck would have it I knew the guy up front, *and* I knew one of the officers walking in, so I bypassed the usual protocol and was escorted straight to Tremelay's desk. I plopped down in a chair and watched him finish typing.

"What's up, Ainsworth? Dragons attacking the city? Werewolves eviscerating prostitutes in the south side? That vampire of yours finally snap and start draining people?" Tremelay's partner, Norwicki, called out from across the room.

"I'm here to find out what's up with the dude who tried to run me down this morning, *and* I've got a lead on the person who shot me yesterday," I told him.

"No shit." Norwicki got up and came over to Tremelay's desk "Is this a lead we can take to the district attorney?"

"Nope. Unless magic is suddenly admissible as evidence in a court of law, that is."

Tremelay pushed his keyboard aside and spun his chair around to face me.

"First, the guy who tried to run you over this morning is some lowlife gang member from DC. He's got a record—no surprise there. He's also lawyered up, so we're waiting for whoever he called to show and hopefully we can continue questioning."

"Think he'll reveal who hired him?" I asked.

"For a deal? Probably." Norwicki snorted. "You've been targeted twice. I'd rather the DA work something out and catch who's behind this before you end up on a slab."

Lovely image there.

"And there's some progress on the shooter as well," Tremelay said. "We found a bullet that wasn't embedded into the pavement and sent it off for analysis. We find the gun, we should be able to link it to the scene."

"I've got something as well. My spell worked and I know who the shooter was."

Norwicki let out a low whistle. "Nice!"

I nodded. "Hopefully you'll find the gun or other evidence and can claim you acted on a tip."

"Tips are not enough to get a warrant and I doubt the shooter has the gun sitting out on his doorstep." Tremelay sighed. "But go on. We'll worry about all that later."

"The shooter's name is Henrietta Aliette. I know what she looks like, too."

He started typing, only to shake his head after a few minutes. "Nothing in Maryland as far as convictions or charges. Nothing at the MVA. If she's a resident, she's clean and not driving with a Maryland license."

I resisted trying to read over his shoulder. "Is there anything you can search nationally?"

"Not on the fly. I can look through Pennsylvania, Virginia, and DC though."

He typed away and I sat back.

"You want a coffee?" Norwicki asked.

I was debating the quality of the station's coffee when Tremelay spoke up.

"We lucked out. She's licensed in the District. I've got an address, although it might not be current. She got pulled over for speeding at K and New Hampshire last week, but beyond that she's got nothing in the system."

I frowned, questioning why a random woman with nothing more than a speeding ticket on her record had been in a bad section of Baltimore, shooting at me while I was out on an early morning jog.

"She's also French, here on a H1B Visa," Tremelay added.

French? That made even less sense. "Does she have diplomatic immunity?" I asked, wondering if she had other types of immunity. Templars got away with a lot because we knew people in high places and were either friends with them, or had dirt on them. Or they owed us big time for something. Either way, we enjoyed the same sort of immunity that diplomats did—actually more than diplomats. And Templars weren't the only organization that had these relationships.

"Nope. Looks like she has a normal passport. And she didn't identify as a diplomat when she got pulled over, from what I can see. The officer let her off with a warning."

Why would a French woman living and working in DC want to shoot me? Did this have to do with the Haul Du situation Reynard had come to me about? Did someone not want me to take my Templar Oath? Was this somehow tied in with Dario or other vampire *Balajs*?

While I was thinking, Tremelay was dialing. Next thing I knew he'd connected with someone in the DC police department and was gathering his coat from the back of his chair.

I stood as well. "Where are we going?"

"It's where Norwicki and I are going, Ainsworth. You're not coming with us."

I rolled my eyes. "Okay, where are you two going then?"

"To talk to a Detective Bromstein in DC, then to hopefully catch this Henrietta Aliette at her home or work. Most likely, we'll end up just letting the patrol cops know that we need to talk to her about an open case, and they'll track her down. But in the meantime, I'll drive to DC and see if I can luck out and find her, and convince her to give us a moment of her time."

It all sounded pretty boring, which I guess was what ninety percent of police work consisted of. Being a Templar wasn't all that different. Knights spent most of their time keeping up with their skills, reading texts, playing tennis and drinking high-end whiskey. Then there was that ten percent of time they were battling a basilisk or a gulon. And hoping they came out of it alive.

"Will you let me know what happens?" Not that I had any intention of waiting. In fact, I was pretty sure Dario and I were going to be taking a trip to DC tonight—after we had makeup sex and I had a chat with him about his smotheringly protective instincts, that is.

"I doubt there will be much to tell you. You know how this sort of thing goes, Ainsworth. We'll talk to her, but without someone putting her in Baltimore with a gun and a motive, talking to her is as far as it's going to get."

"Hopefully we'll catch a break," Norwicki added. "Either way we can have patrol keep an eye out for her car around where you live and work."

As much as Dario's tactics bothered me, I wasn't about to wait around until this woman took another shot at me. Yes, I'd filed a police report and would let Tremelay do his thing, but I needed to know who was after me and why—and stop them before the next hired killer succeeded.

Norwicki went to grab a few things from his desk while Tremelay walked me to my car.

"Don't do anything stupid, Ainsworth," he warned me as I got in.

"Of course not," I told him. Then I drove home, knowing full well that tonight I planned on doing something stupid.

I noticed right away that Buff was no longer lurking outside my door. Instead another man had taken his place—a guy I recognized immediately.

"Answer is still no, Reynard," I told him as I climbed the stairs.

"See, I'm thinking the answer should be yes."

There was something about the smug way he'd said it that made me pause.

"Let's take a walk," he added.

I debated whether I wanted to stroll down a vacant street with Reynard, or risk Gran hearing what I was pretty sure he was going to say to me. Ultimately I decided to keep this outside.

"What'd you do with Mr. Buff?" I asked as we headed down the chipped sidewalk.

"The meathead guarding your front door? He's on a wild goose chase. I figure we've got about fifteen minutes before he figures it out and comes back."

We reached the end of the block and kept going. Silence

stretched on and the clock was ticking. Might as well get this all out in the open.

"I'm not getting involved in Haul Du's internal power struggles," I repeated what I'd told him before. "And as for your threat about civilian casualties, well I'm pretty sure the presence of a Conclave justice will keep things civil between you and this other mage."

"It's the Conclave justice that I want to discuss," Reynard replied. "She's here looking for Dark Iron. It would be a shame if she knew what happened to him."

Was he bluffing? I couldn't imagine he'd found the body, but Reynard was a mage. With appropriate incentive, a demon might have been able to find out what happened, although they generally didn't just come right out with names and details. Maybe he'd hired a medium to contact Dark Iron's spirit, although from personal experience communicating with a spirit didn't often result in much besides odd snippets of not-so-helpful information.

"*Would* it be a shame? From what I heard the guy stole some other mage's property, killed two of his own to cover it up, and was up to his neck in that Fiore Noir business."

"Murder is still murder," Reynard replied.

"You saying you murdered him? Not that I blame you, but that's hardly going to convince me to help you fight off this other mage."

"No, I'm saying *you* murdered him." Reynard halted and pulled something up on his cell phone, turning the screen toward me.

The video was grainy, like someone's cheap doorbell camera, but I knew immediately what I was seeing. I'd been the only other person there at the meeting up with Dark Iron and I certainly hadn't filmed anything. I doubted the mage would have wanted video evidence of his theft and a confession to multiple murders. Watching the video on Reynard's phone, I suddenly realized who'd set this up.

Only one person had known I was meeting Dark Iron. The same person who'd organized the meeting time and place. The same person who'd texted Dark Iron to meet him, then gave me the information to go in his stead. One person.

Chuck.

Bastard. Here I'd been bringing him Fisher's popcorn, playing his little games to get information on what Big Bad might be coming our way soon. He'd become my *mentor*. And the whole time he'd been sitting on a video of me killing Dark Iron—oh *and* the vampires dragging his body away! Was he just waiting for the right time to blackmail me about this, or to sell it to the highest bidder? How much had Reynard paid for this, and how had he even known to reach out to the mage in prison? Chuck must have contacted Reynard. Had he done it before this morning, or had his tantrum over Essie made him decide to turn on me? Either way, I was pissed. That rat bastard.

While all this boiled inside of me I kept my expression blank. "Blurry doctored video. Nice, but it doesn't convince me and it won't convince anyone else."

"It's not doctored and it'll convince Golden Hemlock just fine." He pocketed the phone. "So? Do I send her the video, or do you help me?"

Chuck wasn't the only bastard.

"He stole that soul trap and was in league with Fiore Noir. He killed the two mages in Haul Du that knew about his theft. He killed *Raven*—murdered her and set it up to look like she was a victim of Fiore Noir."

Reynard flinched at Raven's name. "How dare you! You can slander Dark Iron all you want—the guy had his faults, and I know how much you hated him—but don't you dare use Raven to justify your committing murder."

"I'm not lying. I'll swear on my sword right now that I'm telling the truth. Raven found out about Dark Iron working with Fiore Noir. She knew he'd arranged for those two mages to die, that he'd arranged for Bliss to be one of the Fiore Noir sacrifices. They took her *soul*, Reynard. And Dark Iron would have taken Raven's as well if she hadn't safeguarded herself with spelled tattoos."

He glared at me, considering my words. "It doesn't matter. You killed Raven a second time. It was *your* stupidity she was trying to correct when she got herself killed the first time *and* the second time. Nice way to treat your friends, Templar."

It was me that flinched this time. That wasn't fair. He of all people knew how Raven was when she was determined to do something. No one could stop her. Heck, not even death could stop her. I blinked hard, forcing back the tears and glared at Reynard. Damn him. Damn him straight to hell.

"What exactly do you want me to do?" I wanted to wipe that smug grin off his handsome face, but instead I balled my hands up and shoved them in the pockets of my parka.

"Kill Hellfire."

Just because I stabbed Dark Iron in the back didn't mean I was up for being a contract killer. "That's a hard no. Have fun with the video." I turned around and started heading back.

"Then get him out of the country, or at least out of DC." Reynard stepped up to walk beside me. "Ensure Haul Du is mine to lead, and I'll give you the video."

"Until the next time you need something? No thanks. I'll take my chances with the Conclave."

Actually, I'd be taking my chances with the Order. Would they back me up if I took my vow? Did they want me bad enough to give me what amounted to diplomatic immunity?

Reynar moved to stand in front of me. I stopped rather than run into his chest.

"I'll give you my oath. I'll also vow both mine and Haul Du's assistance whenever you need it for the next year."

I hesitated, thinking about Big Bad. The video…well, that was a problem. Chuck could easily sell me out again, and I trusted Reynard's vow as much as I trusted a werewolf not to bite. I was going to need to put some plans in place to face the ramifications of what I'd done. Hopefully I wouldn't be in a Conclave jail, or in a Templar one, when whatever monster Fiore Noir had been spelling against descended on Baltimore.

When the shit hit the fan, I'd need all the help I could get. And a group of demon-summoning mages wasn't help I could lightly dismiss.

"Okay, but if you go back on your vows…" I tapped the phone he still held. "Don't underestimate me, Reynard. Never underestimate me."

Now I was the one who was bluffing. Maybe. I'd changed a lot in the past year, and I wasn't the person I used to be. I'd stabbed a man in the back with my consecrated weapon, killing him. Six hundred years ago that would have been justice, but in a modern world it was murder.

And I was a murderer, no matter what I used to justify it.

From the expression on Reynard's face, he knew it too. "Deal," he said, his voice hitching with uncertainty.

Deal indeed.

* * *

BUFF WAS BACK on my porch when I returned. The man was breathing heavy and looking incredibly relieved to see me in once piece.

"I won't tell if you won't," I said as I climbed the steps.

"Deal."

Yay. Two deals in the last five minutes. I was totally on a roll here.

"Come inside and have a drink," I offered as I unlocked the door. "And some food. We've got leftover Chinese. If Gran's still alive then you should feel safe eating it."

Buff looked out at the horizon. "I shouldn't."

I knew exactly what he was thinking. "Sunset is in half an hour. He's not going to think you're doing me, especially with my great grandmother in the house, and you can guard me better inside than outside. I'll even let you drink your Fireball shot by the window so you can keep an eye out for snipers."

His eyebrows shot up. "Fireball?"

"It's all I've got aside for cheap box wine," I confessed. Well, it was all I had besides my bottles of emergency beer and the expensive wines Dario had bought me for Christmas. Buff wasn't getting any of them unless he got shot while protecting me.

The man glanced over at the horizon once more and sighed. "Might as well drink a shot of Fireball. I'm probably dead come sundown anyway."

"Over a vampire's dead body you are." I held the door open and motioned for him to enter. After a second of standing there, I realized he wasn't going to leave me standing on the stoop exposed, so I went on in, closing and deadbolting the door once he'd entered behind me. Instantly an amazing aroma hit my nose. Goulash. My stomach growled, reminding me I'd had one egg roll since early this morning. A real home-cooked dinner. How long had it been since I'd had that? Probably Christmas.

"Damn. Did you eat an entire cow while you were gone, Aria? You look like a giant bloated tick."

Gran. I could always count on honesty from her. "It's a new bullet proof vest." I took off my parka, then stripped out of the vest. Sadly Gran was no longer looking at me, but the man who'd come in behind me.

"If I'd known *he* was coming inside I would have put on something sexy!"

"You've still got time," I told her. "His shift doesn't end for another half an hour."

Essie laughed. "I know that hot young thing doesn't want to see my saggy ass in a negligee. It sucks to be old, Aria. Sucks."

It wasn't the first time Gran had voiced that opinion. I was beginning to worry about her. She'd always been active and sharp of mind, and I'd never really thought her age was much of a burden for her. I knew she missed her husband, but this last year she seemed to be increasingly frustrated with her incredibly long life. I was worried. Call me selfish, but I'd always expected, and wanted, her to outlive me.

No one lived forever. She'd had a long, full life, but I just wasn't ready to lose her. I'd never be ready, no matter how unrealistic that might be.

"Want a shot of Fireball, Gran?" I headed for the kitchen, sneaking a quick peak into the food cooking on the stove. "I'm getting Buff one." I was planning on indulging myself. I'd just been blackmailed by my best friend's lover. I deserved a drink, even if it was super sweet cinnamon-flavored sorta-whiskey.

"I'll have the Woodford Reserve instead," she called out to me.

I shook my head, wondering if Gran really *was* losing it. That was the whiskey at my parents' house. No way could I afford that stuff here. Swinging open the cabinet door I stared. Next to the bottle of Fireball was Woodford Reserve as well as a bottle of Belvedere vodka and some tequila I'd never heard of. Curious, I opened the fridge and saw several bottles of pricey Sauvignon Blanc and a variety of craft beers. I also saw cold cuts wrapped in deli paper, fresh vegetables, and a packet of three rib eyes.

Gran. Although how either she or the Instacart guy got past Buff was beyond me.

Pulling three glasses out, I poured two fingers of the Woodridge Reserve in each, then went back into the living room.

Gran took her glass, then headed back into the kitchen, muttering something about cheap pours and needing more than a damned splash of booze.

"So what do you do when you're not standing outside someone's house all day?" I asked Buff as I handed him his whiskey. He took a sip and nodded appreciatively.

"Security gigs mostly. I was LAPD after five years in the Army, but quit to move here earlier this year."

"You didn't transfer to Baltimore City? Or one of the county departments?"

"It's a separate hiring, not a transfer. So I'd need to apply to an opening, then go through the process."

It was none of my business, but the guy *had* been harassing me all day, so I was going to make it my business.

"Why didn't you do that before you moved? Or soon after? You've been here a year and I know there have been openings. A seasoned officer would have gotten preference over some newbie, I'm sure."

He actually looked embarrassed. "I…I kinda need flexibility in my schedule right now."

"Because…?" I was envisioning him as a trailing spouse with baby duties that he was too macho to admit.

Buff took another hit of the whisky and let out a long breath. "My mom is dying, and my sister needed help, so I quit and moved back to Baltimore. Mom was all Casey and I had growing up. We've both moved in with her, but Casey needs to work 'cause Mom's social security isn't enough to pay for everything. We figured out a schedule so someone's always home with Mom, and we both can pick up part-time work here and there."

Oh, man. Now I really wanted to make sure Dario didn't fire, or kill, this guy.

"This isn't exactly part-time work, standing outside my house all day long," I commented.

Buff shrugged. "I'm off dusk to dawn. That means it's a 10- or 11-hour shift, and I couldn't say no to the pay."

"Even if getting fired might mean ending up in the hospital or worse?"

Worry flickered across his face, there and gone. Buff forced a grin and raised his glass to me. "Worse means that Casey and Mom get a big life insurance payout. Hospital? Well, let's just say I've got enough faith in my ability to keep you safe that I'm really not worried about either of those happening."

Until he'd realized he was guarding a stubborn Templar, that is.

"You're probably going to need more whiskey when I tell you this, but I went on a jog this morning and someone tried to run me over."

Buff blanched.

"I took care of it," I hastily assured him. "The police came and got him, and he's in lockup now. I just wanted you to know before I told Dario."

"When?" he demanded. "When did this happen?"

"Seven this morning."

He slumped in relief. "Thank God. I didn't get the call to come here until seven thirty. Was told to be here at eight." He suddenly sat up again. "You don't think he'll blame me anyway, do you?"

"He better not," I muttered. "Fair warning, though, he's probably going to make you come here pre-dawn."

Buff downed the rest of his whiskey. "I've got a better idea. I'll jog with you tomorrow. At seven. Between the two of us, we should be able to keep you from getting shot or run down."

I had an even better idea. "Deal, but I need a favor. Can you get a K9 vest to fit my bull terrier Fulk? Just charge it to Dario's account." My dog knew the shooter's scent, and I would feel safer with him by my side than I would with Buff jogging next to me.

"I can definitely do that." Buff set down his glass, then frowned. "You seriously named your dog Fuck?"

CHAPTER 13

*D*ario texted the second the sun went down, then arrived soon after. He and Buff did the typical male sizing up of each other before Buff left, the bodyguard telling me that he'd see me at seven in the morning for our run.

Dario turned to me, his lips curled in a rueful smile. "Figures that's what the security firm sent over. I was hoping he'd be ugly."

"Gran's up putting on sexy clothes right now. She says to tell you thanks for the hottie." I chuckled at Dario's alarmed expression. "I'm kidding. Kinda. He is pretty fine, though. I've been staring out the window drooling at him all day."

"And then you invited him in for a drink?" Dario nudged the empty glass on the coffee table. "The only reason he's alive right now is that you don't smell like he's done more than shake your hand."

"Yeah. Actually, let's talk about that." I motioned for him to sit, then went to let Fulk in from the backyard. Gran was in the kitchen pouring food into Gaia's bowl, a full glass of whiskey in her hand. Noting the alarming amount of empty space in the bottle, I grabbed it and another glass, then went back into the living room.

"First, we discussed this last night. In fact, we argued about it last night." I set the glass down and poured him a splash, adding a bit more to my own glass.

"We did argue about it. And if you'll notice, I did not send a moving crew over to haul you and your household over to my place, nor did I keep you under lock and key. I'm dead all day. You can't expect me to not take precautions to make sure you're alive when I wake up at night."

"The only threat to my life today happened before your rent-a-cop even got here," I told him, not really considering Reynard's blackmail to be in the life-threatening category.

Dario stopped breathing, which would have been alarming had he not been a vampire.

"And I took care of it all by my little lonesome." I pitched my voice high. "Lawdy, I can hardly lift a finger without nearly fainting, but I somehow managed to take down an assailant who was trying to run me over and hold him in place until the police arrived. Aren't you proud, sweetie?"

"Someone tried to run you over?" Dario growled. "I told you not to go for a run this morning."

"And I told you to stuff it where the sun doesn't shine," I snapped back. "I had my sword and my spelled shield. The police have the guy in custody, and the good news is he'll get a plea deal by tomorrow sometime and we'll have a lead on who is hiring these people."

"People? He's not the one who shot you?" Dario's eyes were dark, his fangs sharp as he snarled.

"No. I did a spell this morning and was able to success-fully identify the shooter from the bullet casings." I told him the woman's name and the info that Tremelay had given me on her. "It's been a busy day, what with all that and Reynard blackmailing me into helping him get rid of this Hellfire mage."

I needed to stop because Dario was on the edge of a heart attack—if vampires could even get heart attacks.

"Who do I kill first? Reynard? This Henrietta Aliette woman? The guy who tried to run you down? What was his name anyway?"

"I don't know the guy's name. I didn't ask. Besides, Tremelay is handling that. And don't kill Reynard. It's my own damned fault he's blackmailing me. Seems someone set up hidden cameras and gave Reynard an Academy quality performance shot of me killing Dark Iron and your family hauling his body off to God-knows-where."

"Chuck." Dario's eyes narrowed. "I'm adding him to my list of people to kill."

I rolled my eyes. "Can you not kill anyone? Let's figure out who exactly is trying to kill *me* before we start entertaining that solution. Besides, I already have one murder under my belt. I'm not eager to add to that."

Dario took a deep breath and eyed the whiskey. "Is that for me?" Without waiting for an answer he pounded it. Then pounded mine. I knew that alcohol didn't affect him as far as getting drunk, but maybe it calmed him down?

"Let's start with Reynard. What exactly is he demanding you do?" the vampire asked.

"Kill Hellfire." I shrugged. "I told him that wasn't happening, so I'm supposed to somehow drive him out of town."

"I'll take care of that for you," Dario said. "Just get me a name and an address and he'll never be heard from again."

"Would you cut it with the murder talk?" I went to pour myself more whiskey, then decided not to. "I don't know the guy's real name, where he is, what he even looks like. I'm assuming Reynard will get back to me in the next day or two with a plan, so let's shelve that one for now."

Dario nodded. "And you said the guy who tried to run you over is in the county lockup?"

"Tremelay is handling that," I replied. "And, he's allegedly handling questioning Henrietta Aliette."

"Allegedly." Dario's eyes narrowed.

"A magical spell isn't going to get them a warrant," I told him. "They know where she lives and what she's driving. All they can do is see if she'll talk. If she won't, there's not much they can do but keep looking for enough evidence to get a warrant and make an arrest."

"I can make her talk." Dario's smile was downright predatory.

"Which is why I wanted to invite you to come with me tonight. I'm hoping we can find Henrietta, then find out who she's working for. The big problem is going to be finding her. We can't really stake out her house all night, especially since Tremelay probably has some of his buddies with the DC police force doing just that."

"I can track her down."

Was I weird that this was turning me on? I didn't want Dario to be stuffing me into a gilded cage, but I loved when his take-charge, master-vampire self partnered with me.

"Then let's do it. No killing though." I wiggled a finger at him just to make sure he understood.

"No killing." He stood up and headed for the front door. "Just let me make a few quick calls. I need to make sure things are organized for tonight if I'm going to be out of town."

I got up to go feed Fulk and let Gran know what was going on, not even wondering why Dario felt the need to make his phone calls outside, out of earshot from me. As soon as I entered the kitchen I realized we couldn't leave—at least not right away. Gran had made goulash for dinner. I'd specifically asked her to make it. Dario and I couldn't take off and leave her behind to eat alone after she'd done all this work.

Sheesh. I wasn't used to having a roommate. Luckily Essie was already pulling bowls out from the cabinets.

I shooed Gaia off the table and wiped it off, putting out the bowls and silverware while Gran spooned the food into a serving dish. Dario walked back inside, staring at the place settings. I held a finger to my mouth to silence his question.

"Gran cooked goulash for dinner," I whispered. "I asked her to, but then forgot she'd made it when you came over. We can eat and just do a quick clean-up, then be on our way."

The goulash was amazing with meat so tender it practically fell apart when I stuck it with my fork. The sauce was spicy, peppery and perfect for a cold winter day. We ended up lingering longer than I'd expected, and I thanked Gran several times, knowing she'd put a lot of effort into this meal.

Dario had to step outside for a few quick conversations while I did the dishes and Gran packed away the leftovers.

"I enjoyed this," she commented as she shoved the containers into the fridge. "I don't think I've actually cooked anything in two decades, and here I've made breakfast *and* dinner."

I shook the water off my hands and picked up a towel to start drying dishes. "Well, I loved it. I can barely boil an egg, so anytime you want to cook, you go right ahead."

She sat down at the table and smiled. "I used to make the best biscuits. And when I was a girl, I always loved smoked cod roe on fried bread."

Not exactly a modern comfort food but I was willing to give it a shot. "Well, I may have gotten your magic, but I certainly didn't get your cooking skills."

"Nothing that can't be taught," she told me. "So are you and Dario heading out? I thought I heard you say something about DC?"

I hesitated, not sure if I wanted to let Gran know exactly what I was doing or not. Would she be worried? Worse, would she want to come with?

"We're going to see if we can track down Henrietta Aliette," I told her.

"From the spell this morning? Well, it's good you're taking a vampire with you then." She got up from the table and sighed. "Be safe. Kick some ass. I'm going to take a long soak in that tub of yours then settle in on your couch for a nap and some television. If I'm asleep there when you get home, just let me be. I'll eventually make my way upstairs."

Tub. I shot her a worried glance. "You've got that beeper thing Dad gave you, right?"

She patted her chest. "I'll be fine."

"I know. Just don't go dying on my watch. Dad would never forgive me," I teased.

She chuckled. "Oh, don't you worry. It'll take more than a tub full of water to kill me."

I laughed, knowing she was right. Then I grabbed my coat, kissed her cheek, and went to find my vampire.

* * *

DARIO DROVE TO DC, and I completely appreciated his comfortable SUV with the heated seats. We'd picked up Opal on our way and she sat in the back seat, unusually silent as we headed down BW Parkway. I got why Dario would pick her to accompany us instead of Madeline or Balen. He was the head of his family and he was leaving the city. He needed his strongest vampires there to act in his stead. Opal was young, but had proven herself to be very useful in a fight. Dario knew I liked and trusted her. And she had a way of drawing every male eye in the room—useful if we needed people to not be paying attention to Dario or me.

I got the feeling there would be no passionate makeup sex tonight. Dario was one hundred percent focused on finding whoever was hiring people to kill me, and I can't say I wasn't feeling the same way. With that out of the way, I could focus on things like Reynard blackmailing me, Chuck selling me out, and whether or not I was going to need to take my vow in order to remain out of a Conclave jail for the rest of my life.

Minor stuff like that. But not getting killed topped that in importance.

Henrietta's home was a swank condo in northeast DC. We pulled around the block while I looked to see if I could spot Tremelay's car somewhere near on a stakeout. I didn't, but just in case I stayed in the SUV while Dario and Opal went to the condo building to do some reconnaissance of their own.

Both vampires vanished into the shadows and I leaned back against the leather upholstery, bored. I got it. It made sense for me to stay here and let the two others take this on. They were faster, stealthier, and weren't likely to be recognized by any police watching the building. In addition, vampires had special skills in charming the truth out of humans where I pretty much had to rely on threats and my sword. I trusted that no one who encountered Dario or Opal would suffer any more than slight blood loss and some confusion over what had happened tonight. And if they lucked out and found Henrietta, they were better suited than me to scare the truth out of her.

Still, none of that made me feel any better about sitting in the SUV.

It was an hour before Dario returned.

"Where's Opal?" I asked as he got into the car.

"Dupont Circle." He started the engine and pulled out into traffic. "She had better luck than I did. Seems Henrietta

Aliette runs a furniture import business and is part owner of a nightclub in addition to her side activities shooting at Templars."

I stared at him in surprise.

"I'm kidding about the shooting thing. I've got no idea why a nightclub owner who imports sofas and chairs decided to take up assassination as a hobby."

It did sound weird. Did assassins have day jobs? Was the import thing part of her cover as some sort of foreign operative? Had I been watching too many Bond movies?

"Maybe my spell was wrong," I mused. "It did give me her name, and the image it showed matched the one of the driver's license that Tremelay pulled up. But instead of being the shooter, perhaps the spell showed me that she'd sold the shooter the bullets?"

Dario shot me a quizzical look. "So either she sells bullets to killers on the side, or she takes murder-for-hire jobs on the side. Both sound equally strange."

I frowned. "Either way, let's take a slow and easy approach. I don't want to threaten or scare someone who may have nothing to do with my being shot. Tremelay did say her record was clean, and I'm not one hundred percent on my spell."

"Opal knows we want answers as to who's behind this," Dario assured me. "If she finds the woman before we get there, I promise you they'll be in some back room having a lovely time together. She won't do anything beyond a quick bite without asking me first."

That did make me feel better, although I still worried the entire drive there. Dario parked and this time I came with him, leaving my shield in the SUV but taking my sword. I trusted that Dario could move fast enough to get me out of the way of any bullets. Hopefully my look-away spell would be enough to get me in the door with my sword, because I really didn't want to be completely weaponless against a possible assassin and whoever else at this club that might be armed and working with Henrietta.

The club was in a narrow building about a block away from Dupont Circle itself. The bouncer let us in without so much as a second glance. We walked down a narrow hallway that vibrated with the thump of music, paid a bored cashier ten dollars each, then went down a set of stairs and through a heavy metal door.

The wave of eighties punk music just about knocked me off my feet. Dario winced, and I realized how terrible the sound must be on a vampire's sensitive hearing. Taking my arm, he motioned for me to follow, then headed around the dance floor and toward the end of the bar where I saw Opal sipping a blue cocktail and swaying to the music. She waved to us, then slipped down a hallway behind the bar and into an office. As soon as she shut the door behind us, the music dampened to a moderate level.

"I made friends with the manager." Opal smiled, revealing sharp fangs. "I've had more fun tonight than I have in months. Six meals! And a quickie with this amazing Brazilian woman who bartends on the weekends, and waitresses during the week."

"Opal! Focus!" Dario's voice was stern, but a smile curled his lips.

"Oh! Henrietta had to go somewhere about a shipment." Opal made little quotation marks with her fingers. "Seems she smuggles drugs in her furniture, and was meeting someone about a deal. She left two hours ago and was supposed to be back by now."

I shared a glance with Dario. "You think she skipped town? Maybe she knows we're looking for her? Or that the police are looking for her?"

"I doubt it." Opal shrugged. "Jasper didn't seem too

concerned. He says this happens a lot, and that maybe this thing with the buyer took longer than expected, or she went home afterward."

Crap. "Should we head back to her house?" I asked. "Or wait here for her?"

"Let's head back," Dario said. "Opal, you stay here and text me if Henrietta comes in or you find out anything more."

"Got it, boss."

Just then the door opened and a tall, shapely brunette entered, stopping abruptly when she saw us.

"Ooo, sorry! I was just grabbing my coat," she shouted over the increased volume of the band.

Opal waved at her. "No problem, Lottie. You work tomorrow night?"

The other woman blushed. "I do. Come in to see me. Or call me, okay?"

With a smile, Lottie picked up a black wool coat and left, shutting the door behind her.

"Think I'll walk her to her car," Opal said with a wink, slipping out after the other woman.

"So...back to the house to do a stakeout?" I was at the point of wanting to just go home and let the police deal with it. The idea of sitting in a car outside a woman's house the rest of the night wasn't appealing. And I wasn't even sure at this point if Henrietta really had anything to do with shooting me or not.

Before he could answer, Dario's phone buzzed.

"There's no need for a stakeout," he told me. "Opal found Henrietta Aliette. She's in the employee parking lot out back. Dead."

Crap. I followed Dario out the fire door that seemed to double as an employee entrance, then through a parking area jam-packed with vehicles. Opal waved at us from the far corner and we wove around the cars as we made our way toward her. Sure enough, a terribly mutilated figure was sprawled across the blacktop between a Volvo sedan and a Porsche.

The three of us stared down at the body.

"This wasn't vampires," Opal announced. "I mean, no self-respecting vampire is gonna waste blood like that."

She was right. Henrietta Aliette hadn't been killed by vampires—or by a human without some medieval torture device. No knife or gun ripped the limbs off someone.

No knife or gun left a demon sigil burned into the victim's forehead either.

"Death is the price for failure?" Dario asked.

"Looks like it."

But the question was who? Was the demon mark a red herring? There were plenty of creatures who had the strength and inclination to do this sort of thing, but I didn't know of any who would bother to misdirect potential investigators this way, even if they had the knowledge of sigils. No, a demon had killed this woman—which meant a mage skilled in summoning demons had directed one to kill her.

I snapped a photo of the sigil with my cell phone. "Where's Lottie?" I asked Opal.

The vampire inclined her head. "Over in her car. This really shook her up. I told her I'd call the police."

"You done?" Dario waited for my answer. "Opal, go ahead and call the police. Stay here with the human and go ahead and give a statement. Use my address if you don't feel comfortable using your own."

"Yes, Boss. Do you need me to come straight back to Baltimore, or can I hang out an hour or two?"

Dario glanced over to where Lottie sat in her car, the door open and her head buried in her arms. "Stay if you like, but be back enough before dawn so you can brief me."

"Got it." Opal pulled her phone from her pocket and dialed, walking cheerfully back toward Lottie.

Vampires. Even the most gruesome of murder scenes didn't seem to bother them one bit.

As Dario and I headed back to Baltimore my thoughts churned through the possibilities. Reynard had said Hellfire had killed several Haul Du members. It was a possibility Henrietta was a casualty of that mage war, although that scenario still left the question of her motive unanswered. And more importantly, if she was a Haul Du member, why try to shoot me instead of summoning a demon to do the job? Unless Henrietta wasn't a powerful enough mage to handle bringing a demon outside of a summoning circle for a task.

There were other mage groups besides Haul Du who specialized in Goetic magic, and there were non-Goetic mages who'd studied the art of summoning. I thought of the mage from Argentina whose soul trap I'd disabled and sucked in a sharp breath. Had he discovered what I'd done? Was it him who'd sent Henrietta to kill me and then murdered her when she failed? I'd met that mage, and while he struck me as someone who absolutely wouldn't hesitate to hire a hitwoman, I didn't see him as the sort who'd kill her after one failed attempt. No, he'd want her to keep trying and maybe send in a backup killer just in case.

Also, he'd gone to the Conclave when his soul trap had been stolen rather than go after Dark Iron himself or via a shooter. Was that just a professional courtesy that I wouldn't be afforded as a non-mage, or was it indicative of his desire to follow the rule of law even when something was personal?

"Penny for your thoughts," Dario said softly.

I held out my hand and he dug around in his pocket for a moment before handing me a quarter.

"They're not worth this much," I teased.

"I'm pretty sure they are," he countered.

"Just thinking of who might want me dead and why. Sadly, none of the possible suspects seem to fit the puzzle."

"But clearly it's someone who can summon demons," he said.

I shrugged. "Maybe. Or maybe someone who can summon demons wanted Henrietta dead and her murder is unrelated to my being shot yesterday."

Dario sighed. "I wish we would have found her alive. I guarantee between Opal and I, we would have had answers."

There was a hard edge to his words that made me shiver —and not in a bad way. I was glad this vampire was on my side, even if he secretly owned the house I was renting, hired an ex-army dude as a body guard, and occasionally wanted to haul me off to his home and lock me safely away in a gilded cage.

"We still have that guy in lockup," I told him. "Tremelay should have information from him in the next day or so. And maybe the cops got to Henrietta before she was killed."

Dario snorted. "Then she would have been at the station answering questions, not dead behind a club."

True. "We'll just have to wait," I told him.

"I hate waiting." He growled. "I want you to be careful. I know I can't keep you from going out jogging or working or anything, but please promise me you'll be careful."

I held up a hand. "I promise. Buff is going with me tomorrow morning. I'll have Fulk as well, with his own bulletproof vest. I'll also be wearing the eighty-pound monstrosity you are insisting I wear, be carrying my sword, *and* have my shield with the protection symbols painted all over it."

"Can't you paint those symbols all over *you*?"

I could tell he was only half teasing. Still, his suggestion brought to mind something I'd been thinking about the last few days.

"Does that sound crazy?" I asked. "Because I've been wondering about using tattoos as a focus. I mean, my wrist tattoo isn't much different except it was blessed as it was inked by a Templar artist, but there's no reason I shouldn't be able to charge a tattoo with a blessing after the fact."

"I'm all for making sure you're safe, but the idea of you having a series of landmines all over your skin is more than a bit discouraging. Think of our sex life," he teased.

That *would* suck. That would more than suck. If my wrist tattoo burned him, then what would other blessed tattoos do? I definitely didn't want to inadvertently kill him by having him touch a "sacred space" blessed tattoo while we were getting it on.

"My wrist tattoo doesn't need to be charged," I mused. "I'm thinking these would be just normal tattoos if they're not charged. And I'm not intending on making them all protective tattoos. The first one I'm thinking of getting would be to call my sword into my hand."

He chuckled. "Like Thor's hammer?"

Here we go again. "No, just from the floor or from across the room. I'm thinking it'll be useful in case I'm disarmed—or to even keep my sword in my hand if someone is using a spell to pull it away. I don't think that tattoo would burn or harm you in any way."

"Unless you call your sword through my back into your palm," he joked.

I turned to look at him. "That's an amazing idea! I mean, not through you, but maybe through someone I'm fighting? Except it would come to my hand hilt-first. That wouldn't quite have the same impact as impaling the bad guy."

"A small price to pay for not occasionally stabbing your-self through the hand with your own sword." He smiled and shook his head. "Although taking a pommel to the back at speed might be enough to cause some serious damage."

"You're right, it could."

He reached over and took my hand, entwining his fingers in mine. "Can I admit that I'm kind of intrigued about this tattoo idea? Maybe while you're at it, you can get my name inked somewhere."

I rolled my eyes. "Like on one of my boobs? Inner thigh? Across my ass."

He lifted my hand to his lips. "Mmm, I like that idea. Your ass is mine, Aria. It's even got my name on it."

I laughed because my ass was his. And there was no way I was getting his name tattooed on it.

uff showed up at my house an hour early, just passing Dario on his way down the steps. Both men paused, the vampire saying a few low words to the human before he continued on. I was pretty sure those words were something about making sure I didn't so much as get a split end today.

My guard was carrying a bag which held Fulk's new Kevlar vest. I sent Buff into the kitchen to help himself to coffee and strapped my dog into his new outfit.

Fulk stared at me as if I'd just called him a bad boy and smacked his nose with a newspaper. I'd never seen such a betrayed, accusing look in my entire life

"It's to keep you safe," I told him. "You either wear it or you don't go for a run."

Ugh, I sounded just like Dario. To make up for it, I patted Fulk, slipped him a dog treat, then got the leash. By the time Buff was back with a cup of coffee, I was struggling into my new bulky jogging attire, while Fulk whined and tried to scratch his own vest off.

Buff downed the coffee, and we stopped by his car so he

could suit up as well. I started to laugh, realizing that anyone who saw us was going to think the governor had declared a state of martial law.

Buff must have been thinking the same because he shook his head and sent me a sideways smile. "I'm getting flashbacks of Iraq here."

"Except it's about a hundred degrees colder, and I'm carrying a sword and shield instead of a gun?" I countered.

"And all I've got is a pistol and a Taser," he added.

"Average attire for two people and a dog, exercising in the streets of downtown Baltimore," I quipped.

Buff set up a punishing pace, and I somehow managed to keep up, knowing if I slowed he would as well to stay beside me. My pride won out over the healing bruises on my chest and abs, but at the three mile turnaround, I felt as if I were dying. It was a silent run, mainly because I completely lacked any breath to do anything but keep enough oxygen flowing to my muscles. By the time we broke pace for our cooldown walk, I was silently cursing the man by my side and trying to think of excuses not to run tomorrow morning.

I was off work again today, and thrilled to be greeted by the smell of pancakes and bacon as we entered. I fed Fulk and Gaia, then Gran, Buff, and I had a leisurely breakfast. Afterward, my bodyguard headed outside to check the perimeter while I went up to get my shower.

Today's run had been uneventful, but I wasn't so foolish that I didn't realize this was the calm before the storm. If someone wanted me dead, they were hardly going to give up after two attempts. I was worried that instead of trying to make my death seem like a random act of violence, they might decide to just go all out and just kill me any way they could. I remembered Henrietta's body and felt breakfast churn in my stomach. But I had special skills when it came to demons. In a way, that would be a far less effective way to kill me than having someone unload a pistol into my chest.

How long *would* it take my nemesis to find a different assassin? Or decide to come after me him or herself?

I was just getting out of the shower when my phone rang. It was Tremelay, so I grabbed it then put him on speaker phone while I got dressed.

"Well, we have a written confession and a guilty plea," Tremelay announced. "We also have a prisoner who looks like someone beat the crap out of him with a two-by-four. Any idea who that might be?"

For a second I was confused, wondering why he was asking me about an inmate-on-inmate attack, or a case of police brutality, then I remembered Dario stepping repeatedly out onto my front stoop to make a phone call. While we'd been in DC tracking down Henrietta Aliette, Dario's crew had been beating information out of a man in police lockup.

"I didn't know, Tremelay. I swear."

He sighed. "Whatever. Either way, the guy said he was hired by a man. No name, just cash up front, then more cash after your obituary was in the paper. No contact info for the guy. He said the man was supposed to get ahold of him for the second payment. He wasn't worried about getting stiffed because the initial deposit was more than what the going rate is for running a jogger over."

"But he was supposed to run me over specifically?" I asked. "And why wasn't this man worried that his contract killer would take the money and run?"

"Here's where it gets weird." Tremelay snorted. "Well, weird for most people, not for you and me. The killer said the guy who hired him is some sort of devil-worshipping wizard, just like those people we arrested this past fall."

"Fiore Noir?" In spite of selling me out, I didn't believe

Chuck was trying to kill me, but maybe others with the death mage group wanted me dead?

Or was it Haul Du? They didn't like me, but if they'd wanted to kill me, then they would have done it when I was first kicked out. Reynard had certainly turned into an asshole, but murdering me wouldn't help him get rid of Hellfire. *Could* it be Hellfire? As far as I knew the guy didn't even know I existed. I couldn't think of any reason he'd want to kill me. I couldn't think of any reason *anyone* with Haul Du would want to kill me.

Unless this was someone else who knew what I'd done to Dark Iron and wanted vengeance. Or that mage from Argentina.

"How did he know the guy hiring him was a…a devil-worshipping mage?" I nearly laughed at the term, but I guess someone who hadn't been involved with magic and the supernatural as I had would leap to those conclusions.

"I think he was embarrassed to go into details, because at first he just said the guy had a whole lot of occult jewelry—rings and a necklace. After some talking, he admitted that the guy appeared and disappeared, like he was teleporting. And his eyes glowed red. He smelled like a lit match as well."

A demon.

"And here's where it gets even more woo-woo, Ainsworth. That Henrietta Aliette you pointed me to yesterday? She's dead. And I'm not talking normal DC violence dead either. Looked like someone put her on a torture rack behind a club near Dupont Circle and pulled her limbs off. Oh, and then burned an occult symbol into her forehead. The DC cops are freaking out. They're worried they've got some nutjobs like we had here in Baltimore."

"This nutjob has a different kind of agenda," I told him. Then I went on to describe the potential mage war in DC as well as my sketchy suspect list of who might want me dead.

"So we've got a demon killing one assassin and hiring another. I'm not liking this, Ainsworth."

Neither was I. Using a demon was smart since that meant the police wouldn't be able to trace anything back to the killer. It was also scary, because that meant that not only was the mage skilled in demonology, he was powerful enough to twice bind a demon and send him to do service outside the protections of a summoning circle.

I was no closer to finding out who wanted me dead. I didn't want to rule out someone from Fiore Noir, but I put them at the end of my suspect list since outside of Chuck, mages who specialized in death magic didn't normally have the ability to summon demons. And although Chuck could banish, and I'm sure summon some demons, I honestly felt this would be outside his skill level.

That left someone from Haul Du, this Hellfire guy, or the Argentina mage.

I needed to meet with Reynard and ask him if anyone with Haul Du might wanted me dead, or if there was any reason Hellfire might be targeting me. If he said no to both of those, then my top suspect would be the mage from Argentina—which meant I was *really* screwed.

CHAPTER 15

Reynard texted me before I had a chance to do so, asking me to meet him late afternoon. Eyeing the time, I figured I had about six or seven hours before our meeting. That should be plenty of time to do what I wanted.

So I told Buff to make sure Gran was safe and that no one bombed my house, then I drove to a nearby bakery and grabbed a cup of coffee, drinking as I made about a dozen calls trying to find a tattoo parlor that had an opening for this afternoon. As much as I hated having an unknown artist with some free time on his or her hands putting ink on my skin, I didn't want to wait around on this either. I'd been a fool not to think of this earlier. The tattoo on my wrist had its own magic, powered by my faith and my…Templarness or something. The nail-polish symbol on my neck had worked to sanctify my skin and kill the vampire who'd tried to bite me. The symbols I'd painted on my shield, what Raven had used to keep her soul safe from Dark Iron…it was all based on tattoos channeling magic through them.

Maybe if I had tattoos that meant something to me symbolically, I could charge them as I had the nail-polish symbols, and perform magic that way. It was worth a try. If it failed, then I'd just have a few extra tattoos on my arms— ones that hopefully weren't horribly done.

By the time I'd finished my large coffee, I had list of three artists in Baltimore who had openings today: Kurt Devon, Rob Miller, and Dagger Wayons.

I made my way to my car, thinking I'd try Dagger first. Yeah, his name was cheesy, but one of the tattoos I wanted was of my sword. I figured a guy named Dagger might be able to not make a total mess of that one. I'd check his port-folio, then make a snap judgement. If I felt at all uneasy, I'd move on to the other two on my list. Worst case, I wouldn't get the tattoo today, although I really wanted to get going on this theory of mine and not waste time on checking out every ink artist in the city.

Atomic Charm was a basement shop situated between a vintage vinyl record shop, and a liquor store. The first-floor business was a cigar store—not the ritzy expensive kind of cigar store, but the kind where cheap tobacco smoke oozed from the cracks around the door frame and a yellow-stained sign in the window promoted chew in a tin.

I headed down the chipped concrete steps to a heavy metal door. No windows. Nothing except a sign slapped on the thick black-painted brick proclaiming this to be Atomic Charm Tattoos and Piercings.

The inside was far more professional than the outside. The lighting was bright, the walls a clean dove gray with an assortment of black-and-white nature photos for decoration. Two black chairs sat opposite each other in the middle of the store. A slim elderly man sat in one, receiving a tattoo from a large bearded man who held the gun with a surprisingly long-fingered, delicate hand. A woman with short crimson hair slumped in the other chair, reading a magazine.

The buzz of the equipment blended soothingly with the

alternative rock coming from the speakers mounted near the ceiling. A glass case held a variety of rings, bars, and studs for piercings. Two thick binders sat on top with the artist's name on each book. I glanced at the bearded artist, wondering if he really would have time to fit me in with the elderly client and the woman waiting her turn.

Of course, none of that would matter if his work was scary-bad. I flipped open the book that said "Dagger" on the front and began leafing through the pictures of arms, legs, backs, necks, and other more private body parts, all covered with examples of Dagger's work.

My mouth dropped open. I didn't care how long I had to wait, this guy was going to do all my tattoos. The creativity, the sheer artistry in his work was amazing. Dagger had a distinct style, but put a very personal slant on every bit of ink. Memorial portraits were lifelike and full of emotion. Retro art fully captured the nuances of the period and original artist. One tattoo looked exactly like embroidery, complete with shading on the "threads" that made them seem 3D. Yes, there were the usual tribal symbols, pin-up girls, and skulls, but even they had creative shading, and complex coloring. Every picture made me catch my breath.

"You the walk-in who called around noon?"

As soon as I heard the woman's voice, I realized my mistake. "I am. Are you Dagger?"

Looking up, I saw the crimson-haired woman on the other side of the case. She was tall and incredibly thin and wearing a leather vest that laced up the front and left most of her abdomen visible. The tight skirt that barely covered her crotch was the same color as her hair. Her milky-white skin was oddly free of any visible tattoos. What she lacked in ink, she made up for in piercings, though. The woman had studs and bars all through her ears, her eyebrows, and her nose.

She had two hoops on her lips, and an intricate loop-and-chain piercing through her belly button.

"Yep. You're lucky, you know. I'm booked six months out, but this afternoon's appointment got arrested this morning." She laughed. "Guy gets one phone call from county lockup, and he telephones me to let me know he can't make his appointment."

This wasn't luck, this was fate. And I was going to be completely honest with this woman and hope she didn't kick me out of the shop.

"I'm a Templar, and I'm thinking of using tattoos as a focus and to store energy in working magic." The woman didn't even blink, so I continued. "I've done it before, and it's not unusual for Templars to have blessed tattoos. We all have one on our wrist that acts as a very mild protection against evil. I'm looking to amp that up considerably, and was hoping I could get one or two tattoos from you to experiment with. If they work, I'd like to get more."

Although waiting six months would be a pain in the ass. Also, now that I'd seen Dagger's artwork, I was a little nervous about what this was going to cost me.

She shrugged. "Let me see your ink."

I showed it to her and she took hold of my arm, wrinkling her nose as she looked at the bright red cross on my wrist. I winced. It was basic, but this wasn't meant to be a work of art, just something that committed us to our lineage and gave us some basic protections.

"What are you thinking of?" she asked, releasing my arm.

I took a breath. "First, I want a tattoo of my sword. I'd like to be able to call it to me from across the room, or from the floor at a minimum." There had been too many times when I'd been disarmed, and I'd be damned if I was going to let that be a game-changer ever again.

Dagger didn't seem bothered by that at all so I continued.

"If that works out, then I want a tattoo of a shield, or an armored knight. Or an armored knight with a shield. Basically, I want something I can charge for use in defensive magic."

She nodded. "Like if someone tries to stab you, but you don't happen to actually have a shield handy, or armor on at the time?"

"Exactly. Stab, shoot, turn me into a newt." That rhymed and I hadn't really meant it. Oh well.

"Let me think on that one," she replied. "In the meantime, what sort of sword are you thinking of?"

I pulled it from my scabbard and she jumped back a foot, eyes wide.

"Where the fuck did that come from?"

Crap. I'd forgotten about my "look-away" spell. "I use a magic spell to conceal it from view because people get alarmed if they see a woman walking around downtown Baltimore with a huge sword on her back."

Most times it worked. Sometimes it didn't and I got informed by clerks and bouncers that I had to leave "all weapons" outside. It was telling that none of those people seemed particularly bothered that I was carrying around a sword, or that they had to tell a customer to leave a weapon outside. Baltimore. Go figure.

She held out a tentative hand, and I reluctantly passed her my sword. When I'd first gotten Trusty, it had just been a plain old bastard sword. It had been for practice, for training. I'd always assumed that when I took my Oath I'd get something fancier with precious metals on the hilt and a blade that didn't require constant cleaning and maintenance to keep it sharp.

But I hadn't taken my Oath, and somehow over the years this had become *my* sword. It was plain and utilitarian. Outside of the chipped red enamel cross on the hilt, there were no embellishments. The blade had suffered its share of nicks and dings. The grip was a wire-wrap that smoothed and tarnished over the years to a dull gray. And somehow this all worked just fine for who I was and what I was doing. I wasn't a fancy Knight, I was a soldier of God, protecting pilgrims on the path and living a life of near-poverty in a city filled with crime.

Trusty was a part of me. I'd never want another sword. No other sword could ever take the place of one that had been with me from the age of eight on. None.

"There's a lot of power in this weapon," Dagger commented before shooting me a wry grin. "What? You think tattoo artists don't understand magic? It's what we do. Art. Magic. They're one and the same."

That would make this a lot easier. "Originally this was just a sword, but over the years I've used it for blessings and banishments. It's sanctified. It's a holy object. And in my hands it's a holy weapon."

She nodded. "As a woman named Dagger, I approve. Do you want the tattoo to look exactly like your sword, or have any specific embellishments? Other symbols? What are you envisioning for this tattoo?"

I closed my eyes and thought for a second. "Just like the sword. Dings and chips and all. When I call it to me, I want to be connected to everything this sword is, not some idealized version of it."

"Understood." Dagger gestured toward the chair she'd been sitting in. "Where do you want this tattoo?"

That was something I'd been debating. There was a plus to having my tattoos somewhere hidden so that I didn't worry about someone seeing them and judging me. But there was another part of me that didn't care what people thought. A sword. My sword. Calling it to my hand when needed.

"Can you do a tattoo on my palm?"

"Yeah, but it hurts like fuck," she told me. "They fade fast, so I can't do anything too detailed and you'll need to get it touched up frequently. Solid black or dot shading works best."

"Can you work in the red Templar cross on the hilt?" I asked.

She tilted her head for a second, then looked through her supplies as I sat in the chair. "It won't be very distinct. I can put it in, but it might look like a red blob after a few weeks. Keep in mind this is a small tattoo, and your palm is very calloused—I'm assuming from years of sword play."

"No detail is okay, just two lines of a red cross on the hilt," I told her. "If it fades, I'll get it touched up."

She nodded. "I'm thinking three touch-ups might do the trick for this one. Now, are you right or left handed?"

I didn't feel like going into an explanation that I'd been trained to be ambidextrous when it came to my weapons, and that the best use of a bastard sword was commonly known as half-swording, where I held the hilt in my dominant hand and gripped halfway up the blade with my other hand, turning the weapon into a sort of lance or bayonet. That's why the sharpened part was only on the front half of the blade. I'd also been trained to use Trusty as a sword-and-shield combo with the shield usually in my left hand.

Tattoos took a while to heal, and I didn't relish the idea of trying to fight with Trusty's hilt rubbing against freshly inked skin, so left sounded good. But I'd been carrying my shield, and I always used my left hand for that. It would suck to have to juggle my shield around to call my sword into my left hand when I really needed it in my right.

Ah well. It wasn't like I hadn't dealt with pain before. "Do the tattoo on my right palm."

Dagger shook her head as she set up her equipment. "You guys should really train with rifles and pistols. I totally get the nostalgic appeal of swords, but it's not like this thing is going to deflect a bullet. Or kill someone at any sort of distance."

"But I can majorly eff up some undead," I told her. "Try to kill a vampire with a Glock and it isn't going to happen. Plus if the zombie apocalypse occurs, then I'm your girl."

She laughed. "Got it. Sword it is. Let me prop this antique zombie killer over here for a reference and get started."

I quickly realized that Dagger was right—palm tattoos hurt like crazy. I'd been shot, savaged by a vampire, bruised by a broadsword across the sternum, but nothing hurt like a million tiny needles digging into my palm.

I stared at a black-and-white picture of a dogwood tree on the wall and tried to disassociate from the agony shooting up my arm. When she was finally done, I looked down and was amazed to find a perfect replica of Trusty on my palm, shading and all. She'd even put the red Templar cross on the hilt in beautiful relief. I hated to think that this might blur and fade over the next few weeks, but for now, it was a work of art and I loved it.

"I've got time for the other tattoo if you want to give it a go." Dagger looked up at the clock. "My previous appointment had been for six hours, so I'm all yours."

I noticed the elderly man had left and that the bearded tattoo artist was now working on the back of a blonde woman.

"What do you think about the shield tattoo?" I wasn't sure where I wanted to put it or what exactly I wanted.

"As much as I like the idea of doing a knight in full armor, I think it might be easier for you to spell a shield. I can make the cross match the one on your sword, and do some realistic shading on it. Maybe even put some symbols around the edge if you know what you want."

I thought of the symbol I'd painted on my neck. It

wouldn't work for protecting me against a bullet or a speeding car, but it would help against curses and an attack by undead. "I like that. Yeah. The shield with a ring of symbols around it. But where should I put it?" I mused.

"How about around your wrists, like bracers? The symbols can go all the way around, with the shield on the outside." The woman held her arms up in front of her as if blocking a blow. "You know, like Wonder Woman, only cooler."

It was a good idea, but I didn't want anything to interfere with the cross tattoo already on my wrist. Plus, a shield for me had always been an offensive as well as a defensive weapon.

"How about on the outside of my upper arm?" I pointed to the spot.

"Hmm. That would look cool. Kinda tribal almost." She tapped her chin. "Now that I think about it, neither of those would be what I'd consider the best area for a protection tattoo."

"Really?" I looked down at the one on my palm. That location had been easy since I wanted to call the sword to my hand. I didn't have an ideal place in mind for this tattoo though. It wasn't like I could cover my entire body with it, even though I wanted the protection to include everything from top to toe. "What do you have in mind?" I asked Dagger.

"Well, *I'd* want to line it up with your core power. Ideally you should have a protective symbol on each of your chakras. That would reinforce your aura *and* turn it into a protective shield."

I blinked in surprise. Was Dagger skilled in magic? A spirit worker? I wouldn't be surprised. Lots of people had abilities in that realm of magic, but few developed them.

"My aura?" I hadn't even thought of that. Brilliant.

Although I was reluctant to get a tattoo over every chakra point.

"Yeah. In my opinion, that would create the highest level of magical protection."

I thought about it for a second, then shook my head. "I don't think that would work. I mean, that's a lot of tattoos…"

And I wasn't so committed to this that I wanted ink on my forehead. Or the top of my head. Or between my legs.

Dagger shrugged. "It's your ink and your magic. If you don't want to do all of your chakras, then consider the one that is most connected with safety."

"Which one?" I felt a little nauseous, knowing right away which one she was talking about.

"It's up to you. Put it wherever you want, but if it were me, I'd pick the root chakra.

I shuddered. The root chakra was the base, the conduit between the earth and the self, the regulator of energy throughout the body. It represented safety, security, and stability.

It was also at the perineum.

"Uh…" I knew my face was probably bright red right now.

The woman grinned. "Won't be the first time I've worked down there. You wouldn't believe the places people get tattoos. And the number of genital piercings I've done is in the hundreds. No biggie for me, although it would need to be a pretty small tattoo. While I'm there I can put a curved barbell in your hood."

I was pretty sure she didn't mean the hood of my car. "Uhhh…"

"Come on." She grabbed my arm. "There's a private room in the back in case you're shy and don't want other customers seeing you with your legs in the air."

"I'm not getting a tattoo…*there*. Or a piercing," I stammered.

She let go of my arm. "Fine. Spoilsport. How about a tramp stamp? That *might* be close enough to the root chakra."

I wasn't getting a tramp stamp either. "You know, why don't I just work with the sword one first, before I go getting tattoos on my ass or… anywhere else."

She shrugged. "Suit yourself. Give me a call when you're ready and I'll see if I can squeeze you in."

I paid for the tattoo, nearly fainting at the cost. It was a good thing I didn't get the shield one as well, or I would have been borrowing money from Gran for rent and groceries.

Then I headed toward DC, my new tattoo throbbing. Dagger had smeared antibiotic cream all over it, then covered my entire hand in plastic wrap. It made driving a bit difficult, and by the time I parked my car, I was more than a little worried about how painful wielding my sword was going to be while this thing healed.

I had to meet Reynard at a beer pub in Georgetown. Parking in DC was even worse than in Baltimore, so I had to leave my car nearly four blocks away and hike it to the pub with a sword strapped across my back and my shield looped over my arm. I was getting used to the weight of the new Kevlar vest, but hated how putting a seatbelt on over the thing was like having a wrestling match in the front seat of my car. Getting in and out with it on wasn't easy either, but probably easier than having to take it off and put it on every time I got in or out of the car.

No one gave my sword or shield a second glance in the pub. I put both on the chair beside me, unzipping my over-sized parka to sit down opposite Reynard.

"You going to take out some insurgents on your way home?" Reynard asked.

I ran a hand, the one I hadn't just gotten tattooed, over the Kevlar vest. "It's a long story."

"All right, but what's up with that?" He pointed at my plastic wrap covered right hand.

"Tattoo. I just got it." I really didn't want to explain that one either.

"Okaaaay." He slid a folder over to me. "Here's all the info on Hellfire—his real name, a picture from about six years ago, a list of who he brought over from Italy with him."

"Any info on what sort of magic he can do?"

"Only what he knew before Dark Iron kicked him out. I'm sure he's learned a lot since then. Obviously he was a Goetic mage."

Obviously. "Any idea what exactly he did to get him kicked out? Any specific ritual? Specific demons he was summoning?"

He would have had to be doing something that made Dark Iron uneasy—which meant he was probably summoning higher level demons and having them take care of anyone he wanted gone or punished.

And that sounded uncomfortably close to what had been happening to me lately.

Reynard shrugged. "There were no specific notes in the Haul Du records."

"So what exactly do you want me to do here?" I tapped the folder. "Show up at his apartment and serve him with an eviction notice?"

"First, I want you to come to an induction ceremony tonight and act as a guard—for me as well as the other Haul Du mages. Hellfire has been unusually silent for the last few days, and I worry he's going to pull something tonight."

Something was bothering me about all this. "Why does he want to run Haul Du specifically? I mean, there have to be a dozen Goetic groups in Europe that he could take over. Why come back here for this one?"

"There are some very skilled mages within Haul Du that are loyal to the group no matter who leads it. And whoever leads the group gets access to the library with the grimoires of past leaders, as well as others the group has acquired over the years."

Huh. It sounded like a good reason, but I got the impression there was something more—something Reynard wasn't telling me. Although I was used to Reynard not telling me everything. I wasn't even sure he told Raven everything.

I leaned back in my chair and wondered what a Templar had to do to get a beer around here. Maybe if I had a pint my hand the tattoo wouldn't hurt so much.

"Okay, I get that Hellfire might want to try to kill *you* tonight," I said. "But he'd hardly want to kill the very mages he wants to have in his group. It doesn't make sense to go to all this effort, only to be left with six mages standing at the end of it all."

"You let me worry about that. Just be there to protect me and the others," Reynard snapped.

Got it. Dumb hired muscle. I was beginning to know how Buff must feel sometimes.

"Oh, and you need to wear this." He reached into a shopping bag by his side and tossed me a black robe.

A black robe. Everyone there tonight would have one of these on. I had a sudden flashback to my induction ceremony. I was the only one not robed, and the only face I could see was Dark Iron's as he voted me in as an applicant. Applicants weren't supposed to know the other members until induction. After the ceremony, they'd work with a mentor for eight weeks before being recommended for initiate status. After that, they'd slowly be introduced to members using only their magical names. Even after six months with

Haul Du, I'd only known a handful of faces, and those had been indistinct in the darkness of the ceremonies I'd attended.

I'd completely blend in at an induction ceremony with this robe on. No one would realize I was there, that I was the Templar they'd kicked out. And if Hellfire made a move tonight, he'd assume I was just another mage like the rest.

There was only one problem. The robe Reynard had tossed to me was size small. There was no way I could fit it over the Kevlar vest. I'd be lucky if I could conceal my sword and shield under it.

"You wouldn't happen to have a larger one of these handy, would you?" I asked.

Reynard snorted. "Hardly. If I had realized you were going all SWAT team on me, I wouldn't have grabbed a small."

I'd survived this long without wearing the vest on a daily basis. I guess I could go without it tonight, although there was no way I was going in without anything at all for protection—not against mages who would be far more skilled in magic than I was.

"What's security going to be like tonight?" I asked, vaguely remembering a robed figure wanding me like I was going through the TSA line at the airport.

"The usual. We check for magic. Protective amulets and charms we'll let through, but the guys at the door won't allow anything that could be used as a weapon."

That seemed like an unnervingly loose policy given that pretty much anything could be a weapon in the hands of a mage.

"How about my sword? And shield? I can't exactly protect you and the order with my bare hands."

Reynard nodded. "I'll tell them no guns, or edged daggers, but ceremonial items such as swords and shields should go through. That means I'm trusting you to win if Hellfire sends a bunch of medieval reenactors to take me out."

I nodded. "I'm in one of those groups and beat everyone in hand-to-hand combat to be their next queen, so don't worry about that."

"Good. Then midnight at our lodge. Don't be late."

He went to stand, but I waved for him to stay seated. Then I ordered a beer, because why not.

"Sooo…" I wasn't sure how to segue into this next topic, and decided just to jump right on in. "There's someone who is trying to kill me. I've had two attempts on my life this week by two different people."

Reynard looked shocked. Then he twisted his head around, eyeing the others in the bar nervously. "Are you sure?"

I waited for the waiter to set the pint in front of me and took a quick sip to stall until he was out of hearing. "Well, having someone unload a pistol at me while I was jogging *might* have been just an accident, but the guy who tried to run me down yesterday definitely got paid to do it."

"I had nothing to do with that," Reynard protested.

"Since I'm of more value to you alive than dead, I figured that. I just want to know if there's anyone inside of Haul Du who might have it in for me. Perhaps someone who you showed that video to?"

He shook his head. "I didn't show anyone. And as far as I know, no one within Haul Du gives a crap about you. We kicked you out, and that was that."

"Hellfire then?" I mused.

He pivoted around to eye the door to the kitchen. "I don't know why he'd want you dead. Unless he had issues with Templars over in Italy and figured he'd take you out preemptively."

I frowned. "But how would he know about me?"

It wasn't like I was famous or anything. I wasn't protecting Baltimore in any official capacity, and I'd never had much to do with DC beyond that mess with Fiore Noir.

Reynard shrugged. "Hell if I know. Maybe someone told him. That death mage story got international press. He could have gotten your name from that."

If it was Hellfire who wanted me dead, that meant he'd probably had some run-ins with Templars before. I'd need to check that out, but the very people I would have asked first were out of the country.

In Italy.

I sucked in a breath, wondering if either of my parents had their cell phones with them or if Athena knew how to contact them. Maybe Gran knew how to contact them. Either way, I needed to find out what the Order's take was on Hellfire.

Of course, it *could* be the dude from Argentina that wanted me dead. And if that was the case, there probably wasn't much I could do about it but keep swatting at assassins and hope I got to the mage before he got to me.

Damn it. I really didn't want to kill people, but these mage assholes were making that really hard for me.

Reynard got up and left while I finished and paid for my beer. This was all starting to make sense. Hellfire had been living in Italy. My parents were in Italy on Order business. These attacks on me had started when he'd come to town. The person who wanted me dead had the ability to summon and control demons, and I was willing to bet so did Hellfire. If Hellfire had done something to anger the Templars enough that they'd called in the big swords, then he *would* want to get rid of me before I realized a wanted man was in my area and came after him.

The other question in my mind was why would Hellfire come here? Reynard wasn't telling me the whole truth. I could imagine there might be some internal squabbles over who would lead Haul Du, but an attempted coup from outside the group? From someone who'd been thrown out by their former leader? By someone who might be on the bad side of the Order? Did he think the mages in Haul Du would be able to protect him against the Knights Templar, or was there another reason Hellfire was here, another reason Reynard was afraid of him?

Yes, Reynard wanted to keep control of Haul Du, but he wanted to keep himself in one piece more. I could see him handing over the group to a more powerful mage in return for a favorable spot in the leadership chain. This wasn't about who led the group. No this was about something else, and Reynard's hide was on the line. That's why he wanted me there tonight.

I called both Mom and Dad's cell phones on the way home and left messages. Fulk greeted me with his usual happy self, Gaia wound herself around my ankles, insisting that she needed to be fed *right now*. When I went into the kitchen, I saw Gran and Buff both sitting at the little table, playing Scrabble.

"Who's winning?" I asked as I got the bag of cat food from the cabinet.

"Who do you think?" Buff grumbled. "She's got fifty years of reading shit on me. Course she knows more words."

"I've got more than fifty years on you, young man." Gran wiggled her finger.

"Yeah, well it's not like I sit around reading anything more than the label of prescription bottles lately." Buff put down his letters, spelling "dick."

"I don't think that's allowed, but I'm gotta let it go." Gran set down her letters. "Incinerate. And I'm out. Make sure you add that triple letter score in there."

Buff wasn't listening to her. Instead he was staring at my

hand. "Please tell me you burned that on some hot soup and didn't get attacked this afternoon."

"Tattoo." I held up my hand as if he could see the ink through all the layers of salve and plastic wrap. "I'm going to try to spell it so my sword comes to my hand."

He blinked. "Like Thor's hammer?"

I was getting a little tired of this. "Like Odin's spear or a Jedi lightsaber. Superhero stuff, you know. Because I'm a Templar and that's pretty much like a superhero."

Buff didn't look convinced.

"Look, sometimes a vampire or someone knocks my sword out of my hand. I want to be able to retrieve it."

He nodded. "Why don't you just shoot 'em with a gun instead?"

"Because I'm a Templar and the last time I tried to shoot a supernatural creature with a gun, it didn't even slow him down. *And* I got in trouble for it with the police and wound up having to do a bunch of community service."

"Well, I think the tattoo is a great idea," Gran announced. "Do you want to practice with it tonight?"

I looked at the clock. "I don't have time. It'll be dark soon, and I need to go over to Dario's. Then I've got something I need to do in DC at midnight. I might not be home until close to dawn."

Gran stared at me a moment, then nodded. "If you need me, I'll be there."

I didn't know exactly what she meant, but the idea that my great grandmother might show up at a ceremony with a bunch of mages and potentially a battle involving demons worried me.

"We're still running at seven, aren't we?" Buff asked, interrupting my thoughts and giving me the sort of hard-edged look that I imagined Army Sergeants gave their recruits.

"Well…I do have to work tomorrow." I squirmed, wondering if he was going to tell me to drop and give him twenty.

"When do you go in to work?" The steely glare intensified.

"Eight," I squeaked.

"Then I'll be here at six. We'll do six miles fast, and you'll have an hour plus to shower, dress, and drive to work."

Somehow I found my backbone. "I don't have a buzz cut hairdo, and I need to feed my pets, and eat. If I'm getting home around five or six, that doesn't leave me any time for sleep."

He made a pfft noise. "An hour or two of sleep isn't going to do you any good. Might as well skip it and take a nap after your shift. Tell you what; we'll do three miles. Even if we go slow that won't take more than half an hour."

I wanted to argue, but I realized I wasn't going to win this one. Buff might have given in on following me around everywhere, but he was suddenly determined to turn me into a lean-mean-fighting-machine.

"Okay," I told him. "Six in the morning it is. But only three miles!"

He grinned and I got a bad feeling that my three miles and his three miles weren't the same thing, but I had no time to think about that because I needed to head over to Dario's house, and get ready to sneak into a Haul Du induction ceremony.

CHAPTER 16

"Hey, badass Templar girl!" Opal called to me from Dario's front porch. The female vampire was smoking a joint, holding it in a roach clip accessorized with a leather string that had beads and feathers hanging from the end.

"Hey yourself. So…what's up with Lottie? You think she might be more than a one-and-done?"

Opal had been thinking about settling down with a blood partner ever since she'd seen Dario's and my relationship. Thinking was about as far as it had gone. The girl was enthusiastic, but she was all about fun and a variety of both sexual partners and blood donors. I honestly couldn't see her committing to someone for quite a few years yet.

"I'll admit I'm thinking about it." She took a hit of the joint and held her breath for a few seconds before releasing it. "I don't know, though. She was freaking out over her dead boss. I'm kinda wanting someone with a bit more backbone to her, ya jive?"

I smiled. "Yeah, I jive. Is Dario awake yet?" Duh, of course he was. "I mean, has he fed? Is he ready for visitors?"

Opal winked. "Sister, that man is always ready for you, fed or not. When you gonna give him a taste, by the way? Not that it's any of my business, but I feel like I have to speak up here. The Boss has been really patient."

He had. And I couldn't exactly tell Opal that the few times when in the heat of passion I'd begged him to bite me, he'd refused. His not taking my blood was as much his choice as it was mine at this point.

"I'm a Templar, and that's something that we're looking at long term," I told her instead. "And yes, it's none of your business."

She laughed, then extended the joint toward me. "Wanna hit?"

What did Dario think about his front-door guard lighting up? Although given how little alcohol affected vampires, I was willing to believe this pot had little to no effect on Opal's ability to do her duties.

"I'll pass. I've got a long night ahead of me. Maybe next time?"

She pursed her lips. "You got it girl."

I went through the front door, realizing I had no idea where Dario was. There were the usual groups of vampires and humans clustered around the foyer and the living room. I wove around them to the kitchen where more vampires were playing beer pong, of all things.

"Is Dario around?" I knew he was around, but what I didn't know was if he was indisposed with a blood donor. That wasn't something I wanted to walk in on—not because I was squeamish or anything, but because…well, because I'd be jealous. I remembered the sensation when the narcotic in a vampire's fangs hit my bloodstream. I dreamed about Dario being the one drinking my blood when I had that hit of euphoria. I also had nightmares where Dario vanished and it was Simon drinking from me, Simon enslaving me and torturing me.

I wasn't ready. I wanted to be ready, but I wasn't. And Dario knew it. Still, I didn't want to walk in on him feeding from another.

"He's out back with Balen," Madeline said as she lined up her next shot.

I waited and watched the game, marveling at how vampires could be so adept at everything else, but so incredibly lousy at bouncing a ping pong ball into a cup of beer.

The back door opened with a gust of cold air and Dario walked in followed by Balen. His gaze immediately locked on mine and he smiled.

"Hey, babe."

"Hey, you." I walked over and kissed him. "Your family sucks at drinking games. You know that?"

He chuckled, then grabbed my arm, pulling me into the living room. This time he didn't even need to say anything. The room cleared in a blink, leaving us alone. It was nice how his *Balaj* respected our need for privacy. Although I still didn't want to live here in what had become vampire central.

Dario gathered me into his arms, then his smile dropped as his gaze fell to my plastic-wrapped hand. "What did you do to yourself?"

"Tattoo." I guessed it was okay to take the plastic wrap off now. I didn't want to screw up the new ink, but perhaps it would be okay if I put one of those huge band aids over it with the cream Dagger had given me to keep it from drying out in the cold winter weather.

I slowly unwound the wrapping and showed it to Dario.

"Nice. Looks painful, though. Is this the one you're going to use to call your sword to your hand."

I nodded. "I'm not sure how that's going to work out. It

might take a few tries before I get the spell to work. Heck, I might never get the spell to work."

"It might have been easier to do the protection one," he commented as he gently took my hand and examined the artwork. "You've already done similar spells on your neck and on your shield."

"Yeah, but you wouldn't believe where she wanted to put that tattoo." I told Dario and he burst out laughing. He wasn't the only one. From the kitchen I heard the laughter of half a dozen vampires, followed by equal merriment of their humans as they explained what they'd overheard.

"I'm not getting it!" I shouted to the others. "At least not *there*."

"I'll pay." Dario grinned. "And I'll come watch."

"Perv." I smacked his shoulder, but couldn't help but grin myself. "She offered to throw in a hood piercing while she was down there doing the tattoo."

Dario wiggled his eyebrows. "You *have* to get it done. Please? What do I need to do to convince you to do this?"

"Not happening. Now if you want this artist's number to go in and have her tattoo and pierce behind your balls, you go right ahead."

Dario shuddered. "I'd rather be staked. So how long will it be before you can stop walking around with your hand wrapped in plastic?"

"About four hours. I'm throwing on a robe and hood and attending a Haul Du induction ceremony incognito at midnight tonight. Plastic wrap on my hand might blow my cover."

"A tattoo of a Templar sword on your hand is going to blow your cover," Dario drawled. "Are you going to wear gloves in addition to leather cuffs?"

"A big-ass bandage, and a pair of gloves." Good thing it was winter and my wearing gloves wouldn't seem unusual.

"Won't they notice you've got a sword and a shield under your robe?" he added.

"Reynard told the guard at the door to allow ceremonial swords, just in case my look-away spell doesn't work or my weapons get caught in their sweep."

"So Reynard is expecting an attack," Dario mused. "And you're going to counter that by flinging off your robe, and…what?"

Stabbing Hellfire in the back like I did with Dark Iron. That's what I knew he was thinking. That's what I was thinking as well, and I didn't like the idea one bit.

"What the heck am I going to do about this, Dario?" I plopped down on the sofa and sighed. "I'm not killing Hellfire. You're not killing Hellfire. And much like catching a mouse in a humane trap and setting it free five miles away, he'll be back in DC probably before I will if I just kick him out of town."

"Does your detective pal have any ideas?" Dario asked.

"Chuck's in jail because he won't bother breaking out, and the other Fiore Noir mages are partly because of an agreement, and partly because establishing new identities isn't as easy as television makes it out to be. Hellfire just needs to have one of his buddies or a demon get him out of jail, then he can probably make arrangements to skip the country. Or he can make arrangements for a new identity, or just get a demon to kill anyone who would testify against him." I threw up my hands in frustration. "I'd need a long-term null spell to keep mages in jail. I also need something that can keep supernatural beings incarcerated as well. Right now, there's no way for humans to handle these people breaking their laws that will stick."

Dario shrugged. "Templars do. You said Templars have some sort of prison. And the Conclave as well. Have the Conclave lock him up."

It was a good idea, although I was trying to stay as far away from Golden Hemlock as possible so as to not allow her the opportunity to discover two and two equaled four when it came to Dark Iron's disappearance.

"A power struggle over the leadership of a group isn't breaking any Conclave laws," I countered.

"But killing two mages might be? Attempting to kill the current leader? An attempted coup of an unwilling group? Heck, pin Dark Iron's death on this Hellfire. That'll get him locked up with the Conclave."

That might get him killed with the Conclave. The other things Hellfire had done *might* convince Golden Hemlock to take action. I just needed to prove he was behind the murders.

"Or better yet, claim he's trying to murder you. Won't that get him stuck in a Templar jail for the rest of his life?" Dario added.

"I'm not positive it's him that's trying to kill me," I admitted. "It could be one of Dark Iron's buddies who figured out what happened, or who managed to score a copy of the video from Chuck. Or it could be the mage whose soul trap I disabled getting revenge."

"Or it could be Hellfire." Dario lifted an eyebrow. "There are lots of easy solutions to this problem, Aria. Templar jail, Conclave jail, human jail. Or let me take care of the situation for you."

I shot him a mock glare and pointed at him. "No, you're not killing him. Or Chuck. Or Reynard. Let me think on this a bit. What I decide is going to hinge quite a bit on what happens at this induction ceremony tonight."

"Which is at midnight. Where is it being held?"

"It's at an old dry-cleaning business on Mills just past Rhode Island Avenue in Langdon. And you can't come. The building is warded against non-humans, and I wouldn't be surprised if Reynard ended up having a null spell in the ceremony room."

"So I'll stand outside as backup."

The idea did have merit, but I was too worried some spell would reveal his presence.

"It's okay. I've got this one. I really doubt anything is going to happen tonight anyway."

And now I needed to address the beat-up guy in jail.

"Tremelay called me this morning. Evidently the guy who tried to run me over yesterday confessed. And he was looking pretty worse for the wear today."

Dario stilled, his face that blank mask I'd learned meant he was trying to keep something from me. "I hear inmate violence is brutal."

"Especially when the inmate is roughed up by vampires."

"Did he tell the police that?"

I rolled my eyes. "No, so don't go giving the poor guy a second beating."

"Poor guy?" Dario scowled. "That *poor guy* tried to run you over."

"And the human justice system will take care of it." I shrugged. "It's not like he had much in the way of usable information anyway. Glowing eyed dude who vanished after he paid up front to run me over. That doesn't tell me who is behind all this."

"No, but this confirms we're dealing with the same person." Dario dug in his pocket and pulled out a piece of paper. On it was the same sigil as we'd seen burned into Henrietta's forehead.

"He remembered the sigil enough to write it down?" I shook my head in surprise. "The guy didn't seem all that sharp to me."

"Well when a man with glowing eyes pays you a significant sum of money to run a woman over, then vanishes leaving this sigil burned into the payment, I guess you remember it."

I took the paper from him and stuffed it into my pocket. I hadn't had time to do more than leaf through a few books, and didn't know who this demon was or what to expect if I encountered him. Which worried me because there was a good chance I might encounter him tonight.

CHAPTER 17

I had two leather bracers on my wrists, each of them inscribed with runes of protection, and heavy black gloves that kept my hands warm as well as covered up the huge bandage over my new tattoo. The black cape hid my sword and shield, and the large hood concealed my face. As I walked to the building, I wondered what the neighbors must think of all these hooded figures walking down the dimly lit street in the dark of the night.

Obviously this wasn't the first time I'd been to the old dry cleaners Haul Du used for their meetings, but it *was* only the second time I'd been there in a robe and hood. The group had voted on me after a series of lengthy interviews by Dark Iron and three other Haul Du members who I'd never seen again. I'd gotten the feeling Dark Iron didn't like me, so I'd been surprised to receive the summons a few weeks later. At a ceremony just like what would happen tonight, I'd been voted in, assigned a mentor, and told that if I couldn't make initiate status within a year, I'd be ousted.

I took to the basics of Goetic magic like a duck to water,

and would have been ready to be sworn in less than nine months if I hadn't been kicked out for being a Templar.

Two other robed figures approached the building from the other direction and I slowed my steps so I wouldn't give myself away by being forced into awkward small talk. The dry-cleaning company had moved away at least ten years ago, but the building still wore their name. The large front windows were unbroken with chipped paint announcing the previous clothing services on a background of blackout curtains. I waited for the two Haul Du members to enter, then made my way to the front door. It squeaked just as I remembered. The inside still looked like a dry-cleaning establishment with long counters, a changing room, and framed travel posters from beautiful destinations. Behind the counters was a twisted circuit of metal rod hung from the ceiling, still bearing forgotten suits, coats, and starched shirts from long ago. I pushed past the surprisingly clean, plastic-sheathed clothes and toward the back where the cleaning apparatus and pressing machines had been pushed to the side.

"Password?" the robed person who stood ten feet in front of the staircase asked.

"Prohibition sucks," I replied, grateful that it wasn't something distasteful like "White Power" or "I love Satan." "Prohibition Sucks" had been the password forever, and no one changed it.

This was just a meeting place tonight. Since no magic would be performed, security was relatively lax. As I moved to the staircase, another robed figure held up a wand and traced my outline. I held my breath, wondering if I'd get in with my sword and shield on me.

I must have glowed or something because the guard squinted, then nodded. "Okay."

No wards. No guards beyond the two bored dudes in

robes. No metal detectors or magic detectors beyond the wand, or anything else detectors. I would have thought Reynard would have taken extra precautions, but I guess that's what I was. Of course, what was happening tonight wasn't a big deal in the scheme of things—just members anonymously voting on a potential new mage. Any blatant increase in security probably would have alarmed the members, and as scared as Reynard was, he really wanted everyone to think he had everything under control.

Stairway-guy stood aside and I headed down into the basement, careful not to trip over the hem of my long robe and go tumbling to the hard cement floor. I'd seen that happen before, and had been hard pressed not to laugh when the young guy struggled to get to his feet, hood off and robes twisted around his ankles.

The basement didn't look at all like the meeting area for a magical organization. The tubs of dry-cleaning chemicals had been shoved over to the side, and there were folding metal chairs for members who found standing through a meeting difficult. I took my place smack in the middle of everything so I'd blend in with the crowd, then removed my gloves, folding my hands together inside the bell sleeves of my black cape, and surveyed my surroundings.

It was dark, but that was because the only light came from a naked LED bulb at the top of the steps. Roughly fifty people were crammed into the large room, standing in a half circle facing a rickety table with silver duct tape on one of the legs. Back behind the table was another staircase going down to yet another basement. I'd never been down there, but I assumed the space held additional old dry-cleaning equipment and supplies for meetings and magical ceremonies.

We stood in silence, everyone robed.

"Hope this is quick. Some of us have got to work tomorrow," a robed figure off to my left whispered. The sound seemed deafening. Everyone turned to the offender in one synchronized motion, and I saw him or her cringe.

We faced front again and waited. I was nearly asleep on my feet when I heard footsteps on the stairs and felt the energy shift in the room. All the robed figures straightened, and I did the same, my eyes following Reynard as he circled to the front where the rickety table was.

Reynard wasn't wearing his hood, although he was robed. Anonymity was sacrificed when one became the leader of Haul Du, and right now it was clear Reynard was the leader. It was also clear that none of the other robed figures seemed to care one way or another. Quite a few shifted impatiently. The person who'd whispered before muttered something about needing coffee.

Reynard pounded the flat of his hand on the table. "Meeting is called to order in the matter of potential inductee Silver Rain."

I heard footsteps behind me and another figure appeared, this one in a white robe with no hood. Silver Rain walked with a slight limp as she made her way to the front, judiciously standing a few feet behind and to the side of Reynard. She looked to be a few years younger than me with edgy, short, blonde hair and a jeweled stud in her nose. She was tall and thin, with an angular face and dark brown eyes.

And I recognized her.

Thankfully I held back both the gasp and any telltale muscle twitch that might give me away. Liz Dimond. What the heck was she doing here in DC, attempting to join a magical organization? Last month she'd been given a huge blood transfusion in an attempt to resurrect a famous mage into her body. It hadn't worked—at least I *thought* it hadn't worked—but instead of being up in New England running a family mortuary business with her brother, she was here.

Joining a magical society.

Reynard continued to recite the short list of Silver Rain's qualifications. She'd done some recent study of the Goetic arts. She had a degree in mortuary science and had grown up in the business. She was descended from Edward "John" Dimond, better known as the Magician of Marblehead.

Quite a few in the audience gasped, and I realized her ancestry alone would be enough to vote her in.

Although having studied in another magical system was a plus in being inducted, pretty much the only requirement for the one-year petitioner status was that the applicant have found out about Haul Du and managed to contact one of the members about the organization. That year was the real test, although I wouldn't be surprised if Haul Du extended the time period since Liz came with such an impressive pedigree.

Reynard voiced his approval and ask for recommendations.

These were the individuals who'd interviewed her. Two hooded members spoke up saying that they felt she would be an asset to the organization. We voted, and as usual, Silver Rain received approval.

Then Reynard asked who among the membership would take Silver Rain on and act as her mentor. I'd learned from Raven what an incredible pain in the butt it was to mentor someone. There was the time commitment, and also the risk of having exposed your actual identity to someone who might not make the cut. Plus the mentor revealed their hard-won magic system and secrets to the applicant, allowing them to read the mentor's grimoire and copy spells. Sometimes no one volunteered to mentor and Dark Iron had needed to "volunteer" someone himself. Often times the mentor did a crappy job, basically ignoring their applicant and letting them flounder on their own, or tossing them into the deep end without any tutoring and watching them get burned—sometimes literally—by a spell gone wrong.

This wasn't one of those times. A dozen hands shot up, no doubt everyone eager to claim they mentored a descendant of the Magician of Marblehead.

Without thinking, I raised my hand as well. I really wasn't sure I wanted Liz becoming a part of Haul Du—or learning magic. If something had gone wrong, or rather gone right, at that ceremony two months ago, then I wanted to keep my friends close and my potential enemies closer.

Reynard looked momentarily confused, not sure what to do with so many people volunteering to help the new inductee. Liz's eyes grew wide, and she took a nervous step backward. Finally he pointed at some random robed figure and told them to connect with Silver Rain afterward and arrange for a time and place to begin her study.

Unfortunately that robed figure wasn't me. Not that it mattered. I was going to track Liz down and have a chat with her, and if she continued to want to explore magical study, she was going to need to do it under my very watchful eye. The woman had suffered, and I understood her wanting to explore her family heritage and maybe learn some skills to defend herself if another mage decided to conduct a resurrection using her as the body, but I didn't want to take the chance that maybe someone besides Liz was in there, pushing this course of study with a very different agenda.

Liz was escorted upstairs where, as I remembered, she'd wait among the old dry cleaning for the meeting to end and her mentor to contact her. I'd expected a few other minor matters to be discussed and was surprised when I heard footsteps on the stairs as a middle-aged man with the hood down on his robe entered the basement, several others behind him.

I wasn't the only one surprised. Reynard blinked, then

snarled. That's when I recognized the man from the picture Reynard had given me.

Hellfire was older. Not like my dad older, but more like my brother Roman older. Fortyish, which surprised me. I'd expected someone like one of the Order Elders, bald and wrinkled with a turkey waddle of a neck and bags under his eyes. I wouldn't have called the man attractive with his sallow skin and long, thin face, but he wasn't particularly bad-looking. His thinning dark hair was sprinkled with gray, curly, and trimmed close. A lighter colored beard masked the thinness of his face and gave the illusion of additional years. His eyes were either a very dark gray or brown—it was hard to tell in the dim light. He was taller than Reynard, and from what I could see with the voluminous robe, he was of average weight.

Nothing screamed villain, but then again few monsters actually looked like monsters. Well, except for actual monsters, that is.

This guy has some real balls walking right into a group of fifty mages like this, I thought.

I barely had time for that to race through my head before everyone exploded into action. Several people threw their hoods off, others moved to block Hellfire, raising their hands and beginning to chant. I went to throw off my robe and pull my sword only to find myself knocked into the back wall and pinned there by a rush of people trying to either get to Hellfire or get away from him.

I elbowed people left and right, deciding that getting to Reynard was more important than trying to get this ridiculous cloak off or get my weapons. Before I could get very far, the room filled with a yellow sulfur-smelling smoke.

A demon. I couldn't see him, but I'm sure that's what had just appeared, and I was fairly certain who had summoned him. Screams and shouts filled the room. I hesitated, wondering if I should deal with the demon, or keep going toward Reynard. This was Haul Du, a magical group that specialized in Goetic magic. Surely someone in here was skilled enough to contain and banish this demon without the help of a Templar.

So leaving the demon behind, I punched my way through the crowd just in time to see Hellfire coming toward Reynard from the other side.

CHAPTER 18

Trapped, Reynard took the only way out and ran down the stairway behind him. I shoved two robed figures aside, kicking one out of my way, But Hellfire made it to the steps just ahead of me.

I needed to get to Reynard before Hellfire killed him, and that wasn't exactly easy with people brawling all over the room. Finally I made my way through the crowd and ran down the stairs, not caring how much noise I made. It wasn't like anyone would hear me with everything that was going on upstairs anyway.

Of course, the noise meant that at the bottom of the stairs, I had no idea which direction Reynard or Hellfire had gone. And the fact that it was pitch black down here didn't help one bit. Was this one big room? A hallway leading somewhere? I suddenly envisioned the vampire tunnels that networked their homes in Baltimore and wondered if Haul Du had installed something similar here in DC.

Not wanting to lose precious time waiting for my eyes to adjust, I plunged into the darkness, hoping I didn't run head first into a wall or trip over something and break a leg.

Then there was this stupid robe. I yanked at the clasp as I headed down what I hoped was a hallway, trying to get all the fabric out of the way so I could manage to get my sword out of my scabbard. My shield was a whole other matter. I'd strapped it across my back, and there it sat like a turtle shell that wouldn't budge. With a twist and a yank, I managed to get my sword free. I gave up on the shield, hoping Hellfire didn't shoot me. If he did, then with any luck my damaged Kevlar vest would hold. Or maybe I could spin around fast enough to take the bullets to the shield stuck on my back.

"Where is it?" I heard a voice that must be Hellfire yell. Then I heard the thud of a body against something hard. "Give it to me, or I swear I'll kill everyone in this building. There won't be anyone left for you to lead—if you survive, that is."

"I don't know where it is." Reynard's voice sounded wet and raspy and somewhere off to my left. "Dark Iron never told me. There wasn't exactly a transition, you know. He just vanished."

Another thud. "You've had months to look for it. It's got to be here somewhere."

I slowed and felt my way around toward the voices.

Reynard coughed. "I don't know. I've searched. Can't find it. Killing everyone won't help you find it."

"No, but it will make me feel better."

I rounded a wall and saw two figures faintly lit by a cell phone flashlight that was on the floor.

"Get away from him!" I ran forward, sword out, the cape flapping around my back an annoying hinderance, hoping that I was aiming the pointy end of my weapon at Hellfire and not Reynard.

One of the men turned and I recognized him as Hellfire. His eyes widened, then with a flick of his wrist he had a knife at Reynard's throat. "You're not taking me in," he snarled.

Taking him in where? I advanced carefully, wondering if I could get to Hellfire before he sliced through Reynard's throat. Probably not.

"Put down your sword or I'll kill him," Hellfire shouted.

I kept my eyes on the pair as I slowly knelt down, placing my sword on the ground. Just as slowly I stood.

"Let him go." I raised my hands just to prove I had no weapon.

He hesitated a second, then began to lower his knife. Unfortunately someone chose that time to burst into the room behind me.

Everything happened at once. Hellfire's knife moved upward toward Reynard's neck. A woman behind me screamed. I dropped my right hand and felt a sharp pain as my sword hilt slammed into the raw flesh where my tattoo was. Acting on instinct, I threw the sword as if it were a spear, directly at Hellfire.

In a flash he was gone, but not before his knife sliced a red line across Reynard's throat. My sword clattered against the wall, falling at the same time as Reynard slid to the ground. I ran forward.

"I'm okay," Reynard whispered, his hand pressed firmly against his neck. Blood oozed between his fingers.

"Call 911," I snapped at the woman who'd come down the stairs. "Now."

I heard her footsteps and the beeps of her cell phone as she dialed, heard her shaky voice on the phone. Finally getting the damned cape off, I wadded it up and placed it over Reynard's wound. He was talking. It couldn't have been that bad or he wouldn't have been talking. And if Hellfire had nicked an artery, he wouldn't still have been breathing. Now the question was whether to try to get him up the stairs or wait until the paramedics arrived.

"He's going to kill me," Reynard whispered.

"Hush." I felt his breathing speed up, heard the rush of footsteps on the stairs.

"They're coming," the woman announced. "How is he? What…is he going to be okay?"

That was when I realized that I recognized the voice. Liz. I turned, and she sucked in a breath, recognizing me as well.

"Some people swarmed the building from outside and there's fighting upstairs." She knelt down beside Reynard, putting her hands on top of my cloak. "Go. I'll watch him."

I didn't trust her, which was strange because before tonight, I would have completely trusted her. This was ridiculous. She'd been through a horrible ordeal. I wouldn't blame her for wanting to know more about the magic that had almost taken her life, about what might have been passed down through generations in terms of talent. I wouldn't blame her for wanting to develop skills that she could use to make sure she'd never be in that position again, never be a victim of a mage ever again.

I had to trust her, because I'd heard Hellfire's threat and I wasn't sure he wasn't going to make good on that right now.

Feeling as if there were no good choices in this, I picked up my sword and left Reynard in her care to run up the stairs. I was finally able to pull my shield off my back. It was a good thing too, because I walked right into a firefight.

Reynard's security had clearly been ineffectual, because not only were there guns and knives, but a few people had managed to sneak in magical weapons as well.

Someone shot at me. I knew this because the bullet bounced off my shield with enough force to throw me back off my feet and into two other mages. A knife flashed and I smacked the assailant in the head with my shield, reversing my sword to do the same to the other mage if he attacked. The guy backed up, his hands raised, only for him to go down in a spray of blood as a bullet hit its mark.

Okay, this was getting out of hand. I hid behind one of the vats of dry-cleaning chemicals and hoped they weren't explosive because a few of the mages seemed to know combustion spells and were tossing rune-covered papers that ignited on contact. Although the robes seemed to be somewhat fire retardant, two mages had caught fire enough to employ the stop-drop-and-roll technique.

I wasn't sure who to go after. Everyone was in various stages of robe-wearing, and even without the hoods I didn't know who was with what group. A line of text on a nearby box caught my eye just as another bullet hit the drum of cleaning chemicals.

A foul smell hit my nose and I choked. I couldn't kill everyone and let God sort them out. I didn't know who was on what side. And to make things worse, I saw Liz walk up from the lower basement, Reynard being half supported by her.

What. The. Fuck. The guy had been nearly unconscious with a dangerous amount of blood loss. Even if he'd come to, what had made her think bringing him upstairs in the middle of a fight would be a good idea? I started to race over and try to protect him, when I got an idea.

Looking down at the box, I did the one magic that never failed me, the one I'd been able to do for as long as I could remember.

Fue.

The box burst into flames. I ran toward Reynard, setting other boxes alight as I went. A noxious white smoke filled the air and people began to shout.

"Here." I thrust my shield at Silver Rain. "Protect us." Then I shoved my sword back into its scabbard and bent down to haul Reynard onto my back in a fireman carry.

The dude was heavier than I thought, but thanks to adrenaline and all the training I'd been doing, I barely staggered as I hauled him across the room. My eyes streamed from the smoke. I tried and failed to hold my breath and push past everyone. There was a mad rush toward the stairway, everyone coughing and choking as they covered their mouths and noses with the excess fabric from the voluminous hoods.

My legs and chest screamed in agony as I hauled Reynard up the stairs, Liz in front of us with the shield. The foul stench followed us up from the basement, an actual white cloud that spread its tendrils throughout the first floor, thinning and becoming less noxious. Everyone staggered through the racks of clothes and out the front door to suck in gulps of cold fresh air, yanking the hoods from their heads.

There were the police. Finally. And the fire department, and an ambulance.

"Here. He's been cut across his neck." I knelt down, quads quivering as I passed Reynard off to a paramedic who eased him onto a stretcher."

"Is anyone else inside?" One of the firefighters yelled at me.

I shook my head. "Don't know. Wear a regulator. Drycleaning chemicals on fire."

Just then there was an explosion and everyone began shouting. First responders were shoving people back, dealing with curious onlookers. A paramedic tried to slap an oxygen mask over my face, but I shrugged him off, running toward the door.

"Get back," a guy in uniform yelled.

I should have gotten back, but all I could think about was the injured people who might still be downstairs. I had no love lost for the members of Haul Du, or Hellfire's followers who'd instigated this whole thing, but these were still human beings. They were still my pilgrims, no matter what their sins. And I couldn't let injured people burn to death on my watch.

"I'm a Templar," I shouted back, not sure if the guy even knew what that entailed. Then I grabbed my shield from Liz, yanked the sword from my scabbard, and ran inside.

Idiot. Like I'd be able to use a sword to battle a fire as if it were a human foe. Still, I kept the item in my hand, feeling safer with it near. The upper floor was filled with smoke and I shoved my shirt up over my face, hoping the cotton fabric filtered whatever chemicals were drifting around.

"Anyone here?" I shouted, my voice muffled by my shirt. I heard firefighters behind me, clearing a path and spraying the hanging clothes that were starting to smolder.

"Here!" A faint voice sounded over by the stairway.

I followed the sound, unable to see a damned thing. A hand reached out and grabbed my leg and I nearly cut it off with my sword in surprise.

"Help." I barely heard the whisper. Bending down, I grabbed the arm attached to my leg and followed it up to a shoulder. Groping to find where the person was situated, I once more sheathed my sword, looping my shield up on my forearm, and grabbed the person around what I thought was their waist.

It was incredibly awkward, but I couldn't carry the person out like I'd done with Reynard. The smoke was too thick for me to stand upright and breathe. Actually, the smoke was too thick for me to do this and breathe, but I was determined not to leave this person behind.

In front of me I saw the dim shadows of the firefighters. Then I heard a crack. Liquid poured across the floor and in a flash it had erupted into flames. I don't know what I was thinking, but I kept going, pushing my way through the flames as I half dragged the person behind me. When we got out the front door, I turned to smack embers off the person's cloak as the paramedics ran to take care of him.

Her. I caught a glimpse of long singed hair and a delicate facial bone structure as she turned her head and began to cough.

That was when my brain finally kicked into gear and I decided I needed to leave this to the professionals. Sitting on the curb, I watched as the fire was quickly brought under control and firefighters brought at least eight more people from the building.

I'm sure there would be more coming out of that building later in black bags. Reynard had already been hauled off to the hospital, and I really didn't want to stay around and see what the death toll was.

"Why are you here?"

I turned and saw Liz, her face and white cloak gray with soot.

"I could ask you the same question."

Her chin went up. "I'm interested in seeing if I've got any talent in this or not. I did some research and found this group."

"This probably isn't the best time to join Haul Du," I commented.

"You think?" She sat down beside me. "I don't even know who my mentor is supposed to be. *Or* if he or she's even alive. Maybe I should just go home."

I felt bad for her. And I felt really bad for all the paranoid horrible things I'd been thinking when I saw her as the inductee. Although in my defense, it had been a really diffi-cult week.

"Haul Du isn't that bad," I told her. "And once Reynard gets out of the hospital, he'll help you get a mentor. If not, I know some spirit workers in Baltimore that might be willing to take you under their wing."

She glanced over at me. "You do magic, don't you?"

I laughed. "Sort of. I was with Haul Du for a while before they realized I was a Templar and kicked me out. I've got a lot of magical texts, and of course I have access to all the Templar resource books. My magic is kinda odd though. I can do some Goetic magic, but a lot of what I do is more cleric than mage."

She obviously didn't get the Dungeons and Dragons reference, but she still nodded.

"Could *you* teach me? Just a few of the basics until I can find the right teacher? I mean, I'm not even sure what sort of magic I might be able to do—if I can do any at all, that is."

I stood, noting that my muscles had stiffened up in the cold. "Will you be in town a while? I'm kinda busy right now, but call me and we can get together next week and do a sort of magic 101. In the meantime, I'm going to advise you to give Haul Du some distance. That guy who tried to cut Reynard's head off? The one who summoned a demon into the meeting and whose buddies tried to shoot everyone? He might try that sort of thing again."

Liz nodded. "Got it. And Aria? Thanks. I appreciate it."

I headed off past the crowd of onlookers and the first responders still dealing with the burned building and, no doubt, the dead.

Two blocks down I rounded the corner and edged down a narrow passageway between two buildings. Stepping out into a parking lot, I nearly had a heart attack as a hand shot out and grabbed my arm.

"I'm wondering why a Templar who was ousted from Haul Du is attending one of their meetings," Golden Hemlock drawled.

I took a few deep breaths, trying to get my heart to stop trying to pound its way out of my chest and turned.

"You were asking why Renard had visited me the other

night? Well, this is why. There's a mage that Dark Iron had kicked out of Haul Du years ago, and he's back. Reynard told me he was concerned for his and the others' safety, and he wanted me to come and basically act as security."

She snorted. "Fat bit of help you were. How many died back there? The building was on fire, a bunch of people were shot and/or burned. I saw Reynard being carted off in an ambulance. Remind me never to ask a Templar to act as a bodyguard."

That stung. She wasn't wrong, but I hadn't been given much prep time, or known that Hellfire was going to try to kill *everyone*. Reynard had told me the mage wanted to take over the group, not exterminate them all. And what the hell had he been looking for? Something he assumed Reynard had as the successor to Dark Iron. A grimoire? Special spell components? An amulet? I thought of the soul trap and wondered if Dark Iron made it a habit of stealing stuff from other mages. I'd need to get over to the hospital sometime tomorrow and see if I could pry the answer out of Reynard.

"But all that doesn't matter," Golden Hemlock continued. "I was here hoping to meet with Reynard after the meeting. He's been avoiding me, and that plus a few other things have made me wonder if he's not responsible for Dark Iron's disappearance."

I laughed. "If you knew Reynard, you'd know he lacks the magical skill and the personality to take out someone like Dark Iron," I told her, not sure why I was sticking my neck out to defend the mage who was blackmailing me. "Dark Iron actually liked Reynard and he benefitted from that. He got all the profits without having to take any of the risks. Why would he give that up?"

"Power," Golden Hemlock replied.

I snorted. "Yes, he likes running the group now that Dark Iron is gone, but Reynard doesn't have it in him to assassinate a rival. He's just taking advantage of Dark Iron's absence to step into his shoes. If a stronger mage came along, he'd give up the reins. Reynard is fine with stepping aside and letting someone else do the dirty work, then jumping in to reap the spoils, he won't soil his hands with murder."

Not like me.

The woman fixed me with a hard stare. "Power does odd things to people. Reynard might have decided he wanted more than the scraps Dark Iron threw him. But he's not my only suspect. I find it rather odd how the mage who claimed Dark Iron stole from him suddenly is no longer interested in pursuing the matter."

Now it was me hesitating. As much as I wanted to throw her down the trail to Argentina, that path would lead back to me. And I really didn't want that mage telling this woman that I'd traded the soul trap to him in return for his assistance with a particularly nasty vampire—especially not when one way for me to have gotten the soul trap was to have killed Dark Iron and pried it from his cold, dead hands.

Which I'd kinda sorta done.

Instead I shrugged and kept my mouth shut for once.

"I'm still waiting to hear back from the Order about any official Templar involvement in the matter." Her eyes narrowed. "And then there's my theory that your involvement might be unofficial."

"Nice theory," I said. "Look, it's been a long night. I'm dirty, tired, and stinking of burned dry-cleaning chemicals. If you want to discuss this further, call me and I'll fit you into my schedule."

She stared at me a moment, her gaze unreadable. "I will most definitely be in contact. But not tomorrow. Tomorrow I'm off to speak to someone from Fiore Noir who might be able to tell me what's going on. Maybe you know him?

Charles Jones. He's serving time in Jessup, and I believe he has a fondness for Fisher's popcorn."

I felt as if my entire body had been dunked in ice water. Chuck. She was going to talk to Chuck. He'd sold me out to Reynard, and I wasn't sure he wouldn't do the same with this Justice.

I tried to match her bland expression. "Sounds like fun. Good night."

Golden Hemlock chuckled then spun around. A mist sprang up from the ground and before she was twenty feet away, both she and the mist had vanished. Striding as fast as I could without actually breaking into a run, I went two blocks then turned left.

Then I broke into a run.

CHAPTER 19

I didn't realize I felt the familiar static of a vampire's presence until I was unlocking my car.

"Really, Dario?"

The vampire slid from the shadows, silent and deadly. "And you're just now noticing I'm here? That worries me."

I rolled my eyes, knowing with his night vision he'd see it. Truth was I *hadn't* noticed him. It wasn't because my ability to sense vampires was off, it was because I'd gotten so used to how he felt near me that I didn't even notice it anymore. Another vampire's energy would have been like a splinter under my skin, but Dario…he was like a part of me at this point.

Not that I wanted to admit that.

"Exactly how long have you been stalking me?"

He laughed. "Since you arrived in Baltimore. Oh, you mean tonight? That would be since you left the city."

"So I guess you were there for the shit-show at the dry cleaners?"

"I stayed outside, guessing there might be some wards in place that would alert them that a vampire was sneaking in the back door. Basically I saw a bunch of people running out, smoke, fire. Oh and there were spells and bullets flying left and right."

I smiled, because even in the midst of all that he hadn't come racing in to save me.

Dario held up his hands as if warding off an attack. "You are the most badass human I've known since my days with the maroons. I'll admit that I wasn't comfortable about you walking into a room with a couple dozen mages who tossed you to the curb less than a year ago and who probably wouldn't think twice before siccing a demon on your cute ass, or pumping you full of magic bullets, but I knew you could handle yourself. And look—here you are in one piece."

"Funny how I came out of a firefight between a bunch of mages unhurt, yet I nearly died jogging. And magic bullets? Totally not real."

He pinned me against my car, pressing himself against me. "They aren't? Next thing I know you'll be telling me elves aren't real."

I wrinkled my nose. "Welllll."

Elves…they weren't like what the Christmas stories or Lord of the Rings novels portrayed. But now wasn't the time to get into a discussion of that, especially with the feel of Dario's muscled form against me. He was cool. His breath was cool against my neck. The temperature outside was just below freezing, but thanks to the donor he'd fed from this evening, his body temperature was closer to seventy degrees. A year ago that would have freaked me out, but now it turned me on. I could make him warmer. I could make him a whole lot warmer. Yeah, I needed to get home because Buff was going to be at my house in four hours and it might be good to get some sleep in before he showed up, but I was so tempted. So very tempted.

"You smell like you took a bath in paint thinner."

So very romantic. "Dry-cleaning chemicals. I'll probably get cancer from breathing in that smoke, but at least it broke up the fight and got everyone out of there."

He ran his hands down my sides. "At least you didn't get burned."

I hadn't. Which was weird considering I went right through the fire rescuing a mage. The flames…. They were orange and yellow, but when I'd dragged that mage through, they'd flickered with red, like scales or feathers or something.

"No. I didn't get burned or shot or stabbed." In fact, the only thing that hurt was my palm—which should hurt a whole lot more given that I'd summoned my sword into skin that had just been given a fresh tattoo.

And how *had* I done that? I hadn't charged the tattoo, practiced, worked out any kind of spell or incantation. I'd just panicked, opened my hand, and my sword was there.

"Who was the woman you were talking to a few blocks from here?" Dario asked. "She had some sort of magical device to block my hearing anything. I'll tell you, I was pretty close to jumping in for a few seconds there."

I slid out from between Dario and my car. "That's Grand Magus Golden Hemlock, Justice from the Conclave."

His eyebrows went up. "I thought she'd backed off. Did Reynard sell you out and send her the video?"

"No, but Chuck might. She's due to see him tomorrow." I poked a finger into the vampire's chest. "And no, you can't arrange for his death before that meeting. This is my problem, and it's something I'm going to need to address on my own. Besides, right now her top suspects are Reynard and that mage from Argentina."

He eyed me speculatively. "Think she can help you get rid of this Hellfire?"

I shrugged. "I tried but for someone who is really concerned about Dark Iron's disappearance, she doesn't seem to care one way or another about the mage right in front of her who is actually killing people."

Dario took my arm and led me around to the other side of my car. "You're exhausted, and you've got a long day tomorrow. I'll drive and you can nap.

As soon as he was in the car I snuggled against his shoulder, but sleep evaded me even as he pulled onto the parkway.

"Reynard lied to me, not that I'm surprised," I finally said. "From what I heard Hellfire isn't interested in taking over Haul Du at all. In fact, he wouldn't think twice about seeing them all dead. No, there's something else he wants."

"What? Or Who?"

I frowned. "I think it's a what, but I don't know. Dark Iron had something that Hellfire wants, and he seems to think it gets passed down to the Haul Du leaders, and that Reynard must have it now."

"And Reynard doesn't," Dario speculated. "Because Dark Iron didn't have the time or inclination to transfer leadership."

Nope, he'd died rather unexpectedly. Although with anyone else I would have assumed they would make contingent plans in case the inevitable happened. After all, Haul Du was a magical group that interacted regularly with demons, and demons were always more than happy to kill their summoners if given a chance."

"Hellfire said it wasn't at Dark Iron's house, and I trust that they searched it top to bottom including using a variety of spells and didn't find it."

"And it's not at the dry cleaner?"

I chuckled, envisioning Dark Iron leaving a valuable gem or scroll in the pocket of a jacket he'd taken in for cleaning.

"Not in clear view, anyway. I'm sure over the years the place has been surrounded by wards, so any detection spell from outside the building wouldn't reveal anything."

"And once he was inside?"

"They were wanding us, but clearly a lot got through from what went down after the induction ceremony. If Dark Iron hid something valuable there, he probably would have warded the crap out of it, though." It made sense. That's why Hellfire would have gone after Reynard and tried to beat the location out of him. And kill him once he realized the mage truly didn't know where this thing was.

Would Hellfire go back in later, now that the fire had probably destroyed some of the warding, and search for the object? Would he find it? If not, where the heck would Dark Iron have hidden something valuable that he didn't want anyone to find?

I needed to pick Reynard's brain. He might not know where this thing was, but I was willing to bet he knew *what* it was. And with enough information about Dark Iron, I could possibly figure out where he'd hidden it. Hopefully they wouldn't discharge him from the hospital before I could get over there—which would probably be midafternoon by the time I'd finished with work.

Dario shifted his hands on the steering wheel. "I don't trust Reynard. He's lied to you, blackmailed you, and worse. He'll wiggle out of this promise to help you fight this Big Bad. Or he'll abandon you when you need him most, just like he did during that ritual to get rid of your demon mark."

"I don't trust him either." I sighed and snuggled in closer to Dario. "But just in case he comes through, it would be good to have him and Haul Du on my side."

Dario's muscles tensed. "And what happens when he decides at a particularly important moment that he'd gain more from siding with Big Bad? Aria, he's done this before. He would have seen you enslaved to a demon for all eternity."

"The demon told him he'd resurrect Raven," I argued.

"Yes, he's a sneaky two-faced shit, but I can't completely blame him for that. He loved Raven. Wouldn't you have at least hesitated if you'd been in his position?"

"No. Demons lie. And if the demon *had* kept his word, then any sort of resurrection would have been done with a horrible side effect that would have made me regret the whole thing."

I frowned up at him. "You've had dealings with demons before?"

"Not personally," he admitted. "My mother did and several of the others on the plantation as well. Their religion involved dealing with spirits, some of which your religion would have called demons."

"Dealing with?" I scooted upward a bit so I could see him better.

"All spirits have a good and a bad side," he explained. "My mother told me that you have to keep your wits about you when making bargains with them—or when dealing with them at all. Even encountering one in the woods or fields requires care in both words *and* actions, as well as giving the spirit complete respect."

That was not at all how Templars approached demons. It *was* a bit like Haul Du mages approached Goetic demons though.

"How often did that happen?" I asked. "Your people encountering demons—I mean spirits—in the woods or in their daily life?"

His smile held a hint of nostalgia. "Most times you never knew. That old lady begging on the corner, that crying child, that drunk man brawling down the street? Any of them could be a powerful spirit. Best to always assume they were than to risk offending one and ending up cursed."

I watched him a moment, warmed to see this more

human side of Dario and charmed to hear more about his life before he'd been turned.

"Did your mother ever know if she came across a demon or not?"

"She claimed to have regular conversation with one, that he often came to see her." Dario shook his head, a fond smile on his face. "She said he wasn't so bad as long as you knew how to keep your wits about you when he was there. He liked offerings of tobacco and art. He was particularly fond of drawings or sculpture in his image. My mother never let me know who this spirit was or exactly what they discussed, but she always made sure to have suitable offerings on hand in case he appeared."

The way Dario talked about this demon, he sounded almost like a gentleman caller, a lover, than a tricky malevolent being who wanted nothing more than to take someone's soul and torture it for all of eternity.

Could we Templars have been wrong? We'd been founded in the duality of Christianity, with good solidly on the side of God and evil completely in the realm of Satan. But Dario's mother seemed to have believed the two were merged together. Was she right?

Then I thought of Balsur and shuddered. No, she couldn't be right. There was nothing but evil in that demon. That wasn't the sort of spirit someone would make deals with and give offerings of flattering artwork and tobacco to. No, whoever Dario's mother had dealt with, it must have been an angel and not a demon.

I snuggled back against him and closed my eyes. "Tell me more about your mother."

His voice grew soft and he told me about her beauty and her kindness. How she would always make sure he had enough to eat, even if that meant she sometimes went without. How she'd carried him while working in the fields until he was four, just to make sure he was old enough to keep up on his own. He talked about her friends, about a man she'd loved, who'd become suddenly ill and died within days. He talked about the way her hands, calloused and strong, had gently rubbed his back and held him tight.

I fell asleep and dreamed of a beautiful dark-skinned woman who loved her son, who was kind to friends and strangers and wily enough to negotiate with demons. I woke as Dario was carrying me into the house and heard Essie whisper to take me on upstairs. Then I fell asleep again, safe in Dario's arms, his calloused and strong hands holding me tight.

CHAPTER 20

Dario stayed with me through the night. I woke before dawn and went downstairs, sitting at my kitchen table while he cooked me omelets and made coffee. I didn't want him to leave. I was feeling off balance and numb, my mind whirring with everything that had hit me in the last twenty-four hours.

"I don't want to leave you," he said as he pulled a chair around beside me and sat down.

"Well, *I* don't want you to incinerate at dawn." I took a sip of coffee and reached out to take his hand. "Thank you."

"For standing outside while you dealt with bullets and knives and fire?" He made a low dangerous sound in his throat. "Yeah. Watching while the love of my immortal life flirted with death was not something I want to do again."

I squeezed his hand. "You trusted me. You proved to me that you trusted I could take care of things on my own without you rushing in to save me. Thank you. You've got no idea how much that meant to me. And you were hardly just standing there watching."

After we'd woken in the early morning hours and made

love, with Gran banging on the wall and telling us to finish it off because old people needed their sleep, Dario had confessed that he had found a bomb. He'd not only removed and disabled the bomb, but captured, interrogated, and killed the mage who had been charged with blowing the entire block up once he'd received word from Hellfire.

Dario had shown me one of their cellphones, and indeed the man had received word to blow the "whole mother-fucking place up."

"Don't ask me to do that again, Aria," he told me. "I absolutely respect your abilities. I just can't stand by and do nothing while you're in danger. I want to be in there with you. I want to be fighting by your side."

I slid out of my chair and sat in his lap. "I want that too."

He kissed me and I pressed myself against him, running my hands across his short curly hair and down his neck.

"Love you." I told him, noting that the sky was that ominous gray it got just before dawn.

He stood, placing me down into his chair before kissing me once more. "I love you too. Try not to die today, okay?"

I watched as he headed toward the door. "I'll try."

As Dario left, Buff entered, dressed and ready for our jog. I eyed him with bleary, tired eyes, wondering if I could beg off today and just go back to bed. Fulk racing down the stairs and into the kitchen drove away any thoughts of going back to sleep. The dog was clearly ready to go and eager for a morning run. I hated to disappoint him, and I honestly needed to keep my fitness level up. Last night had totally driven that home in my mind.

I took a deep breath, and realized I shouldn't have been able to do that. Lord knows what sort of nasty toxic shit I'd breathed in last night. I should be in a hospital on oxygen with damaged lungs. I should have been burned to a crisp. I should have had stab and bullet wounds.

The lack of stab and bullet wounds I could thank my blessed shield for. The rest? I had no stinking idea. What protected me from fire and chemical smoke injuries? Maybe I didn't need to get a tattoo on my nether bits after all.

And my palm tattoo…. It still ached, but it should hurt like hell after summoning my sword into my hand last night. It was less than twenty-four hours since I'd gotten the tattoo, and it looked fresh and clean, healed and supple. I'd applied the salve and wrapped it in plastic wrap when I'd gotten up this morning, but it felt better than it should—better than the pamphlet Dagger had given me had indicated.

My morning run was once again uneventful. I took care of my pets, showered and got ready for work, then spent a little time with Gran at the kitchen table drinking coffee and eating leftover bacon before heading in to work.

We had a slow day, and I found myself eyeing the clock every few minutes, eager to get off work. When my shift ended at noon, I picked up subs for lunch and headed home, handing Buff an Italian cold cut with hots on my way in the house.

I was just settling in for a nap on the couch when Reynard texted saying he was home from the hospital and wanted me to come by his house after work.

Which I decided would mean after nap. I told him I'd be there sometime around five or six, then pulled a blanket over me, Gaia curled up at my feet and Fulk lying beside me.

Sadly my nap only lasted an hour before my phone rang. Glancing at the screen, I bolted upright, because this was a call I didn't want to miss.

CHAPTER 21

"Dad?" I was kinda shocked he'd called me back. After leaving a message yesterday on the cell phones of both my parents, I'd figured I wouldn't hear from them until they were back in the states. Templars on assignment didn't have much time to return phone calls. Emergencies would have been routed to the Elders who would take care of any urgent family issues while a Templar was busy.

"Aria. How are you?" He sounded worried, and that in turn worried me.

"Fine. Gran is here with me, in case you didn't know. She went on the lamb from Athena's and came here."

"Oh, sweetie. I'm so sorry. Can Roman take care of her when he and his family get back from Disney?"

I smiled. "It's all good, Dad. I've got a spare room, and I enjoy having her here. But that's not the reason I called. I know you might not be able to give me details of your assignment—if you're on an assignment, that is. But I've got a mage here trying to take out a group in DC, and he spent the last decade or so in Italy. I wondered if there could possibly be a connection. His name is Hellfire."

Dad sucked in a breath. "Aria, be very careful. We're here taking down a group that tried to rob the Temple. They were trying to steal the Ring of Solomon. We've got most of them, but there was a member named Hellfire, along with several other members that have evaded us and are thought to have left the country."

Holy shit. "The Ring of Solomon?"

"It's safe, Aria. They weren't able to get past the second level wards on the Temple."

They'd been after the Ring of Solomon and failed. What the hell did Haul Du have that would be a consolation prize to *that*?

"Dad? What magical item would be similar to the Ring of Solomon? Something we don't have locked away in the Temple?"

"There's nothing like the Ring of Solomon."

"I know, but was there any mage in the last few millennia who may have attempted to do something similar? To create an object that has the power to control a hundred demons or more?"

"Many have tried, Aria. I don't know of any who succeeded, but the world is full of magical items, some of them incredibly powerful, that we Templars do not know about. A mage who succeeded in creating something like that would keep it quiet."

This wasn't making me feel any better.

"This Hellfire is a dangerous mage," Dad continued. "If he's in your area, you need to take care. And you need to contact the Order. One of the Elders will be able to send assistance."

Elders. Crap, Elder Purcell. I'd totally forgotten. Today was Tuesday, and he was supposed to be here in an hour to discuss my Oath. Lovely. I was so not ready to deal with this. Of course, I could hardly duck out on an Order Elder.

And if the Templars were involved in tracking down other members of Hellfire's group, then Elder Purcell might actually be a help.

"Thanks, Dad. Let Mom know everything is okay here. I'll see you both when you get back."

"Make sure you come down for Easter," he reminded me. "Bring Dario if he's available."

My heart grew two sizes at that. He'd explicitly invited Dario. My non-Templar, vampire boyfriend, and this was probably as close as he'd ever come to a "welcome-to-the-family speech."

"I will," I told him. Then I hung up and got ready for my visit from Elder Emmett Purcell.

CHAPTER 22

"Thank you for meeting with me, Aria." The Elder took a seat, and I did the same, the ingrained customs and courtesy from my childhood as automatic as breathing.

I'd sent Buff out with Essie to do some shopping, assuring my bodyguard that I would be safer during his absence than if the entire Secret Service was parked outside my door. Elder Purcell might look like he should be playing shuffleboard in a retirement community down in Florida, but the man could smite like a mofo, even at his age.

"Coffee?" I held the pot over a mug and looked at my guest.

He nodded and I poured him a cup, nudging the sugar and cream toward him as I sat the pot back onto the table. Elder Purcell took his time adding sugar and cream to his mug, stirring it all in, then taking a sip.

"I'm here to discuss your Oath, Solaria."

"I know, but can I ask you something first?"

"Of course." He leaned back on the couch, coffee cup in hand.

I'd met Elder Purcell a few times when I was in school, and he'd always been a stern, imposing, somewhat terrifying man. He looked exactly the same as he had ten years ago, but for some reason I saw him differently. Today I saw a powerful, kind, knowledgeable man who truly seemed to regard me as an equal. It made me feel a whole lot better about this conversation.

"You might not know this, but since moving here, I've taken the city of Baltimore under my wing."

"Go on." He nodded, not revealing if he knew anything about my doings over the last year or not.

"A mage acquaintance from DC alerted me to a potentially violent former member of theirs named Hellfire who was back in the states after many years in Italy." That got a blink from the older man. "Last night Hellfire and some of his associates attacked members of the Haul Du group in the middle of an induction ceremony. They killed several. The leader of Haul Du went to the hospital with a knife wound."

"Yes?"

It was clear that Elder Purcell wasn't going to give me one bit of information until I showed every card in my hand. I didn't intend on showing *every* card, but a few more wouldn't hurt.

"I called my parents who are in Italy on Order business right now, and they said I should talk to you about this matter."

He nodded. "The Order is aware of Hellfire's whereabouts. I was briefed about the incident last night, but not the details."

"I was told that he wanted to take control of the group Haul Du, but last night didn't seem like a coup. I heard him say that it didn't matter to him if every mage in the group died. The actions of his and his accomplices certainly supported that."

"So that is his motive?" Elder Purcell asked. "Revenge? He's looking to kill off the entire group?"

I hesitated, not sure if I should voice my suspicions or not. I didn't always agree with the actions or inactions of the Order, but I *was* a Templar, and the Elders had never given me any reason to distrust them.

"I got the impression that he was looking for something, that the former leader had what I assume was a valuable magical item. From what I overheard, he thought the current leader now had possession of it or knew its whereabouts."

Elder Purcell fixed me with a hard stare. "Does he?"

"I don't know. If he does he didn't tell Hellfire, and I doubt he'd tell me."

The man took another sip of his coffee. "And what is your current relationship with Haul Du and their new leader?"

I was pretty sure he knew that I'd been kicked out for being a Templar, so I didn't bother to go over that.

"I have no relationship with the group. The leader, Reynard, was my best friend's boyfriend. He asked me to be there last night to act as security."

I left out the blackmail and that Reynard wanted me to kill or somehow permanently banish Hellfire from DC, figuring that would be a bit much for this meeting. Besides, he was an Elder, not a confessor.

"But this Reynard still was stabbed?"

"He's still alive. I count that as a win." That was probably a little curt for someone speaking to an Order Elder, but Elder Purcell seemed mildly amused at my statement.

"I count that as a win as well. Now about your Oath…"

I didn't see any way out of this. That video was bound to get out and I needed the protection of the Order. I also was hoping that as a Knight I could plead for some additional help whenever Big Bad showed up. That, and my reluctance to take my Oath was waning. At first it had been an act of rebellion against what had seemed to be a predestined life. This past year, I'd picked up my sword and acted as an Oathless, independent knight, thinking that the only vows that mattered were between me and God. But there was only so much one Templar could do on their own. Just like Dario and his *Balaj*, I needed others. And sometimes they'd need me.

"I'm ready to arrange to take my Oath, Elder Purcell," I told the man. "As soon as my parents return, I'll meet with them and we'll plan the ceremony."

"Is that what you want?" he asked. "A ceremony in front of family and a hundred other knights, all in formal attire?"

I cringed at the thought. When I was a child, Oath ceremonies seemed so regal. Now it just seemed like a whole lot of pomp and circumstance for what was really a very private and holy matter.

"No. I'd prefer just me and an Elder from the Order." My parents would be bummed, but the thrill that I'd actually taken my vows would wash any disappointment away. Besides, they'd had ceremonies with both Roman and Athena, plus big weddings for both. It wasn't like they'd never had a chance to throw a huge party in their lives.

"Would you like to take your Oath now? Or would you like a few weeks or months to prepare?"

No time like the present.

"I'll take it now, if you don't mind."

Elder Purcell stood. I picked up my sword, knelt down on my living room floor, and faced him. The hilt of my sword made a crucifix, pressed against my forehead as my hands gripped the blade.

"In the name of the Father, of the Son, and of the Holy Ghost, I pledge myself into the holy service of the Knights Templar.

"I vow to guard the Temple and its contents from those who

would seek to do others harm, or to establish dominance over others.

"I pledge to aid, defend, and comfort pilgrims on the path, keeping them safe as they complete their life's journeys.

"Any knowledge I have or gain shall be freely given to those who request, and shall be recorded within the Temple libraries for the edification of other Knights and future generations.

"I will submit to the wisdom of the Elders and the rule of the Order, protect my fellow Knights as well as their families with my words, my sword, and my wealth.

"In the name of the Father, the Son, and the Holy Ghost I hereby make this Oath. Amen."

Elder Purcell put his hand on my forehead and murmured a blessing, then motioned for me to stand.

I truly expected a divine rush of power, a feeling of rightness in my soul, at the very least a beam of light through the front window. Instead there was nothing but the sound of Gaia hacking up a fur ball.

I guess that was life. A handful of words and a cat puking, and I was now a Knight pledged to the Order.

Haul Du had worried there would be a conflict of loyalty between them and my Templar duties. I knew Dario sometimes worried the same, only between him and my Templar duties. But the real conflict I feared would be between the Order and what I felt I had to do. In that conflict, I knew which way I'd choose, and I knew very well that choice would have repercussions.

"God will always come before the Order." I felt like I had to tell him.

For the first time I saw the flicker of a smile across Elder Purcell's face. "As it should be, Knight Ainsworth."

He stood, gathered his belongings and headed for the door. "Oh, and I have your first assignment as a knight. As you already know, a group attempted to break into the Temple. They must be brought to justice."

I felt a twinge of irritation. I had a lot going on right now. I couldn't hop a plane to track down thieves with my parents. But I guess this was the trade-off to taking my Oath.

"One of the leaders has been tracked down to this area, and you are the nearest Knight, so I need you to bring him in." Elder Purcell took a piece of white cotton string from his pocket. "Find Randolph Exter, known as Hellfire, and arrest him so he may stand trial before the Order. We prefer he be captured alive, but if that is not possible, then stop him with the point of your sword. He is a danger both to the Temple and Pilgrims on the Path."

Suddenly a whole lot of shit made sense. It had been Hellfire who'd been trying to kill me, and no wonder. He had a dead-or-alive warrant out for his arrest, and I was pretty much the local sheriff. I took the string from Elder Purcell, feeling cold electricity shoot up my fingers as I held it. I'd never seen one of these before, never touched one either. This was the Templar version of handcuffs, and it would absolutely block a mage's powers as well as render him about as physically dangerous as a wet leaf.

Relief flooded me. I wouldn't have to kill the guy, or chase him all over DC as he vanished every time I saw him. All I had to do was manage to get close enough to wrap this cotton string around his wrist, or finger, or neck, or little toe, and he'd be mine. Then I'd turn him over to one of the Elders and wash my hands of the whole thing. One problem taken care of.

And if Reynard proved to be a shit and went back on his word, or Chuck sold me out to someone else, my Oath should protect me. Yeah, I'd face some sort of shit from the Order, but they'd definitely protect me from prosecution by either human authorities or the Conclave.

"I will, Elder Purcell."

He started back toward the door. "Please contact the regional office to fill out paperwork. We'll need your direct deposit information for your stipend and relevant forms for tax withholding. Uncle Sam needs his tithe, you know."

The man sounded downright jolly. It was surreal.

"Oh, and Knight Ainsworth?" He paused in the doorway. "Don't forget to clean up that cat vomit."

CHAPTER 23

I waited for Buff and Gran to get home, sent a quick text to Dario for when he awoke, and headed in to DC. Before I drove to see Reynard, I swung by the site of last night's attack, wanting to see it before the sun completely went down.

It was light as I stood before the burned-out building, but the clouds on the horizon told me it was going to be a dark and probably rainy night. There was all sorts of caution tape around the perimeter of the building, but I ignored it and went in through the smoke-stained doorway.

The place was a mess with heaps of clothes in plastic bags tossed to the side, and cases hacked apart so the first responders could have easier access during the fire. I carefully picked my way through the rubble, stepping over twisted metal racks, burned boards, and chunks of plaster from the stucco ceiling.

Grabbing what looked like the metal stand from a dress-maker's dummy, I used it to prod the floor in front of me, zigzagging to the parts that felt the most stable. It would really suck if after all I'd been through I ended up breaking a leg, or worse, because I fell through the floor.

The stairs were downright terrifying. I managed to make it down, then turned on the flashlight app on my cell phone to look around the meeting space. The cement block walls and tile floors were chipped from bullets, blackened by fire, and stained by what I was sure was blood. Making my way slowly around the room I saw that not all the damage was from the fight. It looked even to my untrained eye as if someone had been down here after the police left, searching for…something.

The door to the storage area had been ripped off the hinges. Boxes full of ritual items and magical supplies had been unceremoniously dumped onto the floor. These weren't cheap supplies, although neither Reynard nor Dark Iron would have been foolish enough to keep the truly valuable items in a storage closet.

It seems the intruders had come to that conclusion as well. A section of the floor had been pried up to reveal a secret space, the blackened symbols along the edges revealing that it had once been magically secured and hidden from view. Two sections along the wall were the same. Scattered near each hidey-hole were the more valuable ritualistic items such as gems, a few grimoires, human skulls, and packets of dried herbs—no doubt those that were nearly impossible to import into the country.

They were all tossed aside. Leaving them where they lay, I headed down the second set of stairs to where I'd confronted Hellfire as he tried to smash answers out of Reynard. That room looked as if someone had taken a wrecking ball to it. I doubted the firefighters had come down here beyond making sure no one needed rescue, or bodies needed to be brought up. Although smoke damage would have been understandable, I couldn't see how the fight or the fire would have caused *this* much destruction. Three holes in the stone walls showed that there had also been magically secured hidden spots down here, but the rest of the smashed walls and stone looked as if someone had suffered a toddler-sized meltdown and taken it out on their surface.

Guess Hellfire hadn't found what he was looking for. I had no doubt that he'd used some sort of spell to discover the magic securing the hiding spots, then used other spells to break those protections. The rest was probably done with a combination of a jackhammer and a pickaxe. He'd probably used magic to manage all that without having the neighbors call the police with noise complaints, unless he'd done it in the middle of the day. Which was a good idea. The scene had obviously been cleared by the police and the fire marshal. Any people coming in and out would have been assumed to be insurance claims adjusters and demolition crew.

Carefully making my way back up to the first floor, I glanced once more around, a bit sad that this part of my short history as a member of Haul Du was now gone. I wondered what Haul Du's insurer was going to think about all this. Somehow I got the feeling they might not be paying out on this claim.

Getting back in my car, I cleaned up as best as I could with some wipes, then headed over to Reynard's house.

I had to text him to get in the place. He'd warded it like Satan himself were after him. It was truly impressive and left me wondering where the hell Reynard had gotten this many magical items. The mage hadn't wanted to bring down his security system, or come to the door, so I was forced to keep him on the line and dance my way around his yard, reciting a bunch of Latin under my breath to get to his house without going up in a puff of smoke.

The door was physically locked, but I used my spelled butter knife to bypass that, and locked it behind me once I'd entered. Reynard was lying on his couch in front of the television, a blanket over him and a pot of what I assumed was tea on the coffee table. He clutched a mug in his hands with a death grip.

I momentarily felt bad that I hadn't brought something. What did one bring to someone who'd almost had their throat slit open and was suffering from a concussion and bruises? Chicken soup? Flowers?

"How are you doing?" I asked, taking a seat in a chair beside the sofa.

"Stitches in my neck, stitches in the back of my head." He took a sip of the tea. "I feel like I got run over by a truck."

"You look like you got run over by a truck."

He held out the mug and I got up to refill it for him. The tea smelled like eucalyptus and pine needles, making me wonder if there was some sort of herbal healing magic to the brew.

"Have you killed him yet?" he asked.

I knew exactly who Reynard meant. "Nope. I have to find him first."

The mage glared at me over his tea mug. "Then go find him."

"If you were upfront with me about things I might be able to help you." I waited, and when Reynard didn't respond I continued. "What's he looking for? What does Haul Du have that Hellfire wants badly enough to kill every member to get?"

The mage didn't meet my gaze. "He wants to kill me and take over the organization."

"That's not what he said when he was banging your head against the wall. He wanted you to tell him where something was, and he said he didn't care if every Haul Du member died for him to get it." I waited for a second to let that sink in. "And judging from his actions last night, I believe him. I'll ask you again, Reynard—what does Hellfire want?"

"Fuck if I know. We've got some gems, some rare herbs, and a few other valuable items. Maybe he wants them?"

I sat back down. "I doubt it. The dry-cleaning place is trashed, and not just from the fight and the fire. He went back in there sometime between last night and tonight and searched. All the secret spots were blown open, the spells and wards broken, the contents thrown around like they were worthless junk. What does Hellfire want? What does Haul Du have that is so valuable he'd be willing to come here and slaughter everyone for?"

"I don't know." Reynard's voice was sullen. "Dark Iron never told me about anything, and you killed him before he could put any sort of transition plan in place. Unless he told you with his dying breath, then no one is going to know where this thing is Hellfire thinks we have."

I didn't believe him, but then I'd come to the point where I pretty much believed nothing Reynard said.

"He's going to come for you," I told the mage. "You can't stay holed up here behind these wards forever. He'll wait, and when you come out, he's going to torture you until you tell him, or kill you out of anger and frustration. You should see what he did to that lower room at the dry cleaner."

He squirmed, then sipped his tea. "You need to find him and kill him. That was our deal. I've still got that video, you know."

What a jerk to move straight back to blackmail. I kept silent for a bit, watching him shift uneasily on the couch before speaking.

"You and everyone else has that video. Golden Hemlock went to see Chuck today at Jessup. How much you wanna bet she's already got a copy? I'm screwed either way, so why should I bother trying to haul your ass out of the fire? Haul

Du never did anything for me. Let Hellfire clean house. There's no dangerous magical item for him to steal. Or if there is, no one knows where it is anyway."

I saw Reynard weighing that. I didn't want him to know I'd taken my Oath, that I'd been tasked with bringing Hellfire in, otherwise he'd have no reason to tell me about this thing the mage so desperately wanted.

If Hellfire had tried to break into the Temple to steal the Ring of Solomon, then what the heck did he think Haul Du had? What was a runner-up to a ring that could command an army of demons? And did Haul Du really have something like that? Dark Iron had stolen a soul trap from another mage. I wouldn't put it past him to have stolen something else—this time with no witnesses.

"Dark Iron hinted that he had something," Reynard finally admitted. "I don't know what it was, but the way he acted, it was something that made him damned near invulnerable."

And the guy didn't have it with him during our fight? I caught my breath, wondering if he had, if somehow this valuable item had been disposed of with the body. Wouldn't that be ironic? I hadn't bothered to go through the man's pockets after I murdered him, although I was pretty sure the vampires would have. I knew Dario would have.

Whatever the heck it was, it hadn't protected him from a Templar's sword. Or that null spell. I frowned, wondering if it was something specific to his practice.

"Something like the Ring of Solomon?" I asked softly.

It was very subtle, but I saw Reynard's shoulders tense. "I've got no idea. And I don't know where he would have kept it. Hellfire ransacked his house. He went through the Haul Du meeting place. I don't know where else it would be."

It was something to do with controlling demons. Fuck, it was something to do with controlling demons. It was diffi-cult enough for a skilled practitioner to manage a demon outside of a summoning circle. The higher level the demon, the longer it was out of the circle, the more difficult it was. That's why the Ring of Solomon was locked in the Temple. An object that would give the wielder power over a hundred or more high-level demons? That was priceless. If this thing Hellfire was looking for would facilitate controlling even a few demons outside a summoning circle, it would still give him immeasurable power. Several demons to kill, to coerce, to steal? And the summoner would be protected from the demons, able to control their actions without the need for carefully worded contracts that always seemed to have unexpected loopholes?

That was worth killing all of Haul Du for. But where the heck had Dark Iron gotten something like that? And where had he hidden it?

Reynard put the tea mug on the table and leaned back on his pillow. "Think I need to call it a night. If I'm feeling better tomorrow, I'll make some calls and look through a few things to see if I have any idea what Dark Iron was bragging about and where he might have it. But for now…"

I stood. "Sorry. I know you're probably feeling like crap still. Rest. I'll call you tomorrow afternoon, and in the meantime I'll see if I can get my police buddy to try to pinpoint where Hellfire might be staying."

"Thanks," Reynard murmured, closing his eyes.

I let myself out, sent a few texts to Tremelay, and another one to Dario. Then I hunkered down behind the tall forsythia across the street from Reynard and waited.

CHAPTER 24

$\mathcal{M}$y legs were falling asleep, and a steady drizzle had begun to fall, soaking through my coat and chilling me to the bone. This sucked. I hated stakeouts.

My phone vibrated, and I took a quick second to glance at it. Dario had sent me the description of a car and the key code for the door. I smiled, then backed out of my spot from the bushes, making my way around the rear of the other house and down a few blocks to where the car was parked.

It was a gray sedan that practically blended into the scenery. I pulled the scabbard from my back, and punched in the code. After putting my sword and shield in the back seat, I climbed in, grabbed the keys from the console, started it up and cranked the heat up to high.

Ah, blessed warmth. Once I felt reasonably thawed out, I texted Dario for an update.

He's working up the nerve to leave.

I put the car in gear and moved it up to where I could better see Reynard's house. There were no lights on inside. Dario was having to keep his distance because of the wards. I concentrated, but couldn't even feel a faint buzz of vampire.

He must be on the other side of Reynard's beefed up wards, his vampire aura blocked by the magic.

On the move.

I still saw nothing but a dark silent house. Reynard's car sat unmoving in the driveway. Asking Dario to help was clearly a good move since by my senses the mage was still in his house sleeping.

Following.

He's taking a neighbor's car two blocks down. Dark green Ford Escape.

Shit. I put the car in gear and got ready. Move too soon, and Reynard would see the car and be suspicious. Move too late and we'd lose him.

Now.

I hit the gas then the brakes when two blocks up Dario jumped toward the passenger door.

"Left at the intersection," he said.

I had the car in motion before he'd even closed the door, turning the corner as fast as I could without squealing the tires or drawing undo attention. The four lane road had a good bit of traffic on it, even at this hour. Six cars ahead I saw the green Escape and resisted the urge to edge closer.

Reynard led us on a convoluted path around the northeastern part of DC, including several stretches on and off the beltway. It was nerve-wracking having to keep from losing sight of him in the traffic, and I was glad I'd asked Dario to borrow an inconspicuous vehicle rather than have to do this in his big black SUV or my car that Reynard probably would have recognized.

"Are we the only ones following him?" I asked as I followed Reynard onto 95 North.

"I'm not recognizing any other cars, but that doesn't mean they're not tracking him another way," Dario replied.

He was right. I couldn't imagine Hellfire staking out Reynard's place like I'd done, although he might have hired someone to do it or even installed a camera. Still, I was sure he wasn't chilling out in some hotel drinking wine while Reynard snuck out of his house. No, he probably had some sort of magical means of keeping tabs on Reynard's movements— something a lot less exhausting and stressful than driving all over the place, trying not to lose track of a green Ford Escape.

Reynard stayed on 95 all the way to Baltimore, ditching the highway for 395, then taking us for a lovely drive around the University of Maryland campus before heading into Little Italy. The rain picked up from a drizzle to a steady downpour and I backed off a bit, feeling more confident now that Reynard was in a section of the city I knew. We spent half an hour meandering around until Reynard finally pulled the car over to the curb. I blended in with the rest of the traffic, passing him and turning right. Dario was out of the car before I stopped, vanishing in a burst of speed. I circled the block and pulled over, eyeing my phone and waiting for any news.

He's out of the car. I'm following.

I got out as well, debating about whether to put on the huge bulky Kevlar vest or not. After a second, I decided not to wear it. I had on the lighter weight vest, the one that had been damaged when I was shot. It was better than nothing, and allowed me flexibility of movement that the heavier vest didn't.

Besides, I'd be battling mages. I doubted a bulletproof vest would do much against spells.

I left the keys on the console and locked the door behind me. That way either Dario or I could get the car if we needed to move fast. Then I followed behind, using Dario's texted directions and keeping out of sight. It took me a few moments to realize exactly where I was and where Reynard seemed to be heading.

Old Town Mall. My skin crawled at the thought. The place had been slated for demolition and redevelopment this year, but paperwork, funding, and the fact that a grisly ritualistic sacrifice had occurred there had delayed the project. Why the heck was Reynard here? Had he known about Dark Iron's involvement with Fiore Noir? Even more perplexing was why Dark Iron would have hidden a valuable magical item *here* of all places. The whole area was going to be demolished. It was far from the best spot to stash something long term.

But maybe Dark Iron hadn't intended it to be long term. He'd been here with Fiore Noir for the sacrifice and soul magic. Maybe he'd kept the item here to have it handy, just in case things went wrong.

And things *had* gone wrong. Maybe he hadn't had time to grab it before getting the heck away from a vengeful angel. Then I'd been here, then the police, then all sorts of media attention. I could see him deciding to just leave the object here until everything died down, and retrieve it later.

But then I'd killed him and he'd never had a chance to retrieve it.

Dario was nowhere to be seen, completely in his stealth vampire mode. I squatted down around the side of an old building and watched as Reynard went into the very place where Bliss had lost her life and her soul. Edging slowly forward, I circled the building and waited, desperately wanting to look through one of the busted-out windows and see what the mage was doing. I couldn't risk being detected. This was one of the reasons I'd asked Dario to come with me. He'd let me know what Reynard did, and what he retrieved from inside.

I heard footsteps and saw Reynard cross the street. Just as

I went to stand and follow, a hand settled firmly on my shoulder.

"Stay here," Dario hissed. "He checked on something then put it back. He hasn't got it."

"Are you sure?" I murmured, knowing that there was a whole host of illusion magic that would make it look like Reynard had left the item when he had actually pocketed it.

"Yes. The thing makes my skin crawl. I thought it was because of the magic that happened here or residual energy from the angel, but it's the ring."

"Ring?" I grimaced, realizing that had come out louder than I'd intended.

Dario nodded. "Gold band with symbols etched on it. Reynard opened the box but didn't touch it. Then he put the box back in the ground and did whatever magic he needed to do to hide it. The spot looks like part of the floor, but I can still feel the ring even through the wards."

Dark Iron hadn't been too creative in his hiding spots it seemed. This sounded like the exact same thing he'd done to hide the valuable ritual items at the dry cleaners. The only difference was no one would have thought he would have hidden something here, in an old store slated for demolition.

"And now we wait," I told Dario, dreading this whole waiting thing. Thankfully we didn't have to wait long. Either Hellfire was especially eager to get this ring, or he was so confident in his abilities that he didn't feel the need to exercise any caution because ten minutes later he appeared. The mage walked down the center of the street, flanked by two people I assumed were mages, and one demon.

The demon was easy to spot even if the aura of his presence didn't make my hair stand on end. He was making no attempt at all to look human.

Dario edged slightly in front of me. "Same one from before?" he whispered.

I eyed the demon. "Think so." I wasn't sure since the demon in the dry cleaners hadn't been eight foot tall with the head of a bull and a scorpion tail. Goetic mages tended to have go-to demons when they summoned. Of course, if Hellfire could control one demon out of a summoning circle, there was no reason to doubt he couldn't control others as well.

"Backup?" Dario asked.

As much as I would like a *Balaj* of vampires helping me out, I shook my head. I didn't want to risk the chance of Hellfire disappearing again. No, I needed him to stick around long enough for me to get the string in my pocket around his wrists...or whatever.

"Showtime." I stood and pulled my sword from my scabbard, sliding the shield down my arm to grip the leather enarmes in my hand. I circled to the right around the building, and Dario went to the left.

Hellfire spotted me as I came around the building and flung out his hands, knocking me backward with some sort of magical energy wave. My back hit the dirt and I rolled, jumping back to my feet. Dario was already engaged with one mage, and Hellfire was running into the building with the demon protecting his back. That left me facing a woman, her black cape pushed back over her shoulders as her hands formed a ball of electricity.

I'd barely taken two steps when the ball in her hands shimmered. I put on a burst of speed and raised my shield, wondering if it would protect me against being electrocuted.

It did—sorta. The shield vibrated. My arm went numb, and I felt as though I'd grabbed hold of a hot wire fence with both hands. I yelped but kept going, reversing my sword as I crashed into the mage. Lifting the shield slightly, I jabbed my pommel under the edge and into her stomach. She gasped, faltering in the spell she was casting and giving me the opportunity to smack her in the face with my shield.

Unfortunately I was too close to get much force behind the blow. The mage pivoted, her cape swirling. With a quick motion, she'd wrapped my sword in the voluminous fabric along with her own arm, stepping into me so my shield was trapped between us.

Stupid cape. I yanked on my sword trying to free it to no avail. The mage began to chant and I saw sparks begin to arc between her fingers. She wouldn't be able to form a ball of electricity with one of her arms caught in the fabric with my sword, but it would still feel like being zapped with a dime-store stunner.

I leaned forward, using all my weight to try to push her off balance and to the ground. She scrambled backward, still trapping my shield and sword as the sparks shot from her fingers into my shoulder. The muscles went numb and I knew if my shield hadn't been squashed between us, I would have dropped it.

Screw this. My eyes met hers and I snarled.

Fue.

Sparks shot from my own hands. The cloak was too tight and thick around my sword hand to allow the fire enough oxygen to take hold, but that wasn't the case for my numb hand holding the shield. Flames licked up around the hem of her cloak and her eyes widened as she realized she'd need to disengage and shake the fabric off, or burn.

Then her eyes narrowed as she realized I'd burn as well. We began an epic battle of chicken as I continued to try to push her off balance and she kept hitting various parts of my body with electric shocks. The smell of burning cotton-poly blend was nauseating, and we both knew it would only be seconds before that would be blended with the odor of burning hair and flesh. Feeling tingled back through my left arm and I made a decision. Abruptly shifting my weight backward, I spun to the right and dropped my shield. As it clattered to the ground, I drove the flat of my palm up into the mage's nose.

Her head snapped back and blood spurted from her nose. I took advantage of the moment to keep spinning, turning my cloaked-wrapped sword into the tail end of crack-the-whip. The mage stumbled, lost her balance, and slammed into the brick wall of the building. Yanking my sword free of the burning cloak, I pivoted, reversing the weapon and grabbing it in both hands like a lance as I plunged it into her chest.

I didn't have much time to think about the fact that I'd just killed someone before the air shimmered with magic. The ground shook, a roaring sound filling my ears. Something slammed into me. Arms came around my waist and we flew to the side, twisting midair so I came down hard on top of Dario. He wasn't much of a cushion, and the impact knocked the breath out of me. His arms tightened and he rolled, flipping me to the bottom as chunks of brick and concrete rained down on us.

Dario grunted and I looked up into his dark brown eyes.

"Hold still." He grimaced, his body shaking with each impact. I obeyed, trying to ease breath back into my lungs.

When the noise stopped Dario stood, taking my arm and hauling me upright and behind him. I looked around in shock. The building across the street was nothing but rubble —and a good bit of that rubble was surrounding us. Dario's clothes were in tatters, his back a mess of torn skin and thick, dark blood. I knew he'd heal, but it was still unnerving to think that damage was meant for me.

The mage I'd killed was slumped against the building covered in brick dust, the fire on her cloak extinguished. Twenty feet away a twisted body lay. Before I could ask who the heck had blown up the other building, the ground beneath my feet began to shake.

"I'll find the third mage," Dario said. "You get inside and take care of the other two."

I grinned, thinking how far we'd come that he was taking on one mage, while I faced a mage and a demon. "Got it."

"Don't get killed," he warned before he took off in a blur of speed.

The tremors grew stronger and I stumbled for the building, grabbing my sword and shield along the way. I realized once I reached the threshold that the mage creating the earthquake was keeping this building out of the spell zone. I guess his boss wouldn't be too happy to have the old shop collapse around his head.

Hellfire must have had great confidence in his mages, because he hadn't put any protective wards around the doorway. He knelt on the floor, chalk in hand as he wrote the glyphs for the spell that would break through the protections surrounding the box with the ring in it. Four candles flickered in a circle around him. And standing between me and the mage was an eight-foot monster with a bull's head and a scorpion's tail.

Who needs wards when you've got a demon standing guard?

CHAPTER 25

*C*learly there was no time to set up a banishing ritual, so I'd need to do this the hard way.

"As a Templar Knight, as the Sword of God, I command you to return to hell," I called out.

It wouldn't do anything besides piss the demon off without the other ceremonial trappings, but pissed off was what I was looking for. If I could manage to strike a killing blow to the demon with my consecrated sword, then I wouldn't need a ritual and an incantation.

My challenge worked. The demon lowered his head and charged me. I set my stance, bracing my back foot against an uneven slab of concrete and readied my sword. The plan was to use my shield to deflect his horns, turn so he went partially past me, cut his scorpion tail off, then proceed to stab him through the back as his momentum carried him past me. Just like bullfighting, only with a demon.

Of course, the plan failed.

Instead of glancing off, the demon's horns punched through the steel and magic of my sword as if it were tissue paper. I yelped and tried to disengage my arm from the leather enarmes as he dragged me forward with him. I yanked my arm free just in time to twist around and barely evade the scorpion barb coming for my head.

I swung my sword, but at that point I was too off balance to do more than smack the tail away as it came in for a second strike. Stumbling back a few steps, I steadied myself and faced the demon. He'd turned, and I nearly laughed to see my shield stuck to his horns, completely blocking his face. With a bellow his shook his head, then reached up to grab the shield, ripping it off his horns.

I mourned for a second. I'd really liked that shield and had spent a lot of time painting all those protective symbols in nail polish on the front. Now it was just a twisted hunk of metal on the ground with two holes poked through it—useless. But I had my sword, and that's the weapon I really needed in this fight.

The demon charged again. I danced to the side, feeling the horns rip through my coat clean down to my skin. The tail stabbed and this time I was ready with a swing of my sword, the barb slice cleanly off, sailing across the room.

The demon howled and spun around, not hesitating before beginning another charge. I waited until the last second, then dropped to crouch, thrusting my sword upward. The blade sliced through leathery skin and a foul green liquid cascaded out of the wound. Holding my breath, I plunged the sword farther in just as I felt something rip through the back of my coat. I tried to roll out of the way, but whatever had stabbed me was stuck in my coat. With another thrust, it came through the fabric just under my arm. Thank God for oversized puffy coats because the thing completely missed jabbing me through the back.

Glancing down I realized it was another scorpion barb. What the heck? Had this demon regenerated that fast?

He went to yank the barb out, no doubt to try again, but it

stuck and instead I found myself hauled out in front of the demon and over top of him. The coat tore free and I hit the ground, right behind the demon. Scrambling to my feet, I grabbed my sword with both hands, and like a lance drove it through the demon's back, pinning its tail in place.

Immediately yanking the sword out, I lopped off the demon's tail before he could strike again, then jabbed my sword through the back of his head.

"*Vade. Vade et amplius iam!*" I didn't continue the phrase to include "and sin no more" since that would be a silly thing to command of a demon. Still, my sword glowed and the demon shrieked, convulsing a few seconds before dropping to the floor. His physical form destroyed, the demon was free from his summoning contract. Go directly to hell, do not pass go, do not collect two hundred dollars. Black smoke rose from the body before dissipating with the stench of sulfur. I waited for a second to make sure the demon was truly gone before turning around to face Hellfire.

He'd broken through the wards and had the box in his hands. It seemed like time slowed as I yanked my sword free. He opened the box and I ran forward, watching him reveal the gold ring with black symbols around the wide band.

Screw the handcuffs. He couldn't get that ring. I had a very bad feeling what would happen if he put it on his finger.

I gripped my sword with both hands, throwing it forward like a spear. This time it stuck in a magical field that surrounded the mage. The sword quivered, and blue cracks spidered out around a sphere of magic. Pulling the blade out, I stabbed the magical ward again and again, watching with horror as Hellfire reached into the box and picked up the ring. In about three seconds, I was going to be surrounded by demons—too many for me to ever hope to banish on my own. I thought of Dario outside fighting the other mage and wished I'd let him call in the rest of his *Balaj* to help.

Although that would have probably done nothing beyond get them all killed.

I redoubled my efforts, panicking as Hellfire placed the ring on a finger and smiled.

"Iam non dico vos mihi. Apparebis in conspectus meo et prae-cepta mea quae praecepero summonds."

Fuck. No. No, no, no, no. I screamed and slammed my sword into the magical barrier with all my might. It finally shattered with a blast of energy that sent me scooting on my ass across the room.

Blue light surrounded Hellfire. I *saw* the veil, saw the demons waiting on the other side to come forth and do his bidding. Gripping my sword tight, I got to my feet and ran, hoping to take Hellfire out before he brought too many of them across the veil.

And then what? I raised my sword to deliver what I hoped was a killing blow, thinking I'd need to battle demons after this, to send as many as I could back to hell before they managed to take me out. Then? Hopefully then Dario could finish the job. He was strong, powerful, and I had no doubt that he'd be properly motivated by my death to plow through half a dozen demons or more before they overcame him.

Erasing the thoughts from my mind, I swung my sword, only to have it pass clear through Hellfire as if he weren't there.

"Apparebis!" he screamed.

I readied myself for the demons about to cross over.

Hellfire screamed again, and this time I turned my attention from the demons who were not moving forward to the mage. He was hunched over, puking blood and chunks of what looked like stomach and intestines onto the floor. His hands withered and blackened, the rot spreading up his arms as he continued to vomit. With a horrible gasping sound, he collapsed into a wet pile of blood and putrefied flesh, the ring sliding off a bony finger to roll a few feet away before settling on its side with a merry chime.

I stared in horror, then glanced over to where the veil had been. It was gone, the doorway completely closed. No demons had crossed over. None.

What the fuck had just happened?

Was this one of those "he wasn't worthy" things like in the Indiana Jones movie? Had Hellfire, a mage able to regularly control a demon outside of a summoning circle, a powerful mage, not been able to handle whatever this ring was dishing out in terms of magical mojo? I looked back at the pretty gold band with the symbols and shivered.

A shadow moved in my peripheral vision and I spun around, sword at the ready, to find Reynard walking toward me, an amulet in one hand and a knife in the other.

"Could have used you earlier," I groused, relaxing my shoulders. "Just like you to show up when I've done all the heavy lifting."

"That was my plan," the mage said. "And now I'll take the ring."

Asshole. The guy didn't even thank me, and if he thought he was getting out of here with that ring, he was wrong.

"Go home and get some sleep, Reynard. Without the ring."

He stepped forward, standing between me and the gold band. "It belongs to Haul Du."

I rolled my eyes. "Right. Just like that soul trap Dark Iron stole belonged to Haul Du? He probably stole this as well. It doesn't belong to you *or* Haul Du."

"Well it sure as hell doesn't belong to you," he shot back. "I found it. It's mine."

I adjusted my grip on my sword and the amulet he held began to glow.

"Put the sword down."

Or what? I eyed the magical device, wondering what it did. Was I about to get a piano dropped on my head? Teleported to the middle of the Bay? Engulfed in flames? Slowly I knelt, placing my sword on the ground then standing up. I was hoping I could call it to my hand again as I'd done before, but if I did this right, I wouldn't need my sword.

I better do this right, because I really didn't want to have to kill Reynard.

"You saw what it did to Hellfire," I told him. "Don't be an idiot, Reynard."

He stepped to the side and glanced down at the ring, his brow furrowed.

"Hellfire was a powerful mage. He tried to use it and it killed him. Don't do this," I urged.

"It'll take research and study," he finally said. "Maybe years of study before I can use it. But I'm taking it with me, and I *am* going to eventually be able to use it."

He didn't even know what the ring was. Reynard's greed and ego was going to get him killed. I frantically tried to think of some way to convince him not to do this, then saw the box.

"Fine, but I'd suggest you don't go handling it barehanded, or carrying it around in your pocket." I picked up the box from the ground, shaking some of Hellfire's goo off it. "Scoop it up with this and keep it in here until you figure it out."

He frowned at me for a moment, then let the amulet hang around his neck and walked forward a step to take the box, knife still in the other hand. Giving it to him, I let go of the box, then quickly slapped his wrist with a piece of string. What looked like white cotton coiled around the mage's wrist and snapped tight. The amulet around his neck went dark and Reynard gave a shout of surprise.

Then he tried to stab me with the knife.

Luckily I had about twenty more years of hand-to-hand combat experience and easily disarmed him, calling my sword to my right hand. Flipping the weapon around, I whacked the mage in the stomach with the pommel. He doubled over and I kicked him backward. Reynard sprawled on the cement floor, gagging and choking as he clutched his stomach.

Reversing my sword, I extended the tip of it outward and scooped the ring up from the floor. Another shadow moved near the doorway and I tensed for a fraction of a second before I realized who it was.

"Looks like you handled this situation fine without me." There was a note of pride in Dario's voice that made me smile.

"Yep. Two mages and a demon, although to be honest the ring took care of one of the mages for me." I shivered, remembering the veil and feeling grateful that I hadn't had to face a dozen or more demons.

"That third mage ran for it. It took me a while to track him down. Sorry I'm late to the party here." Dario stepped forward to look at the ring on the tip of my sword.

"Don't touch it," I warned, even though I knew he wouldn't do anything so foolish.

"You want to put it back in that box?" he asked.

"I've got a better idea." I pulled a little velvet bag out of one of the pockets on my cargo pants and handed it to Dario. "Can you hold this open while I drop the ring inside."

The vampire obviously trusted me because he took the bag without question, opening it up and holding it at the end of my sword. I tipped the blade downward and watched the golden band slide into the null bag. Then just to be safe, I tied the top and whispered a locking ward on the bag before putting it into the box."

"Let's go home," I told Dario. I was tired, filthy, and I

stank of sulfur and putrid rotting goo. My immediate future needed to be a shower, then eventually some sleep because unlike other Templars, I had to be at work tomorrow at the coffee shop.

"What about him?" Dario asked, nodding toward Reynard as we walked to the doorway.

I shrugged. "He'll be fine." As for the Templar handcuffs… well, Reynard could figure out how to get those off on his own. I had no idea how to and I wasn't about to waste any time helping that asshole out.

"Good." Dario put his arm around me. "Think Essie has any of that goulash left over? I'm starved."

CHAPTER 26

I handed the stack of papers over to Elder Purcell. Who knew that taking my Oath would result in so much paperwork? It wasn't just the tax and direct deposit forms either, but health insurance enrollment and life insurance beneficiary forms as well.

If I bought the big one, I'd leave it all to my nephews and niece.

The one thing that differentiated my job from Tremelay's, besides the sword, was that I didn't need to fill out any reports about what went down last night. Good thing too, because I'd lied. I'd lied so much that I wasn't sure I could keep everything straight if Elder Purcell decided to ask questions.

"Soul trap." The elder wrinkled his face in disgust. "And it wasn't even there."

I'd killed several birds with one stone, or rather with one big lie, and told the man that what Hellfire had been looking for was the soul trap that Dark Iron had stolen. I also mentioned that since the rightful owner had been in Baltimore this past November, I'd assumed the rightful owner had tracked down its location and retrieved it. I didn't go into any made-up details on Dark Iron's fate, not wanting to be caught out when Chuck put that video on the internet, or gave it to Golden Hemlock, or when Reynard decided to screw me over.

I also had tried to avoid details on Hellfire's death, unsure whether I should say Reynard killed him or that I'd done it myself. Thankfully Elder Purcell didn't seem to care how the mage had died, or that he hadn't been brought in for justice. I got the feeling he was of the old "let God sort them out" school, and was relieved he wouldn't have to deal with trials and costly incarcerations.

He didn't want to see the body, the scene, anything. Elder Purcell just seemed content with my assurance that the mage was dead.

I don't know why I kept the ring a secret. Something knotted up in my stomach at the thought of turning it over to him, so I kept it in the null bag and put the box in the very back of my bathroom cabinet behind the tampon box. When Mom and Dad got home I'd talk to them about it. Maybe.

Crap, I hope this wasn't like that hobbit ring. Was I going to end up in some damp cave muttering to it and paranoid that someone would steal it from me?

Elder Purcell left and I got ready for work. Buff's assignment as my bodyguard had ended. I hadn't even needed to suggest that Dario pay him through the end of the month, and give him a few leads on other well-paying security jobs. To celebrate, he'd taken Gran out to brunch at some swanky place. She'd left dressed in her Sunday best with her hand on Buff's arm. I'll admit I was a bit jealous that he'd invited her out and not me, but then again it was nice for Gran to have a friend. And it was nice that she hadn't been here when Elder Purcell had come by for our meeting.

We were busy at work. I'd thought briefly about quitting

now that I'd be getting a stipend from the Order, but I loved my job. I'd miss seeing everyone, interacting with customers and my coworkers, making coffee drinks. And the extra money wouldn't be bad either. I might need to reduce my hours a bit if I ended up with a lot of Templar assignments, but I'd cross that bridge when I came to it.

Golden Hemlock came in just as I was ending my shift. I tried to ignore her, but something told me I needed to just get it over with, so I clocked out, had Sean make me a mocha latte, and went to sit down across from her.

"I had an interesting visit at Jessup the other day." She put her phone down on the table and a video began to play. I'd seen it before so I wasn't quite as panicked as I'd been when Reynard had shown it to me.

I took a sip of my latte. "Yes. Very interesting."

But what was she going to do about it? Was I about to be hauled out of my workplace and locked up? Would I get one phone call, and if I did should I call my parents or the Order? Or Dario? Would the Order back me up, or let me hang in the wind until they needed me again?

The mage gathered up her phone and stuck it into her purse. "You could have told me, you know."

I wasn't sure how to respond to that, so I made a noncommittal noise and took another sip of my drink.

She sighed. "I don't know what the hell Dark Iron did to piss off the Order—excuse my language. The guy seemed to have a habit of pissing people off though, so I shouldn't be surprised. I'm just glad I don't have to haul you in because I gotta say I was a bit worried you might put up a fight and I'd end up with a sword through my chest."

I tried not to slump in relief. Elder Purcell had come through. I wasn't sure if he'd returned Golden Hemlock's call before or after I'd taken my vow, but either way I was grateful. This was one less problem I needed to face—unless Elder

Purcell decided my actions against Dark Iron violated the Order's code of ethics and conduct.

But at least the Order wouldn't be executing me, or probably even jailing me. I might end up with some truly shitty assignments, but I could deal with that.

"So where will you go from here?" I asked, hoping that wherever it was it was far, far from Baltimore. She hadn't seemed to care about Hellfire's attacks, or the murder of Haul Du members. I had no idea what Justices did in their free time. Maybe embroidery? Bingeing Netflix? Golf?

"Next is Argentina."

I bit back all sorts of curses that would have been inappropriate for a Templar to think, let alone voice out loud.

"My job is not quite finished. See, the reason I was sent to find Dark Iron was because he allegedly stole a valuable magical item from another."

Golden Hemlock stood, but I remained seated, hiding my expression behind my latte cup. So what if she found out I'd returned the soul trap to its original owner? And if he, or she, found out I'd disabled it, hopefully I could hide behind the Order on that one as well.

I waited until I was sure she was long gone, then finished my mocha latte, and got my sword out of my locker in the coffee shop back room. I'd walked to work today rather than pay for parking. Last night's rain had continued off and on throughout the day but the temperature had dropped making the sidewalks slick with patches of black ice. A shadow detached itself from a building and stepped in front of me.

My heart warmed. "Hi."

Dario wrapped an arm around me, snaking it in between my sword and my coat. "Hello beautiful. We're a few blocks from Little Italy. Dinner at Sesarios'? Or should we head over to Brewer's Art? They've got a new Belgian on tap."

I leaned against him, letting him partially support me as we walked. "Can't. Today's Wednesday."

"Ah, the Anderon game."

"I'm hosting this week," I told him even though he already knew. "Do you want to stay and play with us? Zac can let you run one of the NPCs. Or you can just watch and cheer me on as we battle giants and goblins in the mountains of Pyliamor."

"Think I'll just watch." His arm tightened around me for a quick hug. "So it's pizza, beer, and chips tonight?"

"No, Gran is cooking. She said something about palascinta? Evidently they're a hearty type of crépe with meat and walnuts and raisins. She asked if I wanted the dark chocolate sauce to pour over top of them. That would mean it wouldn't exactly be a finger food, but who can say 'no' to chocolate sauce? I certainly can't."

"Is she going to play in the game?" Dario chuckled. "That would definitely be worth watching."

I laughed. "She rolled up a character, and she's ready to go. A dwarven mage of all things. Should be fun."

He sighed. "You know, I'm going to miss her when your brother comes to get her next week."

"Uh, about that…" I looked up at him and grimaced.

"Don't tell me your brother backed out."

"I'm the one that backed out. Having her here…I don't know, I feel like we've bonded even more in the past week. We were always close, but this is different. I love having her here. She'll go back to Middleburg when my parents get back, but until then I decided I really want her to stay with me."

"And when do your parents come home?"

Dario sounded as if he were pleading, which made me laugh.

"It'll only be three or four more weeks. Two months at

the most. Come on, you love having Gran in the house as much as I do. She cooks, buys booze and groceries, lets Fulk out to pee during the day when I'm working. And Gaia loves her. They both take naps together. She and Buff have this friendship. He's going to take her to meet his mom sometime next week and they're all going to play Scrabble." I stopped walking and looked up at Dario. "I know. Between your house and mine, we don't really have anywhere private right now."

He smiled and shook his head. "We can always get a hotel room for a few hours—or maybe put Essie up in a hotel for the night."

"She'd love that. Get ready for a crazy room service bill, though."

We started walking again. The night was silent except for the smack of sleet against the pavement and the swoosh of tires as cars made their way carefully down the street. The smell of garlic and oregano wafted from a nearby restaurant. A man stood against the side of a building under an awning, hunched into his overcoat and smoking a cigar. A siren sounded in the distance.

Others might turn up their noses at the place I'd chosen to make a home, but Baltimore was my town, and its residents were my Pilgrims.

As for me, I was their Templar—their Templar Knight.

* * *

WANT to know when the next Templar book comes out? Make sure to join my mailing list at: https://debradunbar. com/subscribe-to-release-announcements/

Caden DeSarro is what they call a chubby chaser. He likes his guys with a few extra pounds on them. So when he meets Kevin Dodge in a bar bathroom, he can't help but stare. As far as Caden is concerned, Kevin is physically perfect: a stocky bearded blond. But Caden gets tongue-tied and misses his chance.

When Caden runs into Kevin one night on the el train, he figures it's fate offering him a second shot. Caden manages to get invited back to Kevin's place for a one-night stand that turns into the kind of relationship he's dreamed about.

But the course of true love never runs smoothly—Kevin and Caden's romance is no exception. When Caden returns from a few weeks away on business, Kevin surprises him with a new and "improved" body—one that fits Caden's shallow friend Bobby's ideal, but not Caden's. Caden doesn't know what to do, and his hesitation is just the opportunity Bobby was looking for.

ABOUT THE AUTHOR

Debra lives in a little house in the woods of Maryland with her sons and two slobbery bloodhounds. On a good day, she jogs and horseback rides, hopefully managing to keep the horse between herself and the ground. Her only known super power is 'Identify Roadkill'.

For more information:
www.debradunbar.com
Debra Dunbar's Author page

Northern Lights

Far From Center

Penance

Northern Wolves

Juneau to Kenai

Rogue

Winter Fae

Bad Seed

ACKNOWLEDGMENTS

Thanks to my copyeditor Kimberly Cannon whose eagle eyes catch all the typos and keep my comma problem in line, and to Damonza for cover design.